PERIL IN PICCADILLY

PIPPA DARLING MYSTERY
BOOK 7

JENNA BENNETT

Someone is out to get Pippa Darling.

Or perhaps not. The tumble down the stairs into the underground involved a lot of people, all of whom said someone pushed them, and all of whom, no doubt, had wronged someone, somehow, at some point.

And the Hackney cab that jumped the pavement and tried to run Pippa and her flat-mate Christopher down on their way home... well, it might have been after Christopher, mightn't it?

It might even have been after Lady Laetitia Marsden. She wasn't there, of course, but she looks rather a lot like Christopher in drag, and he was dressed as his alter-ego Kitty Dupree at the time.

Neither Christopher nor Pippa would mind very much if Laetitia were to be run over—it would save Christopher's cousin Crispin from having to marry her—but of course it wasn't either of them in the Hackney. They were too busy getting out of the way of the tires.

If Laetitia was the intended victim, the jewelry theft at Marsden House might have had something to do with it. The Sutherland engagement ring is gone, right out from under Laetitia's nose. She even saw the man who took it. Not to recognize, of course, but perhaps he doesn't know that. So yes, it might have been Lady Laetitia in the headlamps of the Hackney.

Or it might have been Christopher. Or it might have been Pippa.

"Very few of us are what we seem."

AGATHA CHRISTIE

CHAPTER ONE

THE FIRST TIME I almost died, I was a few years old, and stumbled into the Neckar River on a walk through Heidelberg with my mother. A good Samaritan fished me out and handed me back to her, dripping wet and hiccoughing for breath, and I was exposed to several hours of rough toweling and tears, until it all mostly faded into memory. I was more startled than afraid, I think, and while my mother undoubtedly had the shock of her life, nothing terrible happened.

The second time I almost died, I was eleven, and abandoned in the center of the garden maze at Sutherland Hall in Wiltshire by the not-so-Honorable Crispin Astley, also eleven. By then, the Great War had broken out, and my mother had sent me to her sister in England for my safety. I had been folded into the Astley family, and Crispin had taken against me because I had supplanted him as our shared cousin Christopher's best friend. Just as the first time, the experience was traumatic, and much longer-lived, but ultimately no more fatal. Christopher rescued me long before I could starve to death, and Crispin got a talking-to by my aunt, as well as a spanking by his father, which went a long way towards making me feel better (at the time, anyway; even if it makes me feel rather worse about the whole thing now).

After that, there was the time I tried to climb out a second story window at the Godolphin School in Salisbury, which I attended from thirteen to eighteen, while Christopher and Crispin were away at Eton, and while my elder cousins Robert and Francis were in the trenches in France. The ivy wasn't strong enough to hold me, and I dangled for a few seconds before a couple of the other girls hauled me back to safety. The less said about that, the better. That wasn't fatal, either, and probably wouldn't have been even if I had fallen.

After that, a few years passed. The war ended. Francis came home, but Robert didn't. Christopher and Crispin left Eton and went to Oxford and Cambridge, respectively. I went with Christopher, while Crispin, for some reason known only unto himself, seemed to want to get away from us. Eventually, Christopher and I ended up in London. Then came the bullet that grazed my arm during a visit to Sutherland Hall in late April, and a few weeks later, the poisoned cocktail I was served at the Dower House in Dorset. The shot went wide, and Christopher took the cocktail out of my hand and tossed it back himself when he saw that I didn't like the taste. There was enough Veronal in it to put me to sleep permanently, but Christopher—a bit taller and heavier, and with a faster metabolism—merely slept the sleep of the dead for a few days before waking up, none the worse for wear.

That takes us to September, and the second bullet, the one that passed within a foot or so of my head, and that of Francis. We chalked that one up to either a case of mistaken identity—I looked a bit like the Honorable Cecily Fletcher, who was even then fighting for her life upstairs in Marsden Manor—or simply a stray shot from the shooting party in the nearby woods. None of the hunters admitted to firing it, but that was to be expected, really, when it almost killed someone. There was no harm done, so we were all (mostly) happy to relegate it to the past, where it belonged.

And that brings us up to the present day, October 1926, and what I like to refer to, in retrospect, as The Peril in Piccadilly.

Yes, the capital letters are intentional.

I was having a late supper with Wolfgang Ulrich Albrecht, the *Graf von und zu* Natterdorff, a distant cousin and also my sort-of fiancé. We were sharing a table in the Criterion Restaurant, after attending *The Scarlet Lady*—the new comedy featuring Miss Marie Tempest and Mr. Ernest Thesiger—next door at the Piccadilly Jewel Box.

Wolfgang and I (and Christopher) had met a couple of months earlier, in the tearoom at the Savoy Hotel. He claimed to have recognized me from a visit when I was a wee imp in Heidelberg, and I had no reason to doubt him. In the time since, we'd been getting to know one another better. Christopher approves—Wolfgang is quite handsome, as well as a *Graf* —while Crispin and Francis both vehemently disapprove. Francis because he fought the Germans in France, and Crispin for reasons known only unto himself. He wasn't old enough to serve in the Great War (nor was Wolfgang, for that matter), so it can't have been that. But whatever the reason, he despises Wolfgang, a feeling which is decidedly mutual, since Crispin has let no opportunity go by to make himself disagreeable.

I'm still not entirely certain how we ended up engaged, other than that when Wolfgang proposed, I didn't say no. I don't think I said yes, either—my response was something more like, "Thank you, but..." But by the time I got that last part out, Christopher was shrieking, my Aunt Roslyn was whooping, Lady Laetitia Marsden—Crispin's intended—was watching with barely concealed glee, and Crispin himself was scowling. Wolfgang had moved to embrace me, and I couldn't really say that I hadn't meant it, not when everyone was so clearly elated.

In that spirit, I accepted the congratulations—Lady Laetitia practically cried tears of joy, while Crispin's jaw was clenched so tight when he extended his hand to Wolfgang that I feared for the health of his molars—and then I returned to London and went about my business as if nothing had changed.

And nothing much had. Wolfgang seemed satisfied with the semi-positive response to his offer—less than enthusiastic though it was—because he didn't push for anything more definite, and he also didn't bring it up again over the next few weeks. Perhaps he realized that I hadn't said "yes," so much as "I need some time to think about it," and he decided to give it to me. Perhaps he was afraid that if he pushed, "Thank you, but —" might turn into a flat "No."

The thing was, I wasn't in love with him. I wasn't in love with anyone else, either, so it wasn't as if my heart was engaged elsewhere. And I liked Wolfgang; it wasn't that I didn't. But marriage to him came with certain disadvantages. He was a German nobleman, with a title, a *Schloss*, and presumably a fortune to go along with it. All well and good, even if the Weimar Republic had done away with the German nobility in 1919, so the title, at least, was mostly only worth the paper it was written on. The *Schloss* and money were more solid, or so I assumed.

But be that as it may, Germany after the war wasn't a place I wanted to be. Yes, I had been born there. But that was a long time ago now, and I had no fond feelings for the place. My father and mother were both gone; the former in the War and the latter in the influenza epidemic that followed. I had had no contact with any of my German relatives in the past twelve years (or even before that, for that matter). The incident that

Wolfgang recalled, was not something I remembered. I felt thoroughly English now, and there was no part of me that wanted to return to post-War Germany, *Schloss* or no *Schloss*.

And so we limped along for a few weeks, taking tea and supper together in London, spending time together but without touching on any difficult subjects, or for that matter touching much in general.

Until that particular evening in October, at the Criterion Restaurant. The waiter had just served the cheese course when the door to the street opened, and in swept the Viscount St George, resplendent in black tie, with his fiancée hanging on his arm.

Lady Laetitia Marsden is quite possibly the best-looking woman I have ever set eyes on. Or perhaps not: the now-dead Johanna de Vos was also stunningly lovely. But she certainly puts me, and most everyone else, to shame. Tall and willowy, she carries the current tubular fashions off to perfection, while her face is the exact proportion of curves to angles, with big, long-lashed eyes under curved brows, high cheekbones, and full lips.

Just like every other time I have seen her—more frequently than I would wish—she was wearing black: a slinky gown with a plunging V-neck and diamanté embroidery under a black velvet cloak decorated with fur around the neck and wrists. The ostentatious Sutherland engagement ring weighed down her left hand, and the matching diamonds sparkled in her ears.

They stopped just inside the door while Crispin handed off his topper, gloves, and walking stick to the hat check girl, and while Laetitia surveyed the restaurant for, I assumed, familiar faces.

For the record, I would have been quite happy to ignore their presence entirely, and so, I thought, would Crispin be happy to ignore ours.

He saw us, of course. He met my eyes for a moment before he turned his attention to the back of Wolfgang's head—his lip curled—and then he looked away. It was Laetitia who looped her hand through his elbow and towed him across the floor to our table.

"Miss Darling." She gave me the most condescending smile you could imagine, only made more so by the fact that she was standing and I was sitting, and she could quite literally look down her nose at me. Wolfgang, of course, had gotten to his feet, as any gentleman would when presented with a woman of breeding next to his table. "*Graf* von Natterdorff." She fluttered her lashes up at him. He's tall, several inches taller than Crispin, who surely felt like just as much of a child as I did.

Wolfgang bowed over Laetitia's hand, while I managed a smile, or rather a grimace I hoped might pass as one. "Lady Laetitia." I flicked a look at her fiancé. "St George."

He nodded. "Philippa."

My brows arched. I can count the times he has called me by my given name on the fingers of one hand, or at least the times it has happened in the past few years. When we were children, yes. But he stopped sometime around the time he left Eton and went up to Cambridge. Since then, it's been a sneered—or occasionally smirked—"Darling," the way one would address the maid.

"Really," I intoned, "Crispin?"

His given name didn't feel any more comfortable in my mouth than mine did in his. And it must have been obvious, because I saw the corner of his mouth twitch. He didn't comment, however.

"It has been brought to my attention that I've been improper," he said instead, blandly.

"Of course you've been," I agreed, since I had pointed it out to him myself on more than one occasion. "Although that has never stopped you before, has it?"

"I know better now."

I nodded sympathetically. "Of course you do. Someone told you to stop, I imagine."

And not because his addressing me as Darling was discourteous to me, but because his new fiancée wouldn't want him to call someone else something that sounded like an endearment.

"Be that as it may," Crispin said airily, without confirming or denying, "from now on, I will have to address you by your given name, I'm afraid."

"Of course. Am I expected to do the same?"

It only seemed fair, didn't it?

And no, I didn't want to do it. I would much rather have him continue to address me by my last name so I could address him by his title—this given name business was more familiar than I was comfortable with—but I was damned if I would let Laetitia get away with telling him how he could speak to me. If she wanted to stop him from addressing me too informally, she could damn well put up with me returning the sentiment.

Crispin opened his mouth, and then closed it again. Laetitia scowled at him, but there was nothing he could say, after all. We were cousins, or the next thing to it, so if he addressed me by my given name, it only made sense that I would address him by his.

Wolfgang cleared his throat and Laetitia turned to him. "My apologies, *Graf* von Natterdorff."

"No matter," Wolfgang said politely, although he was looking from me to Crispin and back, not at Laetitia.

"We've just come from the theatre," I informed them both. "You never did have anything to do with Marie Tempest, did you, Crispin?"

He stared at me, appalled. "I hope you're joking, Darling."

Laetitia cleared her throat, and he made a face. "Philippa. I hope you're joking?"

"I wasn't," I said. "Why would you hope that, precisely?"

"Marie Tempest is older than my mother, Dar... Philippa. Older than yours, too. Older than Father. No, I've never had anything to do with Marie Tempest. How dare you?"

"I must be thinking of someone else," I said blandly. "Someone whose name and occupation is similar, perhaps."

Someone like Miss Millicent Tremayne—another actress, but a much younger and much less accomplished one—with whom Crispin had had a fling sometime within the past year or two.

Laetitia's lips flattened into a thin line at the reminder. Crispin looked resigned. "I'm not even going to ask how you know about that."

"The same way I know about all of them," I said. "Grimsby the valet's blackmail dossier."

He nodded. "You memorized it, I assume."

"I didn't have to. Your misdeeds are heroic enough that no active memorization was necessary. I was appalled, frankly. So many women, so many drunken nights, so much—mmph!"

"Yes, Darling. Thank you. Ow." He removed the hand that had covered my mouth and examined it ruefully. "Did you have to bite?"

"It seemed appropriate." I pursed my lips and sputtered a few times. "Really, St George. Crispin. Did you have to manhandle me?"

"Of course I didn't have to, Dar... Philippa. But as you said, it seemed appropriate."

"When is it appropriate to put your hand over a young woman's mouth to stop her from speaking?"

"When she's about to share your innermost secrets with

everyone in the Criterion Restaurant?" Crispin suggested, which I suppose was fair.

"Well, I wish you wouldn't do it. It's not as if your misdeeds aren't already known far and wide. Nor will they go away simply because I don't articulate them."

"Of course not, Dar... Philippa. But if you have any love for me at all, I beg you to refrain from rubbing them in my face at every opportunity."

"You know very well that I don't. But since you ask so nicely..."

"Thank you, Darling."

"Philippa," I said.

He nodded. "Of course. And on that note..." He offered his elbow to his fiancée, who latched on with a simper, "we shall let you get back to your supper."

Wolfgang clicked his heels together and inclined his head. "Viscount St George. Lady Laetitia."

"*Graf* von Natterdorff." Crispin smirked, and didn't bother with either the heels or the mock bow. "Darling. Tell Kit I said hello."

"I shall," I promised.

And then Laetitia towed him away, and Wolfgang pushed my chair under me so I was seated, before he walked around the table to seat himself. And there we were, in the same places we had been before the door opened, except now the atmosphere had changed.

"I hate her," I said.

Wolfgang looked at me.

"How dare she tell him that he can't call me what he's been calling me for the past ten years?" Or eight years, or perhaps only six years. But no matter: how dare she tell him that he couldn't call me whatever he wanted? It was none of her concern.

Except of course it was. She was engaged to him, and she didn't want her fiancé to call another woman darling, whether it was her name or not. Had I been engaged to Crispin—God forbid—I would probably feel the same way.

Wolfgang didn't say anything, and I added, "She's going to make him unhappy, the horrible cow."

Wolfgang cast a glance in their direction. They were behind me, so I didn't.

"He doesn't appear unhappy," he said.

"You don't know him as well as I do." Of course he was unhappy. Or if he wasn't yet, he would be. That's what happens when you propose to one person when you know full well you're in love with another.

Wolfgang made a dissenting noise. "She's a lovely woman. He has no reason to be unhappy."

"Surely happiness requires something more than just a lovely woman?"

He didn't answer, so perhaps he didn't think so. And that didn't bode well for the possibility of our union, did it? I wanted a husband who wanted *me*, after all, not someone who thought that I was interchangeable with just anyone else, lovely or not.

He must have discerned the direction of my thoughts, because he glanced behind me one more time before he asked, a bit stiffly, "Is he the reason, then?"

"Is he the reason for what?"

"The reason you won't say yes," Wolfgang said. He dug into his pocket and pulled out something small and glittery that he placed carefully in the middle of the tablecloth, equidistant from both of us. I stared at it the way I would have done a snake that had materialized in the middle of the table.

When I didn't speak, Wolfgang added, "I'm aware that you didn't accept my proposal of marriage, Philippa. I surprised you, and you didn't know what to say. We were in front of your friends and family, and I imagined you didn't want to cause a scene. I behaved as though you had said yes, but I knew very well that you hadn't."

I ducked my head. "I'm sorry. It's not that I didn't appreciate it..."

"Of course not." He flicked another glance over my shoulder. "So it is he?"

"No. Not at all." I had no idea why so many of my nearest and dearest seemed convinced that there was something going on between me and Crispin. "I abhor St George. Not only is he a horrible cad, but he's a horrible human being in general. I wouldn't marry him if he were the last man on earth."

Nor did my affections, such as they were, belong with anyone else. Except Christopher, I suppose, but that was entirely platonic. Not only do his feelings not swing my way, but we're first cousins, so any relationship between us would be ill-advised from the start.

"Then why—" Wolfgang began, and I cut him off.

"I like you, Wolfgang. It isn't that I don't. We could probably rub along together very well."

He nodded, so apparently he felt the same way. There was no declaration of love from him either, you'll notice, glittery ring notwithstanding.

"I'm just not certain that I want to go back to Germany."

He blinked.

"I have lived in England for twelve years now. I feel English, not German. I have no family left in Germany..."

"You have me," Wolfgang said, which only served to illustrate that he didn't understand what I was talking about.

I nodded. "Of course. But—"

But I would have to leave Aunt Roz and Uncle Herbert, and Francis and Constance, and most importantly, Christopher. And—yes—Crispin. Whom I would probably miss, too, if I never saw him again. I had a family and a life here in England, that had taken the place of the one I had had in Heidelberg. There was nothing left of that one, and much as I liked Wolfgang—and I did; I liked him very well indeed—he couldn't make up for everything else I would be losing. It would have been different had I been madly in love with him, but I wasn't.

He looked a bit as if he had bitten into a lemon, and it only got worse when I reached across the table and picked up the ring he had placed there and held it out to him. "I'm sorry I can't accept it. I should have explained up front. It's not you; please believe me when I say that. You're a wonderful man, and a great catch, and I enjoy spending time with you..."

He forced a smile, and I trailed off because he looked pained. When he didn't say anything, I did the only thing I could do, and pushed my chair back. "I think I should go home now."

"Philippa..."

I shook my head. "Thank you for supper, Wolfgang, and for the theatre. It was a wonderful evening. You know where to find me if you want to see me again."

He opened his mouth, and I added, before he could say anything, "I understand if you don't. But I would hate for this to be it. I have enjoyed getting to know you. And I'm not saying I couldn't learn to love you, or perhaps come around to your way of thinking. I don't know how much longer you're planning to stay in London..."

I trailed off for a second to give him the chance to jump in with an answer. When he didn't, I continued, "—but for as long as you're here, I would enjoy continuing to spend time with you. We're family, aren't we?"

It was a rhetorical question, of course—because yes, we were; at least according to Wolfgang—but he nodded, so I nodded back. "Good. Then don't be a stranger. You know where to find me. I'll see you again soon."

I didn't wait for him to speak, or to help me into my coat, I simply snagged it from the back of the chair beside me and threw it over my arm while I hustled for the street. The doorman swung the door open for me, and I burst into Piccadilly Circus in my evening dress with my coat flying like a flag behind me. My heels clicked rapid fire across the cobbles as I skirted the construction zone that would become the updated Piccadilly Circus tube stop, and headed across the street for the entrance to the current underground, dodging motorcars and pedestrians.

I don't normally travel by tube late at night. Christopher would no doubt get on me about it once he found out that I hadn't taken the time to flag down a Hackney for the ride home. But I felt pursued, for some reason. Not physically—there was no reason for Wolfgang to follow me, not after how we had left it in the restaurant, and it was even less likely that Crispin would abandon Laetitia at the supper table to trail me out of the Criterion—but I couldn't shake the need to get out of sight as quickly as possible. And it wasn't as if the underground was deserted at this time of night. Piccadilly Circus is one of the most traveled tube stations in all of London, hence the need for the upgrade.

When I ducked into the entrance and headed down the first flight of stairs towards the bottom, I was surrounded by people. Other women and men in evening kit, domestics making their way home at the end of the day, shopgirls and clerks, we all crowded each other down the stairs and into the curved, tiled tunnel with its white and green stripes.

To the lifts, a sign said, with an arrow pointing the way, and some of my fellow travelers veered off in that direction. I didn't; I continued along the tunnel towards the next flight of stairs.

There was still the need to keep moving, the knowledge—or fear—that if I stopped to wait for a lift, someone—I had no idea who; perhaps just the marriage I didn't want—would catch up to me.

It was ridiculous, and I was well aware of it. No one was chasing me. And if I were wrong, and Wolfgang was behind me, the worst thing that would happen was that I would have to talk to him again. And since I had left the door open to do that at some point anyway, it wasn't as if it would be a problem. But part of me was in flight mode, and I wanted to get out of the West End as quickly as possible. To put some distance between myself and the awkward conversation I had just had—in front of Laetitia and Crispin, no less; had they heard me, from where they were sitting?—and to get back to Christopher and safety and home. My heart was drumming in my chest as I turned onto the second staircase, with its arrow saying *To the trains.*

There was a smartly dressed young woman in front of me, in a brown cloche hat and a matching jacket. Beside me was a man in tweed and a Homburg. In front of the young lady was another man, this one in a black coat and bowler hat, and in front of him again was a young couple of the Bright variety: he in evening kit and she in a fur-trimmed coat similar to the one Laetitia had worn.

When something hit me in the middle back on the third step down, I took out the girl in the cloche hat. She took out the gentleman in the bowler, and he took out both parts of the young couple. And so it went, until we were all piled in a heap at the bottom of the stairs, groaning and whimpering about skinned knees and broken bones.

CHAPTER TWO

"I'M FINE," I said crossly, not for the first time.

It was an hour or so later, and I was seated on the sofa at home with my pyjama trousers pulled up above my knees to accommodate the plasters decorating both my kneecaps, and I was clutching a cup of tea in bandaged hands while I winced at the feeling of heat against my scraped palms.

"You don't look fine," Christopher answered, also not for the first time. He was sitting on the other end of the Chesterfield with a cuppa of his own, over which he assessed me critically. "You look like someone who was pitched down a staircase and who is fortunate to be alive."

Since that was the long and short of it, there wasn't a whole lot I could say in my defense, although I tried. "I'm hardly fortunate to be alive, Christopher. People don't die from falling down stairs."

"Certainly they do," Christopher said tartly. "You're lucky you had a soft landing."

I supposed that was true. My pretty ivory frock was dirty and torn along the hem, and I had scrapes and bruises on my palms and knees, but I had been lucky to get away with no further injuries. The fellow at the bottom of the pile—a young and skinny specimen in evening kit—had, as far as could be determined, not only ruined his trousers, but had also quite possibly broken his nose when he landed face-down on it. It had been bleeding copious amounts, and had looked a bit crooked when he stood up. He had been clutching his wrist, too, so there might have been something wrong with that, as well. And the bloke in the bowler hat had seemed to have trouble catching his breath, so either he might have broken a rib or his heart was acting up.

"How many people were involved?" Christopher wanted to know.

I thought about it. "There must have been ten or twelve of us. I didn't count specifically, but at least that many. Piccadilly Circus is always busy."

"Do you have any idea what started it?"

I didn't, and told him so. "I don't think we ever found out. All I know, is that someone hit me in the back. That's what everyone said, that someone hit them in the back and they fell."

"Someone must have started it," Christopher insisted, and then cut himself off to stare into the foyer as the buzzer beside the front door rang. "Now who could that be, at this time of night?"

I groaned. "If it's St George, please don't let him up. I don't want to have to deal with him on top of everything else. I'm in enough pain already."

"Crispin?" Christopher scooted towards the front of the sofa. "Why would it be Crispin?"

I made a face. "We saw him at the Criterion Restaurant after the theatre. Him and Laetitia."

"Did you really? You didn't mention that."

"We had other things to talk about," I said, indicating my

knees and hands. I hadn't told him about the ring I had turned down either, and that was a much bigger deal than Crispin's presence in the West End.

Christopher pushed to his feet as the bell from downstairs pealed again. "Sadly, I don't think he'll be put off, Pippa. But perhaps you'll get lucky and it won't be him."

Perhaps. Although if it wasn't Crispin, it was likely to be Wolfgang, and I wanted to see him even less. "I've changed my mind. If it's St George, you can let him up." Although it probably wasn't. Laetitia was no doubt keeping him busy. "If it's Wolfgang, lie and tell him I haven't gotten home yet."

"You'll be explaining that to me later," Christopher said, but he strode away from me as the buzzer sounded angrily for a third time. "Hold your horses, I'm coming. Hello?"

There was a faint quacking from the other end of the line, recognizable as the dulcet tones of Evans the doorman, ringing up from the lobby downstairs.

"Yes," Christopher said, "of course, Evans. Send him up."

He replaced the receiver and turned to me across the parquet floor of the foyer. "You were right. It's Crispin."

As if my evening hadn't been traumatic enough. "Listen, Christopher. Before he gets up here, there are a few things you ought to know…"

Christopher sighed. "Tell me later. I doubt he'll stay long."

"I have no idea why he'd be here at all," I said disagreeably. "We conversed at the restaurant. There is nothing left to say. He has been instructed to address me as Philippa, for your information. Just so you're prepared."

"He won't be doing that here," Christopher answered, and unlocked the door. "In front of Laetitia, I'm sure he'll try. In front of you and me, there's no point."

He pulled the door open. From down the hall, I could hear the rattling of the lift, and then the sound of the door gliding open followed by the skitter of the grille being drawn back from the opening. Then Crispin's footsteps. And his voice.

"Evening, Kit."

"Crispin."

Neither of them said anything more until Crispin had passed across the threshold into the flat and Christopher had divested him of his topper, gloves, and cane. "Tea?"

"If that's what you're having."

We were having tea, as it happened, although there was also a little something else in it, to help with the pain. I was getting nicely woozy and ready to sleep.

"Hello again, Darling," Crispin added as he walked into the sitting room, and then he stopped, dead in his tracks, when he got a look at me. "Dear me. Too much time on your knees worshipping Wolfie?"

"Don't be crude, Crispin," Christopher told him, with a shoulder check as he walked past on his way towards the kitchenette for another cup and saucer. "Pippa fell down the stairs to the tube."

"You took the tube home?" He perched on the chair across the table from me, hands in his lap. "At this time of night?"

"I was in a hurry," I said. "Not that it's any of your concern."

He gave my knees and hands one more intent look before moving his attention up to my face. "Yes, I saw you tearing out of the restaurant leaving Wolfie with the bill. What happened?"

"Wolfie—" I grimaced and corrected myself, "Wolfgang was always going to end up with the bill. He invited me."

"That's not what I'm asking, Darling, and you know it."

"Philippa," I said. "Remember your fiancée."

"I haven't forgotten. She isn't here, so I'll call you what I want. Focus, Darling." He snapped his fingers in my face. I scowled, and he added, "What happened with Wolfie?"

"Nothing happened. He offered me a ring, and I had to say no."

He looked blank. "You did?"

"I don't fancy moving to Germany with him."

"You don't?"

"Of course I don't," I said. "Whatever gave you the idea that I would want to leave England?"

"The fact that he proposed and you accepted," Crispin answered. "The fact that you seem to like him rather a lot. The fact that you're always—"

"Shut it, Crispin" Christopher interrupted from the doorway to the kitchenette, where he was leaning waiting for the water to boil again. Crispin looked offended, but obeyed.

"Go back, Pippa," Christopher added. "He offered you a ring?"

I nodded. "A very nice ring, too. A big emerald flanked by baguette-cut diamonds and small sapphires."

"And you turned it down." It wasn't a question. There was clearly no question-mark at the end of the sentence.

I shrugged, and Christopher arched his brows. Before he could speak again, however, Crispin opened his mouth.

"You broke off the engagement." There was an expression halfway between triumph and incredulity on his face.

"No," I said. I'd never actually been engaged in the first place. Not officially. There had been no ring, not until this evening, and no notice in the *London Times*, unlike when Crispin's engagement to Laetitia was announced. So it had never been official.

"But you don't want to go to Germany with him."

I shook my head. "I don't. There's still the possibility that he'll stay in London, of course. And if so, I'll reconsider the ring."

"It's none of your concern anyway, Crispin," Christopher reminded him as he placed a cup and saucer on the table in front of Crispin and lifted the brandy bottle questioningly. "You're engaged to the lovely Laetitia, remember? If you wanted a say in Pippa's future, you should have done something about it before now. Would you like a splash of this?"

"Yes, please." Crispin waited until the brandy was in the tea and the bottle back on the table, before he lifted the cup and saucer and took a sip. "Thank you, Kit."

"Don't mention it." Christopher sank down on the Chesterfield again, and crossed one elegant leg over the other. "To what do we owe the pleasure of your company?"

Crispin leaned back and made himself comfortable, as well. "Well, I saw Philippa tear out of the Criterion like the hounds of hell were on her heels, and I thought I'd see what the problem was."

"There's no problem," I said.

He twitched an eyebrow. "Just a broken engagement and a breach of promise suit."

"I already told you," I said severely, "there is no broken engagement and certainly no breach of promise. Not unless you've decided to call off your arrangement with Laetitia on the strength of it, and she decided to come after you."

He shook his head. "I wouldn't be so stupid."

No, of course he wouldn't.

"I wanted to go after you," he added, "to make certain you were all right, just so you know."

"Laetitia wouldn't let you," Christopher asked, "I suppose?"

Crispin made a face. "Of course not. By the time she had

made that clear, Wolfie had settled the bill and left, too. And at that point, there was no sense in me going."

"He left, as well, did he? Immediately after Pippa?"

Crispin nodded, and I said, "What are you on about now, Christopher?"

"Bear with me a moment, Pippa. Perhaps it was Wolfgang who followed you into the underground and shoved you down the stairs."

"Why would he do that?" I asked, but it was overshadowed by Crispin's louder outburst of, "Someone did that?"

"No," I said. "No one did that."

"Of course someone did do," Christopher answered, indicating my knees. "Otherwise you wouldn't look like you do."

I shook my head. "You're making it sound as if it were deliberate, and it wasn't."

"How do you know that it wasn't?"

Well, I didn't know that, of course. But at the same time, there was no reason to think it had been anything but an accident. There was certainly no reason to think it had been aimed at me in particular if it had been deliberate, and least of all any reason to suspect that Wolfgang had been behind it.

"It doesn't make any sense," I said. "First of all, he isn't mad. He'd have to be mad to try to murder me simply because I turned down his proposal of marriage."

Crispin made a sort of crowing sound, and I added, with a severe look at him, "Not that I did do. I left the door wide open for him to contact me again. He had no reason to want to get rid of me."

Crispin looked truculent. "He certainly didn't look pleased when he left."

"Did he look displeased enough to commit murder?" Christopher wanted to know, and Crispin shrugged.

"How am I supposed to know the answer to that, old bean?"

"We've met our share of murderers," Christopher pointed out, which was certainly true.

"And did you suspect any of them before the fact?"

I hadn't. Or rather, I hadn't suspected any of the guilty parties more than the non-guilty. I had suspected everyone equally, you might say, whether they'd turned out to be guilty or not. I had, in fact, been convinced of Crispin's guilt in at least one case. But in none of them had I done a particularly good job of figuring out whodunit before the denouement at the end.

"Wolfgang had no reason to want to murder me," I reiterated. "Normal people don't go around killing other people over hurt feelings."

His feelings were probably not even all that hurt. He liked me, yes. Admired me, according to what he had said during the original proposal. We got on well enough. I was young and respectable and reasonably attractive, and I could provide him with the heir and spare he no doubt required for the *Schloss* and the other entailments. But he had never professed love, or even deep devotion. His proposal of marriage had come across more as an offer for a friendly business partnership than anything else.

And that was perhaps the biggest reason why I couldn't consider going to Germany with him. Leave out the fact that I wasn't in love with him: had he at least been head over heels for me, I might have considered it. But I'm not upper-class enough to consider marriage solely in the light of a business transaction. My mother had left England and everything she knew to live with my commoner father in a flat on the Continent. How could I make that same trip for the promise of a *Schloss* and a comfortable lifestyle?

"You never know what might be going through someone else's head," Christopher admonished, and I turned to Crispin.

"Tell the truth, St George. Did he appear homicidal when he left?"

"I'm not certain that I would recognize homicidal if I saw it," Crispin demurred, and Christopher chuckled.

"Certainly you would, old chap. You've seen it in Pippa's eyes often enough."

There was no denying that. I had often been possessed of an overriding desire to strangle St George. Although I had never acted on it, so how homicidal was I, really?

"In that case I wouldn't say so, no," Crispin said. "He seemed fairly composed. More so than Philippa. She tore out of there like the hounds of hell were on her heels."

"Hyperbole," I said sourly.

He lifted a shoulder. "He left money for the bill and then strode out. It couldn't have been more than a minute later. Although he didn't appear to be chasing after you, if that's what you hoped for."

"I didn't hope for anything," I said. "Christopher was the one who suggested that Wolfgang would pitch me down the stairs to the underground because I hurt his feelings. Which I didn't do. If *I* had to pick a likely culprit—"

He rolled his eyes. "Let me guess. You think *I* did it."

"You did threaten to shove me down a staircase once."

His upper lip curled. "Did not!"

"Did so. It was at Sutherland Hall in April. Don't you remember? Aunt Roz asked you to escort me downstairs, and you said I'd better be polite to you, or your hand might slip."

Crispin flushed. "Perhaps I did, now that you mention it."

"Hah," I said triumphantly.

"I'll point out that I didn't actually do it, however, even

though you were extremely rude to me. And I didn't lay a hand on you tonight, either. You can ask Laetitia."

"No, thank you." The less I had to interact with the happy fiancée, the better pleased I was. "Besides, it wasn't you I was going to accuse. If I had to pick a likely culprit—"

"It would be Laetitia." He nodded. "And I don't blame you. She would be delighted to pitch you headfirst down a flight of stairs. But she didn't. She was sitting across from me when it happened."

As expected. "You'd swear to that, I suppose?"

He sniffed. "On a stack of Bibles if I had to. Although unless you decide to make something of it, I expect you to simply take my word for it. Neither of us left the restaurant until supper was over. By then, you must have made it home. And I had to take Laetitia back to Marsden House before I could come over. She was displeased that I declined to spend the night, too."

"Of course she was," Christopher said and leaned back languidly. "Hoping to get a head start on that heir and spare, no doubt."

Crispin shrugged, but his cheekbones darkened. "At any rate, she had no opportunity to attack you, Darling."

"Nor did anyone else," I said. "I'm sure it was simply an unfortunate accident. One person lost his or her footing and stumbled into another person, and so forth, until we were all in a heap."

Crispin eyed my bandaged hands. "How bad is it?"

"Not too bad. I took off a layer of skin, and I have some bruises. But I'm sure I'll be right as rain in a few days."

"That's my cue, then." He placed his cup and saucer on the table and made to push to his feet.

"You're not staying the night?" Christopher inquired, looking up at him.

"I don't think I'd better, old bean. My fiancée wouldn't approve."

No, of course she wouldn't. And that, more than anything, was why I told him, "Don't be a goose, St George. It's late, and it's cold, and what Laetitia doesn't know won't hurt her. You can take my bed. I was going to spend the night on the sofa anyway. My knees hurt and I don't feel like moving."

"You're more than welcome to stay," Christopher agreed. "It makes more sense for you to remain here than make the trip to Mayfair at this time of night. We'll get you up bright and early so you can make it over to Sutherland House before Laetitia comes looking for you."

Crispin glanced from Christopher to me and back. "If you're certain you don't mind."

"I don't mind in the least," I said. It wouldn't be the first time he'd spent the night in my bed—without me there, naturally—and at least this time we didn't have to worry about Uncle Harold showing up in the morning to make sure nothing inappropriate was going on. "Run down the street to the call box and ring up Sutherland House, so Rogers knows where you are."

He nodded. "Walk with me, Kit?"

They headed across the foyer and out the door together. I assumed they had something to discuss that they didn't want me to overhear, which was their prerogative. Instead of worrying about it, I took the opportunity to move the teacups and saucers to the kitchenette, and then drag myself down the hallway and into the lavatory to affect my evening ablutions before the boys came back. Makeup removed and teeth brushed, I dug out a pillow and a blanket and wandered stiff-legged back to the Chesterfield by the time they made their way back inside the flat.

"Everything taken care of?"

They both nodded. "Crispin moved the motorcar out of the way of the door," Christopher said, "and we rang up Rogers and let him know what was going on."

"You swore him to secrecy, I suppose? Made certain he won't ring up Sutherland Hall and inform Uncle Harold that St George is misbehaving?"

Crispin sniffed. "I'm not misbehaving. There's no one here that I can misbehave with. If I wanted to misbehave, I would have stayed at Marsden House."

"Of course you would have done." I gave him a patronizing smile, the equivalent of a pat on the head. "My apologies."

He growled. "I abhor you, Darling."

"The feeling is mutual," I told him. "And that's no way to speak to the person whose bed you'll be spending the night in. Now shoo. I want to sleep."

He scowled, but allowed himself to be pulled across the sitting room and into the hallway by Christopher. They both visited the loo, and then shut the doors to their respective rooms —or mine, in Crispin's case. I folded myself into the blanket and tried to ignore the stinging in my knees and hands.

It wasn't easy. The whole experience, from the conversation in the restaurant to hobbling through my own doorway with blood trickling down my legs, had been painful as well as unsettling.

There wasn't any reason to think that Christopher might be right about what had happened in the tube station, was there?

I couldn't believe that there was. Why would Wolfgang want to push me down a flight of stairs? We had parted on somewhat strained terms, admittedly, but I certainly hadn't said anything to upset him to enough of a degree that he would want to hurt me. And no one else wanted to hurt me, either, as far as I knew.

I wouldn't put it past Laetitia, certainly, should the opportunity arise and as long as she could do it without getting herself in trouble. And the same went for Uncle Harold, really. Neither of them liked me, and both would be happy if I were out of the way. The same was probably true for Laetitia's parents. Or her mother, at any rate. Maurice, Earl of Marsden, didn't seem like he disliked anyone in particular, me included, and while I was certain he was pleased about his daughter snagging the future Duke of Sutherland, he didn't seem as invested in it as the Countess Euphemia or Uncle Harold were. Not to the degree that he would hurt anyone over it.

Besides, I'm sure I would have recognized either one of them, had they come up behind me and given me a push down the stairs. As far as I could recall, the people behind me when I headed into the underground had been a middle-aged woman in a dark coat, and a young couple, a few years older than me, on their way home—or perhaps out—for the evening. None of them were people I had seen before, and they had all said the same thing after the accident: that someone had hit them in the back. No one in the pile had been anyone I had ever seen before, nor anyone I had any reason to think wished me harm.

No, it had to have been an unfortunate accident, or if it truly was deliberate, I wasn't the intended target, just an innocent bystander who found myself caught up in someone else's revenge. Perhaps the young lady in the cloche was the former flame of the gentleman behind me, with the other young lady in tow, and she had decided to bump into the older lady, so the older lady would bump into me, so I would bump into the girl with the cloche and bowl her over... all because the young gentleman had once admired the girl in the cloche.

It made as much sense, perhaps more, than that Wolfgang would follow me into the underground and try to shove me down the staircase.

I amused myself with coming up with similar scenarios for

the other people I remembered until the pain in my knees faded to a slow thrum and I was able to fall asleep.

IT FELT like two minutes later when the buzzer rang from downstairs, although when I blinked my eyes open, I could see the thin light of dawn creep in along the edges of the curtains. Elsewhere in the flat, there was the flailing of either Christopher or Crispin coming back to life at the sound of the noise, as well.

I dragged myself into a sitting position, and from there, up to standing. My knees protested, and I bit back a shrill noise before I hobbled around the Chesterfield and into the foyer, towards the front door and buzzer. "Evans?"

"Yes, Miss Darling," Evans's tinny voice said from downstairs. "I'm sorry to have woken you."

"Then why did you?" was at the tip of my tongue. Crispin would have said it. I bit the words back. "What's wrong?" I asked instead, since the commissionaire wouldn't drag us out of bed at the crack of dawn unless something had happened. "It isn't Uncle Harold, is it? The Duke of Sutherland?"

The last time Crispin had ended up in my bed overnight, Evans had let His Grace up to the flat the next morning with no warning. I had had no idea the Duke was even in London until I opened my front door and saw him standing there, looking like a silent movie version of a heavy father, all beetling brows and tight lips. Afterwards, I had told Evans in no uncertain terms to never do it again. If Uncle Harold wanted to come up, he could wait to be announced like anyone else. Being the Duke of Sutherland did not give him automatic access to Christopher's and my home.

"No, Miss Darling," Evans said. And seemed to reconsider the statement. "I don't believe so."

"He's not downstairs?"

"No, Miss Darling."

"Is someone else downstairs?"

"No, Miss Darling. Not any longer. A messenger arrived from Sutherland House with a message for Lord St George, but he has left again."

A messenger from Sutherland House? "Who? And what kind of message?"

"One of the footmen," Evans said, "I suppose. As for the message, Lord St George is to come to Mayfair as quickly as he can make it."

"At this time of the morning?" Under normal circumstances, this was closer to Crispin's bedtime than when he usually gets up. He's much more night owl than early bird, I'm afraid. What on earth was so important that Rogers wanted to drag him out of bed at— "What time is it, Evans?"

It was half four, which at least was morning rather than the middle of the night.

"Did the messenger happen to mention what was wrong?" I inquired. Perhaps Uncle Harold truly was on his way up to Town, and Rogers was trying to avoid the scene that would ensue if the Duke arrived at Sutherland House and Crispin wasn't there.

"A robbery," Evans said.

"A—" I didn't manage to get the rest of it out. The next sentence, "Thank you, Evans," came out garbled, as well.

"Thank you, Miss Darling."

Evans disconnected. I stared at the inside of the door for a few seconds, blinking, before I gathered myself together and plunged down the hallway as quickly as my stiff knees would allow.

CHAPTER THREE

WE MADE it to Sutherland House before the sun rose. Crispin's Hispano-Suiza racing car lived up to its reputation by taking the corners between the Essex House Mansions and Mayfair on two wheels, but we got there without being arrested for reckless motoring, and without picking up the Metropolitan Police Department's Flying Bedstead along the way. We were still on our own when Crispin pulled to a stop under the portico outside Sutherland House with a squeal of brakes, and slammed the gear shift into park. The door to the townhouse flew open, and Laetitia streaked through and into Crispin's arms.

"Darling!"

He caught her, but just barely. She was already hanging around his neck by the time his arms came up to encircle her. "Laetitia?" His voice was muffled in the fur collar of her coat. "What are you doing here?"

"Darling!" She snuffled into his neck. "A robbery! It was terrifying."

On the other side of the Hispano-Suiza, Christopher let

himself out of the passenger seat with an eyeroll, and then pulled the seat forward so I could clamber out. I did it with less than my customary grace, given the stiffness of my knees. In fact, I needed a hand to haul myself out of the motorcar onto the cobbles.

"Oh," Laetitia said when she caught sight of me—or of us, I suppose I should say, although it was probably just me. She doesn't have much of a problem with Christopher. Her tone indicated deep disappointment.

Crispin glanced over his shoulder. "Right. I spent the night with Kit and Pippa."

Laetitia looked betrayed. I thought about mentioning whose bed he had spent the night in—nothing wrong with speaking the truth, after all—but before I could, I noticed something that drove the inclination right out of my mind. "What happened to your engagement ring?"

She had stopped clutching at Crispin now, the better to impress upon him her level of disappointment, no doubt, but her left hand was still splayed on his shoulder, and the ring finger was bare.

"What happened to yours?" Laetitia shot back.

I eyed my ringless finger. "I turned it down. Although if you're wondering about these—" I displayed my bandaged palms, "I fell down the staircase to the underground on my way home from Piccadilly last night."

"I..." She stopped, and turned to Crispin, teeth in her bottom lip. "Darling, I'm so sorry. There was a robbery, and..."

Crispin cut her off with a quick and concerned, "Are you all right?"

From what Evans had said earlier, I had gotten the impression that the robbery had been at Sutherland House, but it appeared as if it had been Marsden House that had been violated, and Laetitia had made her way here for comfort and companionship, only to find Crispin gone. It was pretty typical, really. Everything that could go wrong, did go wrong.

"Did you call the police?" Christopher wanted to know.

Laetitia flicked him a glance. "Thompson did."

The butler, one presumed. "Did they come?"

"I don't know," Laetitia said. "I left."

She turned back to Crispin. He glanced at Christopher and me—it was obvious to all three of us what had to happen—before turning back to the Hispano-Suiza. "Let's go."

"We'll take the backseat," Christopher said, and opened the motorcar's door again with a nod to me.

"But—" Laetitia blinked. "I want to stay with you."

"We're all going," Crispin assured her, as he escorted her around the H6 to the passenger seat. Meanwhile, Christopher handed me into the backseat and crawled in behind me.

"Tom?" I asked him, *sotto voce*, as Crispin busied himself with getting his fiancée situated in the front of the H6.

Christopher shook his head. "I don't know, Pippa. It's possible. He mentioned a jewelry theft in Mayfair a few months ago, during that time when Flossie Schlomsky was missing, if you recall..."

Tom—Detective Sergeant Thomas Gardiner with Scotland Yard—was my cousin Robbie's best friend at Eton, and after Robbie died in France, Tom transferred that loyalty onto Robbie's little brother, and to a degree onto his elder one, although Francis was less in need of rescuing than Christopher was.

I wasn't quite sure how Tom and Christopher had ended up meeting one another again. But Christopher and I had only been in London for a few months the first time I saw Tom in the foyer of our flat, having a low-voiced but intense disagreement with Christopher about the latter's penchant for attending drag balls and the former's need to keep him from being arrested for doing so. I ought perhaps to find out how it had happened, although if I had to guess, I would say that Tom had most likely recognized Christopher during one of the raids —quite an accomplishment on his part if so, because Christopher in his guise of Kitty Dupree looks very little like himself and quite a lot more like Laetitia Marsden, as it happens.

At any rate, Tom had become a regular part of our lives over the past six or seven months. Christopher kept him busy with rushing to the rescue every time Christopher found himself in trouble, be it another drag ball, another murder investigation, or that time he drank the cocktail meant for me, and ended up sleeping for several days.

"What are you whispering about back there?" Crispin wanted to know as he made himself comfortable behind the wheel of the H6. He pulled on his driving gloves and cranked the key over in the ignition.

"Tom," I told him over the sound of the motor.

He glanced at me over his shoulder. "Is he involved in this?"

"We think it's possible. There was a jewelry theft in Mayfair in August that he investigated. If there's a connection..."

I let the sentence trail off, since his guess was as good as mine.

"There was a robbery last week, as well," Laetitia volunteered, and we both—we all, Christopher included—turned to look at her.

"How do you know?" Crispin wanted to know.

Laetitia looked guilty. "It was at the Cummingses. I didn't mention it because..."

Because Lady Violet Cummings had been an old flame of Crispin's, and his current fiancée hadn't wanted to bring her up.

Crispin didn't say anything, but Christopher and I exchanged a look that said it all. "What happened?" he wanted to know.

Laetitia sniffed. "The same thing that happened to me. I was asleep. I had taken the ring off because I didn't want anything to happen to it..."

That was certainly understandable. The Sutherland engagement ring is obscenely large and gaudy. One could easily take out someone's eye with it. Laetitia could have taken out her own, had she been careless in her sleep. Had it been mine, I would have taken it off to go to bed, as well.

"It was on the makeup table," Laetitia added, wretchedly, "along with the earrings and the string of pearls I wore last night."

The earrings were also part of the Sutherland parure, and correspondingly ostentatious and gaudy. The diamonds were enormous, and would undoubtedly fetch a pretty penny for whoever had stolen them. And while long strands of pearls are everywhere these days, this strand was probably made from real pearls, instead of the kind of cheap costume jewelry that us non-titled girls have to settle for.

"What happened?" Crispin inquired, his voice soft and sympathetic. I don't know what amount of effort it took—perhaps it required none at all. It seemed as if the loss of the Sutherland diamonds was of less consequence to him than his concern about his fiancée's wellbeing.

Which would have made sense if he were in love with his fiancée, but since I knew that he wasn't...

Laetitia sniffed. "I was asleep. I didn't hear the door open. He was very quiet. It wasn't until he was at the toilet table, and something—perhaps the pearls—knocked into something, perhaps a perfume bottle..."

She took a hitching breath and tried again. "I heard a click.

When I turned to look, someone was standing beside my toilet table. I thought at first that it was Geoffrey, but of course..."

Yes, of course. There was no need to spell it out. Lord Geoffrey Marsden, Laetitia's brother, was in prison, waiting for the next session of the Western Circuit of the Assizes, to be tried for his involvement in the death of the Honorable Cecily Fletcher. He hadn't killed her—someone else had been responsible for that—but Geoffrey had played his part, and had to answer for it. Buying an abortifacient with the intent of administering it is still a crime, even if the unborn child was the only one he intended to kill.

So no, this hadn't been Geoffrey. Although it was possible that the thief had looked like him.

Laetitia shuddered when I asked for details. "He was tall, dressed all in black. He had a scarf tied over his nose and mouth."

"So you wouldn't recognize him."

She shook her head. "I only got a glimpse."

"Did he run when he realized you were awake?"

I pictured the scene, like something out of a silent film: Laetitia sitting upright in bed, in a drippy negligee of the type I had seen her wear during other weekend parties, screaming her head off, while the servants appeared from all corners, dressed in their pyjamas and carrying meat cleavers and fireplace pokers with which to overcome the burglar.

"No," Laetitia said, and her flush was obvious even in the low light before dawn. "I hid. Under the covers."

I blinked. So did Christopher. Crispin might have done, too, although I couldn't tell from looking at the back of his neck.

I had no idea what to say. On the one hand, it was rather cowardly on her part, wasn't it? The thief was stealing her jewelry, including the Sutherland engagement ring. The least she could have done was put up a fuss, it seemed. I would have liked to think that I'd be out of bed and on the attack as soon as I saw him, screaming like a banshee the whole time.

On the other hand, she had been taken by surprise, and she had undoubtedly felt at a disadvantage, in bed in her night-things. Hiding might have been the safest course of action, and perhaps a natural inclination, at least for some. I had never found myself in that position, so what did I know? Perhaps I would have done the same thing.

"You must have been terrified," Christopher said sympathetically.

Laetitia sniffled, and nodded.

"What happened then?" I wanted to know. My understanding only extended so far, and I'm at any rate less inclined to coddle people than Christopher is. "Did he realize that you had seen him?"

She hesitated. "I don't know. I pulled the counterpane over my head and waited. I was afraid that he would come over to the bed and—"

She made a hiccoughing little sob, and Crispin slanted her a look from behind the wheel, "—and touch me."

There was silence in the motorcar for a moment while we all contemplated this confession, and yes, I'll admit it, the thought of it sent a chill down my spine. Perhaps I ought to be a bit more empathetic to her actions. It must have been terrifying to lie there and wait for the blankets to be pulled away and then —God knows what else.

"And did he do?" Crispin asked. His voice was tightly controlled.

Laetitia glanced at him, bottom lip quivering. She shook her head. "I waited until I heard the front door close. When I was certain he was gone, I called for Thompson."

That was a bit less understandable, and not really admirable at all. She might at least have called out as soon as she heard his footsteps on the stairs, once he was far enough away that he couldn't have come back before she had a chance to lock the door against him, but before he was outside in the street and away.

It wasn't my place to say anything about it, however, and by then we had reached Marsden House anyway. I put it out of my mind. Crispin pulled the Hispano-Suiza to a stop under the portico outside the front door and turned off the motor. Blessed silence descended.

Like Sutherland House, the Marsden family's Town residence was a Georgian monstrosity of three stories or so that took up quite a large part of a city block just around the corner from Park Lane. And like Sutherland House, it looked staid and conservative. Or it would have done, were it not for the fact that every light in the house was on, and that the front door stood wide open. At the bottom of the steps stood what was easily recognizable as a police issue Crossley Tender.

A tall, rather handsome individual of around fifty years of age stood in the open door. "Miss Laetitia." He inclined his head. "You're back. And with Lord St George."

He bowed to Crispin, as well.

"Hullo, Thompson," the latter said blithely, while Laetitia nodded.

"Yes, Thompson. I went to fetch Lord St George."

"The police are here," Christopher commented, and Thompson turned to inspect him. It took him but a second to peg Christopher as being related to Crispin—they look enough alike to be brothers—and another to figure out exactly who he was.

"Yes, sir, Mr. Astley. They arrived a few minutes ago."

"May we come in?"

Thompson glanced at Laetitia, who nodded.

"Of course, Mr. Astley."

Thompson stood aside. Crispin presented Laetitia with his elbow, and she latched on and swept past Thompson into the house, quite as if they were entering some ballroom somewhere after being announced as the guests of honor. Christopher watched, and then turned to me with a smirk as he presented his own elbow. I placed my fingers on his arm in the same manner Laetitia had done, and we breezed past Thompson with our noses in the air. Christopher winked at the butler on his way past. "Thank you, Thompson."

"Of course, Mr. Astley."

Thompson shut the door behind us.

The foyer was tall and lovely, with a checkerboard marble floor and a two-story ceiling. To the left and right were hallways reaching into the back of the house. Sutherland House was set up in a similar manner, and I assumed that the formal rooms were down one corridor while the servants quarters and kitchen were down the other. The family's bedrooms and sitting-out room would be upstairs, along with the guest rooms.

That was also from whence the sounds were coming. And when I say sounds, I mean footsteps and voices, at least one of them recognizable.

"Tom," Christopher said.

I nodded. "I assume the police are upstairs in Lady Laetitia's room, Thompson?"

"Yes, Miss Darling," Thompson said. I hadn't been introduced, of course, nor had I ever been here before, but he must know the Astley family tree, and its assorted hangers-on, well enough to have placed me.

Or perhaps Laetitia had mentioned me. I wouldn't put it past her to grouse about me to the servants; she had certainly done so to her mother, who had taken against me long before we'd been privileged to meet face to face.

"Would you mind if we went upstairs?" I inquired politely.

Thompson hesitated. Perhaps he was unused to being asked for permission, or perhaps he simply didn't want us wandering anywhere unsupervised. He slanted a look at Laetitia, but she had pulled Crispin into a room to the right of the foyer—somewhere with a bar cart, at a guess—and was of no help.

"We'll only be a minute," Christopher said persuasively. "We just want to say hello to Detective Sergeant Gardiner."

"Of course, Mr. Astley." Thompson didn't sound certain, but he did, at least, not try to stop us.

"It really will only be a minute," I told him, as Christopher tugged me towards the staircase. "Could we have some tea for when we come back down, Thompson? It's a bit early for spirits."

"Of course, Miss Darling." Thompson moved towards the hallway on the left, washing his hands of us as we headed up the stairs.

The first floor consisted of a long hallway with doors on both sides, and at the end, another, less ostentatious staircase up to the second floor, where there were more servants' quarters and perhaps a nursery and such. We didn't bother with that. A door stood open halfway along the hallway, whence the voices came. We made our way there and peered inside.

I hadn't taken the opportunity to look at Laetitia's bedchamber at Marsden Manor when we'd been in Dorset last month. I had, however, seen Constance's room, which was lovely, and Christopher's and Francis's shared room, which was also lovely, and my room, and Cecily Fletcher's room, and Dominic Rivers's room—all of which were lovely, as well. It came as no surprise that this bedroom was lovely, and approximately twice the size of my bedroom in the mansion flat at the Essex House.

Laetitia had spent the night, what there was of it, in an

intricately carved four-poster with gauzy hangings and a pale pink counterpane over what was undoubtedly a goose-feather mattress. There were Persian rugs on the floors, and landscapes in gold frames on the walls, and a matching toilet table—matching the bed, I mean—that also matched a marble-topped tallboy and armoire in the corner. Last night's black evening gown was thrown negligently over the back of the toilet table chair, while a pair of lovely T-strap shoes lay on their sides below. The matching silk stockings lay in wadded-up balls beside them.

Two men were inside the room: one compact and muscular, with brown, wavy hair and a handsome face, the other taller and thinner, with fair hair and a rabbity chin.

"Tom," Christopher breathed, while I said, a bit more politely, "Detective Sergeant Finchley. How nice to see you again."

Finchley—the blond—nodded. "Morning, Miss Darling. Mr. Astley."

"Kit," Tom said. "Pippa. What are you two doing here?"

"We came with Crispin and Laetitia," Christopher said, looking around the room.

"The butler said that Lady Laetitia decamped for Sutherland House."

I nodded. "But St George spent the night with us. When Rogers sent one of the footmen to the Essex House Mansions, he didn't make it clear that the burglary had taken place here and not at home. We assumed it had been at Sutherland House, so we thought that St George might need the moral support."

The look that Tom gave me was jaundiced. He knew as well as I did that I rarely go out of my way to provide Crispin with support in any way, shape, or form. In this case, it had been curiosity as much as anything else that had caused me to accompany him, and Tom knew it.

Christopher, of course, loves his cousin. And I love Christopher, so I had gone along for that reason, as well.

"Laetitia said there had been a burglar," I added brightly, as I eyed the toiletries table.

Tom nodded. "That's what the butler said. Lady Laetitia is downstairs?"

"We brought her back with us," I confirmed. "I have no idea why she thought it made sense to leave the house before you got here. It's not as if Crispin could do anything about the situation whatsoever, even if he had been at Sutherland House."

"Shock?" Detective Sergeant Finchley suggested, and I snorted.

"An excuse to check up on him and make certain that he was snug in his bed and not out gallivanting, more like."

"She must have been disappointed, then," Tom said dryly. "I'll go talk to her, Finch."

Finchley nodded. "Better you than me. You're familiar with this group. I'll finish up here."

"Is it just the two of you?" I asked, as Tom made his way towards the door. Christopher followed him, naturally, and I was alone with Finchley.

He nodded. "No fatality this time, so no need for Doctor Curtis. And we thought we'd let the Chief Inspector sleep for a few more hours."

He might as well do. There was nothing he could do here that Tom and Ian Finchley couldn't do without his presence. They were both, if not seasoned veterans, at least experienced hands at this, and if Laetitia was right and the Cummingses had been burgled too, this was at least the third scene of its kind in a few months.

"Any fingerprints?" I inquired. That's Ian Finchley's

specialty on CID Arthur Pendennis's team. Tom is the crime scene photographer.

Finchley shrugged. "Plenty of them. Miss Marsden's, I assume. The maid's. Nothing that looks like a man's hand."

After a moment he added, "Every criminal these days has the good sense to wear gloves."

"Laetitia told us that there had been another jewelry theft a couple of weeks ago. At the Cummingses. And Tom told us that there had been one in August, as well. While Flossie Schlomsky was missing, do you recall?"

"There have been more than those two," Finchley said. "Or three, now. There's been a burglary in Mayfair or Kensington almost every weekend for the past month. If not on Friday night, then Saturday."

"Interesting," I said. "How many altogether? Burglaries, that is?"

Finchley didn't have to think about it. "This is number five. I can't tell you their names—these are people whose names you would recognize if I did do—but unfortunately, that information is confidential."

Of course it was. "That's all right," I said. "If I wanted to find out, I'm sure I could."

Aunt Roz used to sell gossip to the tabloids, so I'm sure she has a solid pipeline—not that I've ever tapped it—and of course there's Crispin, who knows everyone who's anyone in London society.

Ian Finchley made a face. "Don't get involved in this, Miss Darling. Just because this character hasn't hurt anyone yet, doesn't mean that he wouldn't take that step if he felt it necessary."

"I didn't plan to threaten anyone," I said lightly. "Besides, I'm not likely to ever come across him, am I? I don't own anything worth stealing—unlike Laetitia, I don't have an engagement ring, and my pearls are paste—and besides, I live with Christopher, with Evans downstairs in the lobby. No one is likely to try to make it inside my flat to raid my jewelry box."

"Miss Marsden was surrounded by servants," Finchley pointed out, "and Cummings House had a full contingent of staff as well. It didn't matter."

No, I suppose it hadn't done.

"Out of curiosity," I asked, "what did he get away with in the Cummings robbery? Here, Laetitia startled him by waking up, it seems, so he only got away with the few pieces on her toilet table. Did he do better at the Cummings's?"

Finchley hesitated.

"You can tell me," I said persuasively. "Laetitia or Crispin probably know the answer already, and will tell me if I ask. And it's not as if I'm going to talk to anyone else about it."

Finchley relented, as I figured he would. "In the Cummings household, the jewelry was all kept in a safe in the study. The thief got away with all of it, as well as quite a bit of money. Nobody even realized he had been there until hours later, the next time they opened the safe and realized it was all gone."

"Ouch."

Finchley nodded. "On the positive side, nobody was frightened out of their wits that time. Back in August, Lady Latimer's butler died when Latimer House played host to this character."

My eyes widened. "That's terrible. What happened?"

Had the burglar committed murder? If so, Laetitia truly was lucky to get away with her life.

"Heart attack," Finchley said. "He was nearly as old as Lady Latimer, who's eighty if she's a day—"

I nodded, I was familiar with Lady Latimer.

"—and he must have come upon the chap either coming or

going. Or so we assume. Lady L found him in a heap in the foyer when she came home from supper."

"How awful."

Finchley agreed. "There were no marks on him, so we don't think it was deliberate, but it's still death during the execution of another crime. But at least this bloke doesn't seem inclined to violence unless it's absolutely necessary. Hopefully that won't change."

Hopefully so. "Do you think this will happen again?"

"No reason for him to stop now," Finchley said cynically. And added, "And now, if you don't mind, Miss Darling, I should get on with my job."

"Of course." I took myself off towards the door. "I'll be downstairs with the others. It was nice to see you again, Detective Sergeant."

"You, as well, Miss Darling," Finchley said politely. He had already turned back towards the toilet table and the fingerprint powder. I headed back down the stairs to where the others were gathered.

CHAPTER FOUR

THEY WERE CLUSTERED around a small table in the
parlor when I came down the stairs. And instead of the tea I
had requested, someone must have asked for coffee, because
that's what everyone was drinking. I suspected that at least
Laetitia's beverage was laced with something stronger, even if
the others' probably weren't.

Tom and Christopher were sitting on one side of the table,
with Laetitia and Crispin on the other. She was plastered to his
side. There was an empty cup and saucer on one of the short
sides, and I headed for that. Perhaps it would fall to me to
referee.

"Tea or coffee?" Christopher asked as I made myself
comfortable in the green velvet chair.

"Tea, if you don't mind. Thank you."

Tom watched as Christopher poured and doctored a cup,
and then handed it to me. I balanced it awkwardly in my
bandaged hands.

"What happened to you?" he wanted to know.

"I fell down a flight of stairs at the underground last night." I leaned back and attempted to cross one knee over the other, and remembered, only when it was too late, why that was a bad idea. Instead, I took a sip of the genial beverage and flapped a hand. "Don't let me interrupt the conversation."

Tom watched for a moment, but he didn't comment, just turned back to Laetitia. "So you don't know what woke you. But when you opened your eyes, he was already in the room with you."

Laetitia shuddered delicately. "Yes. He stood beside the toiletries table. I think he had the ring, or perhaps the earrings, in his hands. Something that sparkled."

"You may have heard him pick it up?" Tom suggested, and Laetitia nodded. "Had you closed the door when you went to bed? Do you know how he made it into the house?"

Laetitia shook her head. "The windows in my room were shut, so I know he didn't come in that way. The door to the hallway was closed but unlocked. He must have come from there."

Tom nodded. He scribbled a few words in the little notebook that was open on his knee. "At what time did you come home last night?"

Laetitia looked at Crispin. He looked back at her.

"I took the underground home," I said into the silence. "When I got to the flat, it was after eleven. St George showed up perhaps thirty minutes later."

Christopher nodded, his eyes limpid, even as he smothered a smirk. "I agree with Pippa. It was close to midnight when Crispin arrived."

"You must have dropped Lady Laetitia off around eleven-thirty, then, St George? Unless you stopped somewhere on the way to the Essex House Mansions? No? What did you do when you arrived home, Lady Laetitia?"

"Thompson opened the door," Laetitia said. "I said good-night and went up to my room. The maid was already in bed—I thought I would be home later than I was, so I had told her not to wait up for me..."

She directed a look of deep disappointment Crispin's way. He pretended not to notice.

"I undressed on my own and went to bed. I left my frock on the chair and my jewelry on the toilet table for the maid to deal with tomorrow morning. This morning now."

Tom took the statement down, dutifully. "Is there a clock in your room, Lady Laetitia? No? How long would you say that you had been asleep when you were woken up?"

Laetitia shook her head in a very desultory, helpless fashion.

"Evans rang up our flat at half four," I contributed, "but I don't know how long it would have taken the footman to make it from Sutherland House to Bloomsbury after Lady Laetitia arrived. I suppose that depends on how upset she was."

The look she sent me could have peeled the skin from my bones, and her voice was crisp when she told Tom, "It was perhaps forty-five minutes from the time I was woken up until I made it to Sutherland House and discovered that Crispin wasn't there."

Disappointment and blame curdled around every syllable of those last few words. Crispin looked like he had taken an arrow to the heart, or at least to the belly.

"Buck up, St George," I told him unkindly. "All is well that ends well. Your fiancée is fine, and now you can buy her a prettier engagement ring than that monstrosity that's been passed down in the family for the past five centuries."

"The Sutherland engagement ring is an irreplaceable heirloom that dates from 1682, I'll have you know, Darling."

Laetitia looked at him, and he added, "Philippa."

"I'm well aware of it," I said, "Crispin."

We both wrinkled our noses and I added, "I've seen it in half the portraits in the portrait gallery at Sutherland Hall. And it's an ugly, heavy thing. I'm certain Laetitia would prefer something less likely to give her muscle strain every time she lifts her hand."

Crispin twitched a brow, first at her and then back at me. "It doesn't matter now, does it? It's gone, along with the matching earrings."

Laetitia looked wretched. "I'm sorry, darling."

"It's not your fault," Crispin told her. "Philippa is simply being her usual ray of sunshine."

He patted her hand, right where the engagement ring would have been, had it still been on her finger. I smirked and turned to Tom. "Sorry to take over the conversation."

"No matter." He barely spared me a glance. "So, Lady Laetitia, it is your statement that the break-in might have happened around three or three-thirty."

Laetitia nodded. "I'm sorry I can't tell you more specifically."

"Very few people can," Tom said calmly, "when they're woken up in the middle of the night. I'm surprised this chap was here so late, frankly. He usually visits in the evening, when the occupants are out to supper and the staff is busy."

Neither one of us said anything, and he added, "Would you tell me about the staff, Lady Laetitia?"

She did, a bit desultorily. Perhaps she wasn't certain who was who at the Marsdens' London house. I wasn't surprised. Laetitia wasn't the type to notice the servants.

"Do you know whether anything else was taken?" Tom wanted to know, and Laetitia admitted, a bit shame-facedly, that she hadn't stopped to check. Her only concern had been to get to Crispin.

He looked a bit uncomfortable at that admission, and who could blame him? The last thing he wanted was a wife who was a limpet. I had always known that it would be a bad idea to propose to Laetitia. She was obsessed enough with him that at this point, there was nothing at all he could do that would make her relinquish her hold.

"Was anything else taken at the other burglaries?" I wanted to know. "Other than jewelry and money, I mean?"

"A few small things," Tom said. "An enameled snuff box, a gold cigarette case, other trinkets of that sort... small, valuable things that would fit easily into someone's pockets."

Yes, of course. Our burglar probably wasn't walking around with a suitcase.

Unless, of course, he was.

But no, Laetitia shook her head when Tom inquired. "I didn't notice anything like that. All I saw was that he was holding my engagement ring."

"Finch said that there have been five burglaries in all," I said. "Has anyone else seen this character?"

Tom shook his head. "So far, the burglaries have all taken place while the houses were empty—of anyone but the servants, that is—or while the occupants were asleep. He's not inviting attention."

"But the one time someone noticed him—Lady Latimer's butler—he ended up dead."

Laetitia squeaked and turned pale. "Well done, Darling," Crispin told me, in a tone that indicated the opposite of approbation.

I smirked. "Sorry, Laetitia. I didn't mean to imply that you were in any danger."

Laetitia turned enormous, fear-filled eyes on Tom. "Detective Gardiner?"

"Detective Sergeant," Christopher muttered.

Tom flicked him a look but didn't respond. "Pippa is winding you up," he told Laetitia instead.

"So it isn't true?"

"It's true that Lady Latimer's butler is dead—"

Laetitia squeaked again, and grabbed for Crispin's hand.

"—but it was not something that the burglar did. The chap's heart gave out. He was an old man, and the stress was too much for him."

"So you don't think that he'll come after Laetitia because she saw him," Crispin said, patting Laetitia's hand.

Tom opened his mouth, but I got there before him.

"If that was going to happen, I'm sure it would have happened already. He was up there alone with her, after all. There was no one to stop him if he wanted to strangle her."

Laetitia whimpered.

"Thank you, Pippa," Tom said, in much the same tone that Crispin had employed earlier. "Let me handle this, please."

"Of course. Be my guest." I made a gracious gesture to cede the floor to him.

"Lady Laetitia." He turned towards her. "Pippa's right."

Hah, I thought. Christopher glanced at me and smirked. I smirked back. Crispin, meanwhile, rolled his eyes hard enough that he practically gave himself whiplash.

"If this bloke had a problem with you seeing him," Tom continued, "or he were inclined to violence, it would likely have happened before now."

Laetitia nodded and sniffed. She was still clinging to Crispin's hand while she used his handkerchief to dab at her cheeks.

"Now, you say you didn't see him well, that he was wearing something over his nose and mouth, but every little bit helps. For instance, you would definitely say that the burglar was a man, wouldn't you? No question about that?"

Laetitia shook her head. "Certainly not. And dressed in black with a scarf over his face and head. I couldn't see his face aside from his eyes, or his hair."

"Height?" Tom asked. "Weight? Age?"

"Tallish?" Laetitia ventured, although she didn't sound certain. "Youngish? But it was only a glimpse. I..." She flushed, "I hid before I could notice much."

"That was probably the safest thing you could do," Tom told her, kindly. "We'll check with the neighbors, in case anyone else saw him arrive or depart. If you could do me the courtesy of having a look around, to see whether you can spot anything else that might be missing? You would know where the small and valuable objects are, I assume."

Laetitia nodded.

"Finchley started fingerprinting Laetitia's toiletries table," I told Tom. "Is there anything you want us to do that would help you?"

He eyed me for a moment in silence. "I don't suppose you know anything about any of this?"

"Nothing whatsoever," I said cheerfully. "You told Christopher and me about the burglary in Mayfair in August. That would have been at Lady Latimer's, I assume. Laetitia told us about the Cummingses being robbed. Finchley said there have been five burglaries altogether, but he wouldn't tell me who the other victims are. He said I would probably recognize the names if he did do, though. Based on that, they're clearly people of quality, although that goes without saying, really. If you're going to steal, you go where the money is."

Or in this case, the jewelry.

Tom nodded. "You and Lady Violet Cummings are friends, aren't you? She was there at your engagement party."

This was directed at Laetitia, not me. Lady Violet and I are certainly not friends. Nor are Lady Violet and Laetitia.

Friendly acquaintances, perhaps, in the way that all Bright Young Things are friendly acquaintances, but the only reason that Laetitia had invited Violet Cummings to Marsden Manor for the party, was that she had wanted to rub her engagement to Crispin in Violet's face.

Laetitia nodded, if reluctantly.

"Do you also know Lady Latimer?"

"I think my mother does," Laetitia said. "Or her mother did. Lady Latimer is *old*."

Tom's lips twitched, but instead of saying anything else, he turned to Christopher and me. "You two should go home. You know nothing about this, and can't be of any more help to me."

I'm sure I looked mutinous. I had hoped he would ask about the other victims of the burglaries, and now I had missed out on that knowledge. Christopher looked reluctant—he would much rather be where Tom was, and in a house this size, it wasn't as if we'd be in the way—but he nodded.

Tom turned to Crispin. "I don't need you to stay any longer either, although I would like to ask your fiancée a few more questions in private. You're welcome to stay for that, and then, if you wouldn't mind, if you would take Kit and Pippa home?"

Crispin nodded. "Of course."

He glanced at Laetitia, who looked at him with huge, limpid eyes. Crispin turned back to Tom. "After your questions, would it be acceptable if I took Laetitia back to Dorset? We didn't come prepared for a long stay, and I don't think there's much more she can tell you."

Tom nodded. "I don't see why not. We can reach you by telephone if we have any more questions."

He wiggled his fingers at Christopher and myself. "Out you go. Wait by the motorcar. Your cousin will be there to take you home in a minute."

"Don't do us any favors," I said sourly, because my knees hurt getting up, and Crispin gave me a look.

"You're as stiff-legged as a wooden board, Darling."

Laetitia cleared her throat, and he added, "Philippa. The less you walk and irritate those scabs, the sooner they'll heal."

"Yes," Tom cut in, "tell me what happened to you again, Pippa?"

"I fell down the stairs to the Piccadilly Circus tube stop," I said, as I moved carefully towards the foyer, with Christopher's arm for support. "After supper and the theatre last night. There was nothing sinister about it, everyone's suspicions to the contrary. Someone stumbled and took out the rest of us like ten-pins."

Tom winced. "But you're all right?"

"I'm fine. Give me a week, and I'll be back to normal."

"Well, you definitely shouldn't take the tube home. Let St George take you."

"I wasn't going to take the tube," I said irritably. "I thought we might find a Hackney. It's late enough now that I'm sure London has woken up."

There was daylight creeping in around the edges of the drapes, so the sun had risen in the time we had been sitting here, and there was sure to be a Hackney somewhere on the street.

"Why would you pay for a Hackney," Crispin wanted to know, "when the motorcar is right outside and I can easily take you and Kit home on my way?"

"I'm sure what Pippa meant," Christopher said, supporting me carefully for the walk across the slippery marble floor of the foyer, "was that we'd be delighted for the lift. Thank you, Crispin, for being willing to go out of your way."

"Of course, Kit. We'll be right there." He turned to Tom. "Let's get these questions over with, Gardiner, so I can get my fiancée out of her night clothes and into something decent for the drive. And then we'll get out of here."

By that point, Christopher and I had reached the front door, which Thompson held open for us. "Miss Darling. Mr. Astley."

"Thank you, Thompson," Christopher said. "We're just going to wait right here until the others come."

"Of course, Mr. Astley." Thompson inclined his head. "Good day to you, Mr. Astley. You as well, Miss Darling."

He closed the door behind us. I gave it a disgruntled look.

"You just wanted to hear the names of the other burglary victims," Christopher told me as he guided me slowly towards the Hispano-Suiza.

"And you just didn't want to leave Tom," I shot back.

He didn't answer, and I blew out a breath. "I hate being kept out of things."

"I know you do." He smirked. "But all you have to do is wait for the others to come out, and then ask Crispin. He'll tell you."

"Laetitia won't let him," I said morosely.

"I'm not sure it's up to her, Pippa." He stopped beside the Hispano-Suiza and attempted to prop me against the wheel well for support. I snorted at him, and he added, "Why do you want to know, anyway?"

He pulled open the door and then moved the seat up before gesturing to me.

"No particular reason," I said as I made my slow way into the backseat. "I just like to know things."

"Of course you do." He climbed in after me. "Unless you think you know who the burglar is, I doubt it matters."

"Of course I don't know who the burglar is. How would I know something like that? It's just interesting to speculate, is all."

"Of course it is." He leaned back against the seat. "It's been quite an eventful morning, hasn't it?"

It certainly had. "An eventful evening yesterday, too. I'm ready for a nap, I think."

"When we get home," Christopher said. "Or you can put your head on my shoulder and try to sleep now, if you'd like."

"With the way St George drives? I wouldn't dare."

Although I did put my head back and close my eyes while I waited for Crispin and his fiancée to come out of the house.

When they did, Laetitia was appropriately dressed in a day frock—black, of course, with white embroidery—and her effects were packed into a weekender bag that Crispin stowed in the boot of the motorcar. That done, he assisted Laetitia into the passenger seat and slid himself behind the wheel.

"Everything all right?"

"She's tired and in pain," Christopher answered, so Crispin must have looked at me, I supposed. I opened my eyes, in time to see Laetitia direct a gimlet stare at the side of his head.

"I'm fine." I sat up. "Who are the other families that were burgled?"

Crispin arched a brow in the mirror. "Really? You couldn't even wait until I started the motor?"

"You have the answer," I said, "and I want to know. So spill."

He sighed, but turned the key in the ignition. "Hasn't anyone ever told you that you'll catch more flies with honey, Darling?"

"Philippa," I said. "And I believe you have told me that, actually. Repeatedly. If you would like me to coo at you—"

Laetitia made a protesting little noise, and Crispin said. "Please don't. In fact, I'll tell you just so you won't coo at me. I don't think I could survive it."

Christopher snorted, and Crispin shot him a look, but

didn't say anything. Not to him. To me, he said, "I don't think you know them, anyway. In addition to the Marsdens and the Cummingses, there have been the Wickstroms and the Harrimans."

"I don't know either of them," I said.

"Just as well," Crispin answered. "Now close your eyes again and let me concentrate, Darling."

"Philippa," I said, and closed my eyes.

IT WASN'T A LONG DRIVE. The Marsden Town house was located in Mayfair, just a few blocks from Sutherland House. Christopher and I can't afford Mayfair—or perhaps it would be more accurate to say that Uncle Herbert can't, since he's the one footing the bill for our flat.

Although that's not entirely accurate, either, because of course he could afford it if he wanted to. Or if we wanted to. The Astleys have plenty of money. We had even been offered lodging in venerable Sutherland House when we first started talking about going up to London to live. Christopher and I had agreed, however, that Mayfair wasn't necessary, nor was it desirable, and we certainly didn't want to live anywhere where the Duke of Sutherland might show up without notice, or where the staff answered to him. We, or perhaps more specifically Christopher, would prefer something a bit less staid and stuffy, with rather less supervision. He had, after all, gone up to London in the hope of a different life than the one Wiltshire could offer him.

Again, not that we hadn't been perfectly comfortable at Beckwith Place with Aunt Roz and Uncle Herbert and Francis. There was no question about that. But rural Wiltshire isn't exactly Soho, and the village charm—and village morality—was chafing a bit at a young chap who wanted to spread his wings and fly.

At any rate, we had compromised on the Essex House Mansions, a short drive from Mayfair in Crispin's H6. London had woken up while we had been inside Marsden House: the sun had risen and the streets were full of pedestrians and other motorcars. Even so, it couldn't have been more than fifteen minutes or so—fifteen mostly silent minutes—before Crispin pulled up in front of the Essex House Mansions and opened his door. "Out you come."

He extended a hand to Christopher, who let himself be pulled from the backseat of the car in the manner of a cork from a bottle. Crispin turned to me, but when Laetitia cleared her throat, he took a step back, albeit not without a small grimace.

"You had better do it, Kit. I don't want to get in trouble."

"Nobody had better do it," I said irritably as I hauled myself from the backseat and onto the cobblestones with no help. It hurt, and the pain made me irritable enough to tackle the issue head-on, in front of Laetitia. "Although I will say, St George, if this is how you're going to treat your female relatives from now on, I'm not looking forward to it."

Laetitia made a face, and so did Crispin. "Don't worry about it, Darling," he told me. "You won't be here to see it, will you?"

"I won't?" This was news to me, frankly.

"Of course not." He curled his lip in a sneer. "You'll be a distant memory soon. That German girl who spent some time with the family before she snagged herself a German nobleman and went back to Germany to live in luxury."

For a moment, time itself, as well as my breath, suspended. My mouth dropped open as if he had socked me in the stomach. And it wasn't only the accusation of being a gold-digger, to be clear, although that was bad enough. But beyond that, this came very close to the argument we had had (by letter) back in August; the argument that had culminated with me telling him to go cry on Laetitia's shoulder, because he and she deserved one another. And while he was at it, he might as well propose to her, because I certainly didn't care what he did.

Which he had then proceeded to do, instead of taking a step back and a moment to realize that we were both angry and that, after four months of telling him not to, I probably hadn't really changed my mind and suddenly thought it was a good idea for him to throw his life away.

And now here he was again, the absolute tosser, throwing the land of my birth in my face and ripping open those wounds that had only just started to heal.

My hands curled into fists, in spite of the abrasions on my palms. My voice was breathless—with anger, I assure you—when I told him, "Go to hell, St George. And take your fiancée with you. And don't show your face here again. How dare you accuse me of settling for a title and money, you bastard, when you—"

But by that point Christopher had grabbed me around the waist and had hauled me to the door of the mansion block, which Evans was holding open. His eyes were wide as he took in the spectacle of Christopher having to hold me back from throwing myself bodily at St George and throttling him.

"Is everything all right, Miss Darling?"

"Fine," I snarled as Christopher wrestled me across the threshold into the foyer. "Stop it, Christopher. You can put me down. I won't go after him."

I wanted to, but I wouldn't. I wouldn't have done it in the first place, curled fists notwithstanding.

My feet touched the floor of the foyer and Christopher removed his hands from my person. He smoothed down his jacket while I turned to Evans. "Everything is fine. Lord St George and Lady Laetitia were just leaving. And the next time he shows up here, you have my permission—no, the absolute privilege—to tell him that we're not in to him."

I stalked across the lobby towards the lift while Christopher headed back outside to bid his cousin and cousin-to-be goodbye.

CHAPTER FIVE

BY THE TIME Christopher made it upstairs—he had to wait for the lift to come back down after I had used it—I was standing in the kitchenette watching the kettle boil while I muttered darkly under my breath. Christopher placing an envelope with my name on it on the counter in front of me didn't improve my mood.

I slanted him a fulminating stare. "Where did you get this?"

"Evans gave it to me on my way in," Christopher said as he began to unbutton his jacket. "I imagine you went by him too fast. Or perhaps he was afraid you would take his head clean off if he attempted to interfere with you."

Perhaps he had done. It was a not invalid concern. I had been angry enough to commit violence five minutes ago, and I wasn't much better now. I eyed the envelope with my name written across it in Wolfgang's snarly *Kurrentschrift* with a furrowed brow. "He didn't waste any time, did he?"

It was a mostly rhetorical comment—it wasn't even seven in the morning yet, so clearly he hadn't done—but Christopher shook his head. "He sent the messenger as soon as it was light outside, I imagine."

I flicked him a glance. "What do you suppose he wants?"

"Open it and see," Christopher said, shrugging out of the jacket and draping it over the back of a chair before reaching up to dig around in the cabinet for cups and saucers. "Although five quid says it's an invitation to supper so he can make another attempt to talk you into marrying him."

I could always use five pounds, so I unstuck the envelope flap and pulled out the short note with the Savoy Hotel insignia in the corner. "You owe me five quid," I said a few seconds later.

He stopped what he was doing, which was placing the saucers on the counter and the cups on top of them, to look at me. "Truly?"

"He invited me to tea, not supper."

Christopher rolled his eyes and turned back to the task. "A technicality."

"A technicality still counts. You said supper, not tea."

He huffed and turned his attention to the cabinet. "Orange Pekoe all right?"

"I would rather have English Breakfast," I said, "but I suppose Orange Pekoe will have to do, if that's all we have."

"We'll pick up some English Breakfast the next time we do the marketing." He put the tin on the counter and popped the lid off. And flicked me a look. "I notice you don't deny that he will give talking you into marriage another go."

I made a face. "Most likely, yes. Although I don't know, Christopher. He's never been pushy about it. When he proposed at Marsden Manor and I didn't immediately say yes, he wasn't difficult about it. He isn't trying to force me into accepting him."

"He'd better not," Christopher said, in a tone that hinted of danger should anyone try. He's approximately as dangerous as a kitten in a snit, so I paid it no attention beyond an eyeroll and a, "Yes, yes."

"Shall you go?"

"Tonight, do you mean? I suppose so. We're not doing anything else, so why wouldn't I? It's one more meal your father doesn't have to pay for, isn't it?"

"My father can afford to feed you," Christopher said, with the magnificent disregard of someone who has never had to worry about where his next meal will be coming from. "Aren't you afraid that he'll make another attempt on your life?"

"Are you still on about that?" I shook my head. "He hasn't made the first attempt on my life, Christopher."

"You don't find it suspicious that you tell him you don't want to go to Germany with him, and five minutes later, you plunge headfirst down a staircase?"

"No," I said firmly. "It sounds coincidental, I'll give you that. But why on earth would he want me dead? If he wants a wife who'll go to Germany with him, and I don't want to do it, he can just find someone else."

"Perhaps he doesn't want anyone else."

"That's fine, then. But killing me won't get him what he wants, either. I'll be dead, but he'll still need a wife. And if that's the case, he might as well just find one without killing me first."

"Perhaps he was trying to scare you," Christopher said, "so you'll accept the protection of his name."

"The what, now?" I shook my head. "That doesn't make any sense, Christopher. First of all, me falling down the stairs has got nothing to do with me needing the protection of anyone's name, but if I did do, I've got the protection of yours. Being attached to the Astleys, and by extension to the Suther-lands, goes a lot further than being the fiancée of the *Graf von und zu* Natterdorff. At least for as long as I'm here in England."

Christopher didn't quibble with that, most likely because he recognized that I was right. "Perhaps he was trying to give the impression that you were in danger, then," he said instead, "so he could swoop in and save you. And then you might go to Germany with him out of gratitude, or to get away from whoever is after you."

It made more sense than the 'protection of his name' thing. But nonetheless—

"That's ridiculous," I said. "No one is after me. It was an accident. Nothing more."

Christopher looked mutinous. "It won't seem ridiculous when you're rolling around on the floor of the Savoy with your heels touching the back of your head."

I stared at him. "What on earth has gotten into you, Christopher? You like Wolfgang! Or at least I thought you did."

"That was before he tried to take you away," Christopher said mulishly.

I blinked at him for several seconds before I found my voice again. "I didn't realize you felt that way."

His eyes flashed. "Of course I feel that way! You're my best friend, and he wants to marry you and take you to Germany with him!"

"Yes," I said, "but you never said anything."

He threw his hands up. "What was I going to say? 'No, don't marry this man you seem to like, whose proposal you accepted, because I don't want to lose my best friend?' What kind of friend would I be if I did that?"

"Someone who cares that I stay," I said. "And I didn't, you know."

"Didn't what?"

"I didn't accept his proposal." I thought back to that

moment in the Marsden Manor foyer, and added, "What I actually said, was, 'Thank you, but...' But then someone squealed, and everyone started cheering, and at that point I couldn't really say no. But I never actually said yes, either."

"Laetitia," Christopher said.

"I beg your pardon?"

"Laetitia was the one who squealed. Crispin squeezed her hand hard enough for that stupidly ostentatious Sutherland diamond ring to make a bruise."

"Good grief," I said, "why?"

Christopher rolled his eyes, hard enough that they seemed to be in danger of vanishing into the back of his skull. "I'm just going to say it, Pippa. I promised I wouldn't, so I haven't, but this is getting painful."

"What is getting painful?" Other than Laetitia's bruised finger, although there had been no bruise on it this morning, and also no Sutherland engagement ring, so that point was now moot, in more ways than one.

His eyes narrowed. "Your obliviousness, you daft cow."

I sniffed, offended, and he added, "He fancies you. Has done for years."

I opened my mouth and then closed it again when nothing came out.

"He took one look at you on the train platform in Salisbury when we came home from Eton that last time," Christopher continued when I didn't speak. "You were all grown up, in heels and bobbed hair and lipstick, and he made a sound like a dying duck. When I looked at him, he told me he'd kill me if I said anything at all about it, so I didn't."

I shook my head, finally finding my voice. "That's mad, Christopher. He might have been surprised that I wasn't the same snotty-nosed girl in pigtails that I'd been the last time he saw me—" Over Christmas holidays, that would have been, almost six years ago now, "—but he certainly wasn't struck by..." I wrinkled my nose, "—by fancy."

"Shows what you know," Christopher said. "This level of thickheadedness isn't an attractive trait, Pippa. Everyone else knows. How could you not have noticed?"

How could I not have...?

"Because there wasn't anything *to* notice!"

My voice was shrill, and I made a concerted effort to calm down and sound less like something only dogs could hear. "Have you lost your mind, Christopher?"

"No," Christopher said.

"You must have done! This is your cousin you are talking about, correct? Just to clarify? Not some other chap you may have been sharing your train compartment with on the last ride home from school?"

He gave me a look, one that said clearly that I was pushing him too far, and I raised my hands in pacification. "You can't blame me for wanting to be certain, Christopher. Not when you're standing there telling me that the then-Honorable Crispin Astley, current Viscount St George, future Duke of Sutherland—that's him, correct? Same chap?—that he... that he... fancies me!"

My voice rose incredulously on the last part, and Christopher winced but persisted. "Not just fancies you, Pippa. But yes, the same chap. The one who's in love with you."

The ground did a little shimmy, and I did my best to ignore the unsteadiness under my feet. But truly... love, and not just fancy? "How can that be, pray tell, with the way he has always spoken to me?"

"Ugh," Christopher said with feeling. He reached up and pinched the bridge of his nose as if I were giving him a headache. "I really don't want to do this, you know. Not only did I promise him I wouldn't do—and no, that time on the train wasn't the only time it came up; we've actually discussed it more than once, so I'm not simply imagining things—"

Well, that took care of that objection, and before I could voice it, too.

"If he's in love with me," I said, and my face twisted involuntarily as the words came out, "why would he propose to Laetitia?"

Christopher stared at me. "Because you told him to, didn't you? Slapped him down and told him he might as well marry Laetitia because he didn't deserve any better. What did you think he would do?"

"Not that," I muttered. I had thought he had a better sense of self-preservation that that, frankly. I mean, we both knew he was in love with someone else, didn't we?

"Do you mean to tell me," I said for clarification, "that all those times when I told him he ought to man up and tell the girl he was in love with that he fancied her..."

Christopher nodded. "You were talking about yourself."

"And when we discussed it with your mother and father before going to Dorset for the engagement party last month, and I suggested that we find her and put her wise..."

"Still talking about yourself."

"And Aunt Roz and Uncle Herbert knew it?"

"Of course they knew it," Christopher said. "Everyone knows it, Pippa. Mum and Dad, Constance and Francis, Laetitia..."

That explained the animosity, at any rate. I had wondered about that.

"Uncle Harold?" I asked. "Aunt Charlotte?"

Christopher nodded. "Them, too. Grandfather, before he died. All the servants. Tom, of course. It's not a secret."

"So when we listened to Uncle Harold rant at Crispin that weekend in April..."

"Grimsby had just informed Grandfather of Crispin's many failings," Christopher said, "and Grandfather called both Uncle Harold and Crispin on the carpet. Crispin didn't want to listen, it seemed, and his father followed him to his rooms to, I assume, try to talk some sense into him."

And we had heard them screaming at one another when we came out of Christopher's room to go outside for a walk.

"Uncle Harold called me a common chippy," I said, thinking back, "and a foreigner to boot."

Funny how I had never connected those words to myself. I had racked my brain trying to think of other women of Crispin's acquaintance who might fit the criteria, and had mostly come up empty, at least after Johanna de Vos bit the dust. It had never once occurred to me that I fit the parameters myself.

Christopher nodded. "He also said that Crispin should marry someone else and keep you as a mistress. As I recall, Crispin didn't like that much."

No, he hadn't. "So when Aunt Charlotte put me as far into the west wing at Sutherland Hall as she put you into the east wing..."

"It wasn't me she was trying to keep you away from," Christopher said.

"Would that be why she hid the pages from Grimsby's notebook in my room, too, do you suppose? So I could see all of St George's misdeeds in black and white, and I would detest him all the more?"

"I wouldn't be surprised," Christopher said. "You've never pretended to like Crispin, but I suppose she thought it wouldn't hurt to make sure that you continued to despise him."

No doubt. I shivered, and then folded my arms across my chest to hide how the thought made me cold all the way down to the marrow. Never mind the fact that she had tried to kill me; what parent does something like that to her only child?

Then again, we were talking about the upper crust, weren't we, with their titles and estates hanging in the balance, and it wasn't as if Uncle Harold and Aunt Charlotte had been a love match, was it? I supposed they both felt that if they could deal with each other for the sake of the reputation and fortune of the Sutherlands, then so could Crispin.

And at least he was allowed to keep me as a mistress on the side, the lucky boy.

"Do you think he would have done it?" I asked.

Christopher squinted at me. The water had finished boiling now, and he was dealing with the strainer and tea leaves. "Done what?"

I made a face. Now that I had to deliberately articulate what had fallen out of my mouth more or less without input from my brain, I wished I had kept my mouth shut. "Married Laetitia and tried to keep me as a mistress."

Christopher turned to me. His eyebrows rose. "Are you mad?" he wanted to know.

I opened my mouth and then closed it again when he continued. "Entirely aside from the fact that he's in love with you, and that he wouldn't insult you that way, or for that matter use you that way—"

He had better not.

"—is there anything about your relationship with Crispin that would indicate that you would allow him to survive after coming to you with such a suggestion?"

I had to admit that there wasn't. "I would eviscerate him. After I finished laughing myself sick."

Christopher nodded. "And I'm sure he knows that. Besides, he isn't that sort of a person."

I opened my mouth, and he waved me to silence. "Don't,

Pippa. You know he wouldn't marry Laetitia and then carry on with you behind her back."

"Tell that to all the girls he's bedded in the past couple of years," I said.

"But he wasn't married to any of them. Nor in love with any of them, either."

"But according to you he was in love with me. And it certainly didn't stop him from spreading his favors to all and sundry."

"Because he couldn't have you," Christopher said, heading out of the kitchenette with both the cups of tea and a toss of his head indicating that I should follow. "You'd never agree, and Uncle Harold would never allow it, anyway."

I trailed after him, out of the kitchen and into the sitting room. "I don't know if I can trust this, Christopher. Are you certain you haven't lost your mind and he's simply pulling your leg?"

Christopher snorted as he placed the cups and saucers on the table and dropped down on one end of the Chesterfield. "Mine and everyone else's, I suppose?"

I opened my mouth to say that I wouldn't put it past him—Crispin, that was—and Christopher shook his head. "Don't bother, Pippa. I'm not the one who has lost my mind. You're the one denying what everyone else can plainly see. Bloody hell, it's not as if he's been exactly discreet, is it? He's called you darling for half a decade. I can't believe you haven't caught on."

"Yes," I said, "but..."

"But nothing. Everyone else can see it. Why can't you?"

I thought about it—not that I was convinced, mind you, but if Christopher was right and Crispin did nurture fond feelings for me... why hadn't I noticed?

"I suppose because he behaves as if he despises me," I said, honestly. "He always has done."

"He doesn't," Christopher said. He had picked up his Orange Pekoe and was sipping with every appearance of enjoyment, while I still sat with my hands in my lap while my tea turned cold on the table. "Although the fact that you so obviously despise him doesn't make him any more likely to be vulnerable with you, I'm sure you'll agree."

Yes, of course. And the idea of Crispin being vulnerable made my face pucker.

After a moment's silence, Christopher added, thoughtfully, "Although at this point I'm not certain what difference it makes, anyway. He's marrying Laetitia, isn't he, however he might feel about you."

Yes, he was. "Serves him right," I said, "if he couldn't even be bothered to tell me."

Christopher smirked. "I don't imagine he had much hope that you felt the same way. Might as well save himself the embarrassment, if you were just going to laugh in his face."

"Perhaps I wouldn't have done," I said, and picked up my own cup of tea at long last. "Perhaps I would have been sympathetic and understanding."

I tried to keep a straight face, the way someone who was sympathetic and understanding would do, but I couldn't maintain it, and Christopher grinned. "You wouldn't have done, Pippa. You would have seen an opportunity to gloat, and you would have taken it. We both know it, and so does he."

We did both know it, although having it pointed out didn't make me feel very good about myself. "Are you absolutely certain about this, Christopher? You wouldn't joke about it, would you?"

"I wouldn't," Christopher confirmed. "And yes, I'm absolutely certain. We talk about it occasionally. Obliquely, of course. He isn't the type to cry over a girl..."

No, of course not.

"—but I keep him up to date on what's going on with you. I rang up Sutherland Hall the same day we met Wolfgang, if you'll recall."

Yes, of course I recalled. "He showed up at the Savoy the next night to take me home," I said. All the way from Wiltshire. Although he had intimated, on that occasion, that he was really in London to see someone else and I was just an afterthought.

But when I mentioned that, Christopher set me straight. "The only reason he motored up was because I phoned him and told him about Wolfgang. Laetitia Marsden wasn't even in London that weekend."

"There are other women," I said.

He shook his head. "Not lately. After Francis's and Constance's engagement party, Uncle Harold made it quite clear that he expected Crispin to fall in line and propose to Laetitia."

Of course he had done. The Earl and Countess of Marsden were Constance's aunt and uncle, so the occasion had created a perfect meeting of the minds for the Duke of Sutherland and the Countess of Marsden to put their heads together and matchmake their children.

"I fail to see why *I'd* be such a terrible wife," I said with an offended sniff.

Not to Crispin, obviously. I didn't want to marry Crispin. I just didn't like to be told that I wasn't good enough for him.

Most of Crispin's conquests had been higher-born, admittedly—Lady Laetitia Marsden, Lady Violet Cummings, the Honorable Cecily Fletcher, and the Honorable Gladys Long. Even Millicent Tremayne was the granddaughter of someone or other. On the other hand, I wasn't as objectionable as that waitress he had dallied with back in June. I was young, healthy, and reasonably attractive. My hips weren't any skinnier than Laetitia's, and she was expected to produce children. I was the ward of the brother of the Duke of Sutherland, and my mother had been an Honorable. It wasn't as if I were a street urchin.

"It's the German thing," Christopher said apologetically.

Yes, of course it was. Although it wasn't as if my country of origin was *my* fault. I hadn't asked my mother to marry a foreigner, nor had I asked to be born. If Francis, who had fought the Boche, could forgive me for my birth, then surely Uncle Harold, who hadn't lifted a finger in defense of his country, should be able to do the same. Half of me was very respectably English. And if Crispin didn't mind—

At that point, my brain rebelled, as it was borne in upon me just how much Crispin apparently didn't mind.

I shook my head, as if to dislodge the thought. "You can't be serious about this. *He* can't be serious about this. It must be a joke. Otherwise, it's... it's madness, Christopher!"

"Believe me," Christopher said, "I have told him so. More than once. How he imagined he was going to win you over behaving the way he does is beyond me."

"That's not..." I shook my head in frustration. "Never mind. Just... let us never speak of it again, please. I won't bring it up, and you won't either."

"Fine by me," Christopher said easily. "It brings me no pleasure to imagine my cousin and my other cousin going at it like rabbits."

My face puckered. "That's foul, Christopher. I beg you won't put that kind of image in my head again."

"It's in mine," Christopher said, "and you can't blame me for wanting to share the misery."

I absolutely could, and told him so. "All of this aside, I don't see any reason why I shouldn't have tea with Wolfgang later. St George is marrying Laetitia, and wouldn't have been allowed to marry me anyway, and that's assuming I would have wanted to marry him..."

Christopher opened his mouth, and I waved him off. "I might as well reconsider Wolfgang's proposal in this new light. Perhaps going off to Germany with him would be the best thing for everyone."

It would keep me from gnashing my teeth for the next half-century while I watched Laetitia make herself at home as mistress of Sutherland Hall. And if Christopher wasn't pulling my leg and Crispin truly did have more than familial feelings for me, getting out of his way so he could find whatever happiness he could with a woman he didn't love, might be the kindest thing I could do for him.

"Not for me," Christopher said.

Well, no. Of course not for him. But— "Do you foresee us staying together for the rest of our lives, Christopher?"

Didn't he want a life and a relationship of his own at some point? With someone like—say—Tom Gardiner?

"I foresaw you doing as you promised," Christopher said severely, "and marry me if we are both still single at thirty."

Well, yes. I had promised that, hadn't I? Although that had been before anyone else had wanted to marry me. Or at least before I had known about it.

"After all," Christopher added, "it's the only way I'm likely to get an heir, isn't it?"

An heir? "I didn't know you cared about having an heir."

He huffed. "A child, then. You know Mum and Dad care about grandchildren."

"Of course. But surely Francis and Constance have that in hand? If anyone has child-bearing hips, it's Constance."

"Now, now," Christopher said, albeit not without a twitch of his lips, "don't be unkind, Pippa."

"I'm not being unkind. I love Constance. But you have to admit that she's not exactly the Roaring Twenties ideal of woman."

Quite unlike Lady Laetitia, who had the appeal of the decade down to an art.

Constance had the bobbed hair and the lipstick, of course. Everyone did these days. But she was an old-fashioned girl in that all she wanted to do, was marry Francis and settle into being a wife and mother. No cocktail parties and cigarettes for Constance.

And yes, her hips were more ample than my own, and for that matter than Laetitia's. Everything about Constance was soft and warm. She'd be a wonderful mother when the time came.

"I suppose," Christopher admitted, a bit reluctantly. I could tell that he still felt as if he were being disloyal to his brother's fiancée.

"Besides, even if we were both still single at thirty, and we did marry one another, did you really want to...?"

Christopher's face twisted. "Bloody hell, no. No offense, Pippa, but that's vile."

I wouldn't go as far as to use that particular word, but then I had precious little experience with which to reason. The idea of kissing him passionately was certainly off-putting—who wants to kiss their own brother, and that's basically what he was to me?—but surely something like that, or worse, would be required?

"Well," I said, "then how did you think we would manage to make an heir? Through immaculate conception?"

"I rather imagined," Christopher said, with no shame whatsoever, "that by then Crispin would have talked you around, and I'd help you bring up his children. It's not likely that anyone would be able to tell the difference."

It was my turn to pucker. "If anything is vile, Christopher, that is. You'd marry me while I was carrying on with your cousin—your married cousin—and between us, we'd bring up the illegitimate children? And you thought Laetitia would accept this? Let alone that I would?"

Because that would never happen. I didn't want Crispin in the first place, but if he wanted me, he'd damn well better be willing to give up the title and fortune for me, rather than marry Laetitia and try to talk me into his bed on the side. It seemed like the least he could do.

"I'm meeting Wolfgang for tea," I said firmly. "And you'll do me the favor, Christopher, of not ringing up Wiltshire and dragging St George back up here for it. He has enough to deal with without that."

"Probably won't end up in Wiltshire anyway," Christopher said, and he was most likely right about that.

CHAPTER SIX

WOLFGANG WAS WAITING at the table when I walked into the Savoy tearoom later that afternoon. He got to his feet when the maître d' escorted me across the floor, but he didn't circle the table to pull out my chair. Perhaps I no longer merited the courtesy of his personal attention now that I had announced my opposition to moving to Germany. Or perhaps he simply felt that we were past the stage where he had to exert himself to impress me. Either way, I wasn't certain I liked the portent.

I didn't make a fuss, of course, because that would have been improper. Instead, I thanked the maître d' graciously and smiled at Wolfgang as he sank back down on his chair again. "Good afternoon."

He smiled back. "Philippa."

If he was upset with me, it was not immediately visible.

"I didn't think I would hear from you again so soon," I said.

He looked politely confused, as if he couldn't imagine why. "Because we parted on uncertain terms yesterday, do you mean? Of course not, *mein Schatz*. Cold feet are normal."

He reached for my hand across the table. When I extended it to him, he looked down upon it with every appearance of shock. "What happened to you?"

The last half a day had been so eventful that it honestly surprised me that he didn't already know. Last night felt so long ago. But of course it had all happened in the less than twenty-four hours since I had last seen him.

"I fell," I said. "On my way home last night."

"My dear." He squeezed my fingers gently before letting go again. "I hope it wasn't a motorcar?"

God forbid. I would have looked a lot worse had that been the case.

"Not at all," I assured him. "A mishap on the stairs into the underground."

He eyed me. "I wish you wouldn't take the underground by yourself at night, Philippa."

"It's perfectly safe," I said. "Not to mention a lot cheaper than a Hackney."

And while Uncle Herbert seemed happy to provide, there was no reason to squander his money unnecessarily.

"I would have been happy to escort you home," Wolfgang said. His tone held a subtle implication that the only reason he hadn't done, was because I had left the restaurant in a snit, but it was mostly left unsaid. Or perhaps I imagined it, and there was no subtext whatsoever.

"I know you would have done," I said peacefully, "although you don't have a motorcar of your own either, you know, Wolfgang. There was no point in you paying to take me home and then going back to the Savoy. I was closer to home in Piccadilly, and you were closer to the Savoy."

"A gentleman—" Wolfgang began stiffly, surely preparatory to telling me that it was his job to see me safe home, useless female that I was. Luckily, the waiter appeared before he could tell me what a gentleman should or shouldn't do—as if I didn't know the answer perfectly well already—and we ordered tea and cake. The waiter withdrew, but by now Wolfgang had wound down, and didn't seem inclined to pick up the issue again.

"How bad is it?" he inquired instead, eyeing my hands. "Is that the only damage?"

"That and my knees. Although speaking of damage... you'll never guess what happened last night."

He arched his brows, and I went on, since he truly wouldn't be able to guess. "Rogers rang up from Sutherland House at half four this morning and told us that there had been a burglary at Marsden House. Laetitia's engagement ring is gone."

I couldn't quite keep the glee out of my voice. Wolfgang was silent for a moment, probably placing the locations of Sutherland House and Marsden House, and the persons of Rogers and Laetitia, into their proper slots in his head. "Does that mean that the engagement is over," he asked, "as well?"

Oh, if only.

I snorted derisively. "Hardly. The only way Crispin gets out of marrying Laetitia at this point, is if he drops dead, and I wouldn't put it past her to try to wheel him to the altar then, too."

Although that was perhaps a touch unkind of me. She really did seem to want him for himself at least as much as she wanted the chance to become the Duchess of Sutherland later.

Wolfgang nodded. He looked as if he were thinking deeply. "Why would... Rogers is part of the staff at your cousin's Town house, I suppose?"

Crispin wasn't my cousin, of course, unless Wolfgang was talking about Christopher. But— "The butler," I confirmed, "yes."

"Why would the butler contact you?"

"Oh." Valid question. "Lord St George spent the night with us."

Wolfgang's facial countenance underwent a change. "With you and your cousin Christopher?"

I nodded.

"In your two-bed, one-bath flat?"

"Yes," I said. It should be noted here that Wolfgang had never been to the flat. But I must have described it in enough detail that he knew what it consisted of. "He's done before. One of us sleeps on the sofa in the sitting room."

I couldn't share a bed with Crispin, after all—that would be beyond inappropriate—and given Christopher's sexual orientation, I suppose that the two of them sharing might be equally awkward. Not that there had ever been a question of it. Crispin usually ended up in my bed, while I slept on the sofa. The Chesterfield fits me better—he was taller and broader—and besides, I have never felt comfortable asking the future Duke of Sutherland to bunk down in our sitting room.

Of course, knowing what I knew now, Crispin had probably been delighted to end up in my bed, even without me in it. Although that concept brought up some concerns which I had no intention of dwelling on at the moment. I'd deal with them the next time I had to put him up overnight. Instead, I focused my attention back on Wolfgang, who looked contemplative.

"A burglary," he said, in the tone of a man who was trying the concept on for size.

I nodded. "The Sutherland diamond ring is gone. And the matching earrings. And apparently the necklace Laetitia was wearing yesterday—I don't know if you noticed it. I didn't, although if she said she was wearing one, there's no reason to think she would lie about it."

"Unless she lied about the whole thing," Wolfgang said, "because she wanted to make herself out to be a victim."

I looked at him for a second, blankly, before I caught on to what he was implying. "You mean, no one was there, and Laetitia pawned the diamonds herself? Or plans to?"

Wolfgang lifted an elegant shoulder. "Who knows?"

I did, I suspected. "I doubt she would do that. Not only has she worked very hard to get her hands on that diamond ring," and what it signified, "but it's not as if she needs the money. Her father is the Earl of Marsden."

Wolfgang shrugged, just as the waiter appeared with the teapot and cups, the cake, the little crustless sandwiches, the creamer and sugar pot. We sat in silence while he distributed it all across the table, and then he took a step back and asked whether there would be anything else.

Wolfgang shook his head, and the waiter withdrew. "I'll pour," I said, "shall I?"

That seemed acceptable—he probably felt it was my feminine duty. I rather thought the waiter ought to have done it, since we were paying customers. But I suited action to words: filled Wolfgang's cup with the genial beverage, and then my own. While I did so, Wolfgang let his eyes wander around the room. I was just putting the pot back down when he said, "Isn't that...?"

I positioned the hot teapot carefully on the trivet before I raised my eyes to his face, and then turned my attention in the direction he was looking, at the door to the lobby.

No one was there, or no one that shouldn't be. The maître d' was standing beside the door as usual, and was looking into the restaurant, but there was nothing noteworthy about that. I gave him a politely dismissive smile when he glanced at me, and then squinted past him into the lobby. "Who?" Or whom.

"Never mind," Wolfgang said, hands busy with sugar and milk. "I must have been mistaken."

"Did you see someone you knew?" I turned back to the door for a more thorough look. The maître d' had turned away now, back to his podium, and was fiddling with what looked like paperwork, marking it with a fountain pen.

"I thought I saw your cousin," Wolfgang said.

I flicked him another look, just as he pushed my teacup across the table at me.

"Christopher, do you mean?" It wasn't likely that Francis would be here. He doesn't much like London these days, not since he stopped coming up here to carouse with his friends from the trenches. These days, he prefers to stay sober, and to stay in Wiltshire with Constance, and with Uncle Herbert and Aunt Roz.

"The young popinjay with the motorcar," Wolfgang said and sat back on his chair.

"Crispin? He's not my cousin. And he wouldn't be here. He and Laetitia headed back to Dorset this morning. They must be there by now."

Wolfgang threw a doubtful glance at the door. "Are you certain? I could have sworn..."

Well, it certainly wouldn't be the first time that Crispin lurked in the lobby while I was enjoying a meal with Wolfgang —and after Christopher's revelation this morning, suddenly a lot of small things like that took on a new significance in my mind. But he had sounded fairly serious about taking Laetitia home. She had sounded rather serious about wanting to go. He wouldn't have had time to motor to Dorset and back, although I supposed it was possible that they had changed their minds and were still at Sutherland House.

I glanced again at the door, doubtful now too. "I wouldn't

think so, although I suppose it isn't impossible. I don't see anyone who looks like him, at any rate."

Wolfgang shook his head. "Most likely just my imagination."

"Certainly," I said, although I wasn't sure I believed it. He had seen Crispin enough times by now that he should be able to recognize him. If Wolfgang thought he had seen him, then I was inclined to believe he had done.

Unless Christopher had decided to check on me, of course. In the beginning, he had insisted on escorting me to the Savoy for my dates with Wolfgang himself, and on handing me over with a warning to behave. That had stopped after the first few times, once Christopher became more comfortable with Wolfgang and trusted that the latter wasn't going to chloroform me and take me off to Limehouse (or to his room upstairs) to do unspeakable things to me. But my tumble down the stairs last night seemed to have brought Christopher's latent protective instincts to the fore again, and perhaps he really had decided to loiter in the Savoy lobby to keep an eye on me. From a distance, he and Crispin look very much like one another, and under the artificial lights of the Savoy, Crispin's platinum hair might very well look more like Christopher's sunny blond, or vice versa.

Naturally I didn't say anything about it. If Christopher was hanging about because he was afraid that Wolfgang was trying to murder me, it wasn't a subject I wanted to broach with Wolfgang. Nothing good comes from telling a man that your family suspects him of trying to do away with you.

I turned back to him with a smile. "I'm sure it's nothing to worry about. If something was wrong, someone would let me know. And if you truly did see Crispin, he's most likely just escorting Laetitia somewhere. Just as last night."

Wolfgang drew breath. "About last night..."

"Please, may we forget it? I'm sorry for becoming emotional."

He blinked at me, and I added, "Won't you tell me about *Schloss* Natterdorff? I should at least not reject the idea until I know what I am rejecting."

He stared at me for a second, intently, as if he were trying to determine whether I was telling the truth or not. Just as it was getting uncomfortable, his expression melted into warm eyes and a wide smile. "*Mein Schatz*."

He reached across the table. I lifted my hand to meet his. We were just about to clasp hands when my teacup upended with a *clink* of porcelain on porcelain, and brown liquid soaked into the tablecloth and approached the edge of the table.

Instead of clasping Wolfgang's hand, I pushed my chair back. I had destroyed one evening gown by tripping down the stairs to the underground yesterday. I wasn't about to ruin my favorite afternoon frock by soaking it in hot tea.

Wolfgang jumped to his feet, too, of course, and the waiter as well as the maître d' descended at a run. The waiter gathered up all the flatware and silverware, and the maître d' whisked the tablecloth off and draped it over his arm before escorting us to another table. It was only a minute or two before the waiter had supplied another teapot, two more cups and saucers, and more cake and sandwiches. I poured again, and then sat back on my chair.

"That was exciting."

Wolfgang nodded, looking around, but of course no one was uncouth enough to be watching us.

"Where were we?" I prompted, and he gave me a rueful smile. In case I haven't mentioned it thus far, Wolfgang is exceptionally good-looking, with wavy, golden hair and midnight blue eyes. Even the Mensur scar that bisects one cheek isn't enough to destroy the appeal.

"I believe I was about to attempt to take your hand," he told me with self-depreciating humor. "I won't make that mistake again."

"I would hardly call it a mistake," I demurred, since it hadn't been my trying to get out of holding his hand that had caused the mishap. I wasn't exactly sure what had happened, to be honest; I had just noticed the result. It may have been my hand that knocked the cup from the saucer. Then again, it might have been his. "Perhaps, for now, we ought to forego the hand-holding and instead focus on tea and cake while you tell me about Germany."

He beamed, and while I dumped sugar and milk in my new cup of tea and transferred a fresh cucumber sandwich onto my plate, he proceeded to do just that.

"I don't know how much you remember from being a child in Heidelberg—"

"Not much," I admitted. "And I remember less and less every day, I'm sorry to say. Although I was eleven when I left Germany, not a small child, so I do remember a few things."

He nodded. "*Schloss* Natterdorff sits some thirty kilometers from Heidelberg. I don't think you visited as a child."

"I don't imagine so," I agreed. I'm sure I would have remembered, if so. A castle is the sort of thing that sticks with you. Instead, my memories were of the small flat we had lived in in Heidelberg, and the streets of the town, and the river.

"It sits on the outskirts of the village of Natterdorff," Wolfgang said, and went on to describe something that, frankly, sounded a lot less like Mad Ludwig's Neuschwanstein, and rather more like Sutherland Hall or Marsden Manor. Not a fairytale castle with towers and turrets against the picturesque backdrop of the Hessian highlands, but more like a manorhouse in the style I had become used to.

Of course I didn't show my disappointment, just kept him

going with smiles and encouraging noises. We had moved from the orchard and stables past the number of bedrooms and baths, and he was describing the wallpaper in the formal ballroom when the maître d' materialized beside the table.

He stood there politely, without clearing his throat or interrupting, but of course he was impossible to ignore. Wolfgang tried, I'll give him that, but it was only fifteen seconds or so later that he interrupted his own description of the damask to look up. "Yes?"

"A message for *monsieur*." The maître d' held out a small envelope on a tray, like Tidwell was wont to do at Sutherland Hall.

Neither he nor Wolfgang were French, but perhaps the maître d' did not want to sully his mouth with the German, and let's be honest, English simply doesn't have the same snooty flair.

Wolfgang eyed him for a moment before plucking the note from the tray. The maître d' withdrew, with a polite clicking of heels, and Wolfgang glanced at the envelope in his hand. His stare was intent enough that it seemed he might be trying to see through it to the message inside.

"Go ahead," I told him. "It could be important."

He hesitated, but after a moment he unsealed the flap and pulled out a small notecard from within. The message written on it was short: I saw his eyes flicker for just a second, over what was surely only a line or so of script. His jaw tightened and he glanced over at the entrance to the restaurant, to where the maître d's podium stood beside the door to the lobby. Perhaps he was hoping to catch a glimpse of whoever had left the note. If so he must have been disappointed, because the maître d' stood alone, and wasn't looking our way.

"It isn't St George," I inquired, "is it?" Just in case Wolfgang was right, and he actually had seen Crispin in the lobby earlier. Or Christopher, I supposed.

His lips stretched into a semblance of a smile, although it didn't quite reach his eyes. "No, no, *mein Schatz.* Merely a business matter that needs my attention."

He slid the notecard back into the envelope and put the whole thing in his pocket.

I watched it disappear before I asked, "Is there anything I can do?"

He shook his head. "I'm afraid not. I'll deal with it later. Now—" he gave me another smile, this one a bit more natural-looking, "where were we?"

"In the ballroom," I said, "with the pale blue damask wall-paper and crystal chandeliers."

He nodded, and went back to describing *Schloss* Natter-dorff and its many delights.

He spoke glibly and at length, but nonetheless, I did get the impression that he was distracted. He fidgeted on his chair almost as much as Crispin had done on the rather memorable occasion when I had dropped a handful of rose hips under his collar just before luncheon.

The Honorable Mr. Astley, all of eleven or twelve years old at the time, had lasted through the meal under his father's disapproving eye, although it had taken days before he deigned to speak to me again. I still wasn't entirely sure that he had forgiven me. On this occasion, it was only five minutes or so later that I felt I ought to offer to take myself off and so give Wolfgang the opportunity to deal with the piccontents of his message. It wasn't as if he could jettison *me*, after all. A gentleman can't do that sort of thing, at least not to a lady he hopes to see again.

"I should be making my way home," I said with a smile.

I won't go so far as to say that Wolfgang looked relieved—he did put up the token protest: "Already? Are you certain I can't talk you into staying for a bit longer?"—but he got up without demur and offered me his arm for the walk into the lobby.

"Don't feel as if you have to take care of me," I told him as we passed through the door and onto the black-and-white marble floor. The maître d' bowed unctuously as we passed. "You said you thought you saw St George, didn't you? Or perhaps Christopher? I'm sure either one of them would be happy to see me home."

I scanned the lobby for a head of fair hair. I had found them both here once before, taking up a corner of the lobby, waiting for me, but the armchairs were empty this time. Or empty of Astleys, at any rate. There were plenty of people around, albeit no one I recognized.

"Don't be silly," Wolfgang informed me. "Of course I shall see you home if you want me to. Or I'll put you in a Hackney, at the very least. No more tube rides for you." He squeezed my elbow.

I smiled back. "It's perfectly all right, Wolfgang. I can see myself home. There's an entrance to the underground right down the street, and it's still daylight. Nothing would happen to me."

I had taken the underground to the Strand, as a matter of fact. I had deemed it a good idea to get back on the horse, so to speak, so I wouldn't develop some inconvenient phobia of the tube forever, out of fear that something might happen to me. I had perhaps been a bit extra careful on the stairs going down into the tunnels, but nothing had occurred, and I had made it here in one piece. I could just as easily make it back to Bloomsbury.

"Nonsense," Wolfgang told me, and nudged me out the front door, past the doorman, and towards the first Hackney waiting in the queue. "In you go." He opened the door for me.

"Thank you." I climbed in, docilely, even as I wondered whether it was my own cynical nature throwing up suspicions, or whether he really was trying extra hard to make sure I was away from the Savoy before he dealt with his note. "I'm perfectly capable of taking the tube home, you know."

"Not after yesterday." He brushed his lips over the back of my knuckles carefully before he shut the door behind me. "Safe home, *mein Schatz*."

"Where to, guv?" the cab driver inquired, and Wolfgang gave him my destination and enough coin for the fare before stepping back and raising a hand.

"Right you are," the cabbie said, and off we went, down Savoy Court towards the Strand. I turned my head and peered out the back window in time to see Wolfgang lower his arm. He did an about-face towards the door to the hotel just before we turned the corner, and then we were out of sight down the Strand.

I leaned forward. "Pull over at Charing Cross station, if you please."

The driver peered at me in the mirror. "You don't want to go to Essex Street?"

I shook my head. "I realized I left something in the tearoom at the Savoy. I want to go back there and get it."

"I can take you back to the Savoy and then on to Essex Street."

"That won't be necessary," I said. "Keep the money the gentleman gave you," because that was more likely than not the problem here, not so much that he particularly wanted to make the drive to Bloomsbury, "and set me down at Charing Cross. I'm sure you can find another fare there."

He squinted. "You sure about this, miss? Seems the least I can do is take you back to the Savoy."

"That's all right," I said, "just pull in here, and... thank you." We rolled onto the cobbles beside the Eleanor Cross. "I'm just going to hurry back to the Savoy and pick up my... um... my gloves, and then I'll take the tube home. You just stay right here and find another fare. The gentleman will never know the difference."

There was a twinkle in his eyes. "Afraid he's got something going on the side, are you?"

"Something like that," I agreed with the best humor I could manage. Certainly a lot more than if there had been any truth to the suggestion. "There was a note delivered over tea. I'm just going to keep watch for a bit. See whether someone stops by, or whether he goes out somewhere, or something like that."

He nodded. "But you don't need me for it?"

I shook my head. "Oh, no. No, you stay out of it. Get another fare and get paid twice." I pushed the door open. "Good evening, sir."

He didn't stop me when I swung my legs out of the Hackney, or when I shut the door behind me, or as I scurried away across the cobblestones, back in the direction of the Savoy, but I could feel his eyes on me until I had turned the corner and was out of sight.

CHAPTER SEVEN

THE SAME DOORMAN was still on the door when I got back to Savoy Court, and he arched his brows when he saw me. "Back already, Miss Darling?"

"I'm afraid so," I said. "I realized I left my gloves inside the tearoom."

The lie came more glibly this time, having already been told once. He might even have believed me.

There were no gloves, of course. I hadn't wanted to aggravate the plasters any more than I had to, so I had done without them today, in contravention of the usual, but I went to the door of the tearoom anyway, to keep up appearances. The maître d' was away from his podium, but one of the waiters took pity on me. He went so far as to go back into the tearoom and peer under the tables we had sat at—both of them—and came back to inform me that no, no pair of gloves had been found. I thanked him and turned to contemplate the lobby.

There was no sign of Wolfgang, nor of anyone else I recognized. If the correspondent had been out here when the note was delivered, he or she must have gone somewhere else by now. Or the note may have specified a different meeting place, and Wolfgang had hied himself there as soon as I was out of sight.

After making sure that I was out of sight, in fact, by putting me in a Hackney and paying the fare and telling the driver where to take me, so as to make certain that I wouldn't be here to see what was going on.

Unless I was being unduly distrustful, of course, and Wolfgang had simply been behaving like a proper gentleman. It was possible, even if his behavior had sent up a red flag for me.

"So suspicious, Darling," Crispin's voice murmured in my head. "Always sticking your nose into other people's affairs."

And while I didn't appreciate his voice being where it didn't belong, I could hardly quibble with what it had said. I'm curious by nature, and I don't like secrets. I wanted to figure this one out.

An assignation might be exactly what it was, of course. The Crispin in my head hadn't been talking about that sort of affair, but it seemed like a distinct possibility. Wolfgang was young and healthy and wealthy and handsome, and I knew for a fact that he was attractive to women. He might be upstairs in his suite right now, going at it—as Christopher had so charmingly put it—like a rabbit.

If Wolfgang were involved with someone else, though, why would he propose to me? And once he had proposed to me, oughtn't he to have stopped the correspondence—and the rabbiting—with anyone else?

Or the note might have been something else entirely. Wolfgang had called it a business matter, and that might be all it was. A summons to the German embassy, or the bank, or—who knew—the front desk of the Savoy. It could be anything at all.

I shook my head. This had been an ill-advised impulse on my

part. There was nothing for me here. I likely wouldn't recognize the note-writer even if he or she were standing right in front of me —and he or she might be; there were plenty of people in the lobby at this time of day—and the last thing I wanted, was for Wolfgang to come out of whatever hole he had tucked himself away in, and find me standing here. The best thing I could do, was remove myself from the Savoy before he could come back downstairs and realize that I was back, and more importantly, the reason why.

I headed for the front door for the second time in ten minutes, and let the doorman open it for me. "No luck?" he inquired, when he noticed that my hands were still bare.

I shook my head. "It's not important. I have other gloves."

That didn't explain why I would have bothered to come back for this pair, of course, but the doorman was kind enough not to point out the discrepancy. Perhaps he had already realized that I was lying through my teeth.

"Is the *Graf* von Natterdorff still inside," I added, "or did he leave, too?"

"The *Graf* von Natterdorff has not left through this door," the doorman informed me, "although there are many ways into and out of the Savoy."

Yes, of course there were. The hotel is quite large with plenty of exits and entrances.

"Does the *Graf*..." I hesitated, considering how to express what I wanted to ask, and came up with, "—receive a lot of visitors?"

"Not aside from yourself," the doorman said with a little bow. "Although the *Graf* von Natterdorff is no longer a guest at the Savoy, of course."

"No longer...?" I blinked, while the thoughts reordered themselves in my head. "How long... I mean, when... where did he go?"

"I was not informed of the gentleman's current where-abouts," the doorman said.

"When did he leave?"

He thought back. "The gentleman stayed with us for approximately two weeks before he left again. That was at the end of August."

Was it, really?

I had met Wolfgang a week or two into August, while having tea with Christopher at the Savoy. He had recognized me across the lobby and half the tearoom, not to mention across the best part of two decades, and had stopped by our table to introduce himself. And I had run into him again by coincidence a week or so later, so he must still have been staying at the Savoy then, or he wouldn't have had a reason to loiter in the lobby. But the times we had seen one another since then, he had lived elsewhere, it seemed.

During the engagement party in Dorset last month, he had lived elsewhere.

When he proposed to me in the Great Hall at Marsden Manor, he had lived elsewhere.

Last night, during supper at the Criterion, he had lived elsewhere.

At no point had he said anything about it.

And that wasn't all: this morning, when the note had arrived inviting me to tea, it had had the Savoy logo in the corner.

"He must have taken a supply of stationary with him when he left," Christopher said an hour later, when I was back home and was sitting on the edge of my bed, watching him put on his face in my toilet table mirror.

"That's obvious," I answered. How he had come to have the stationary wasn't the concern here. The fact that he had been using it was. Or the fact that he had taken it with him with malice aforethought, perhaps. Part of a plan to do... something.

"Why wouldn't he tell me that he had moved somewhere else?" I continued. "Why make it look like he was still staying at the Savoy?"

"Perhaps he was ashamed," Christopher said. He leaned forward to perfect the curve of his right eyebrow. His eyes met mine in the mirror. "Perhaps he couldn't afford the Savoy any longer, and he didn't want you to know about it."

"That's silly," I said. "He's the *Graf* von Natterdorff. Of course he can afford it."

Christopher arched his drawn-on brows. "How do you know this? Have you contacted Germany and inquired about the state of the Natterdorff holdings? Things are tough in Germany these days, you know."

Of course I knew that, and no, I hadn't inquired. Christopher continued, triumphantly, "You don't even know that there *is* a Natterdorff estate!"

"Wolfgang told me—" I began, and then stopped when Christopher quirked another brow. "Why would he lie to me, Christopher?"

"Why would he move out of the Savoy and not tell you?"

There was nothing I could say to that, of course, since it was the crux of the problem. Christopher waved an expansive hand, the one with the eyebrow-pencil in it. "I don't know why he'd lie, Pippa. Perhaps he didn't do. Perhaps the Natterdorff estate is doing very well indeed, but he simply didn't want to live in a hotel forever. Perhaps it wasn't about cost but about comfort."

"But the Savoy Hotel is comfortable, wouldn't you say?"

"I'm sure it is," Christopher said. "The Schlomskys certainly had a very nice suite. So perhaps it wasn't about cost or comfort, but about privacy. Perhaps he simply wanted a space of his own."

Perhaps so. There's not much privacy in a hotel, with maids coming and going at all times of the day and night. Then again, that describes every noble house in England, and probably in Germany too, so he ought to be used to it.

"What do you suppose he's doing, for which he requires privacy?"

"The same thing every young man does," Christopher sighed, "I presume."

"Carousing? Women, wine, and song?"

"I suppose," Christopher said, and then seemed to think better of it. "No, wait. He proposed to you. There wouldn't be any of that. Or oughtn't to be, at any rate."

Certainly not. However—

"He received a note while we were sitting down to tea. The maître d' delivered it to the table."

"Perfumed?"

I wrinkled my brows. "Not so as I noticed."

The envelope hadn't reeked of anything, I did know that much. But I may have missed a subtler scent in the other odors of the tearoom.

"Did you get a look at it?" Christopher wanted to know. He had put down the eyebrow-pencil now, and had picked up his lipstick instead. Christopher *au naturel* has soft coloring: pale skin, sunny blond hair, light eyelashes and brows. His alter ego, Kitty Dupree, looks quite a lot like Laetitia Marsden, with her glossy, black Dutch Boy bob—which in Christopher's case is a wig, of course. He darkens his brows and lashes to match, and he also uses strong color on his lips. Tonight's lipstick was blood red.

I shook my head. "He opened it at the table, but didn't say a word about what was in it, other than that it was to do with a business matter. He lasted another five or ten minutes before I suggested that we should call it a night."

"You suggested it? He didn't?"

I confirmed that I had done, not Wolfgang. "He fidgeted a bit," I added, "so I thought he would welcome the chance to leave. And he didn't try to get me to stay longer. In fact, when we walked out, he put me into a Hackney and paid the fare."

"As if he wanted to be certain you left," Christopher said.

He's quick on the uptake, my cousin.

"Precisely. By the time I made it back—"

He grinned. "Of course you went back."

"Of course I did. It took a few minutes. I couldn't get the cabbie to set me down until we got to Charing Cross. By the time I got back to the Savoy, Wolfgang was nowhere to be seen. I thought he might have gone up to his room, so I asked, and that was when the doorman told me that the *Graf* von Natterdorff isn't a guest of the Savoy any longer."

"So he wouldn't have a room to go to," Christopher nodded. "Although I suppose he might have gone up to someone else's room."

He might have done, at that. "I thought about sticking around the lobby for a bit, just in case he came back, but I didn't want to risk him seeing me there and thinking I was spying on him."

"Probably a good decision," Christopher agreed. "If he's up to something, he wouldn't want you to find out what it is. If it was something he had wanted you to know, he would have told you."

So one would think. "Speaking of..." I said, "you didn't stop by the Savoy at any point this afternoon, did you?"

"I would have told you if I had done," Christopher answered, turning back to the mirror for the final adjustments to his—or Kitty's—face. "And also I would have waited, to take you home. Why do you ask?"

"Wolfgang thought he had seen you. Or perhaps Crispin. But he must be in Dorset by now, surely."

"Hours ago, I'm quite certain," Christopher agreed, pushing his chair back. "It wasn't me, and I can't imagine that it was him, either. He has a distraught fiancée to make feel better, and an engagement ring to replace."

I made a face but didn't comment, since I didn't want to prolong the conversation about that particular subject. Instead, I watched as Christopher headed for my wardrobe, his size forty-two T-strap shoes clicking against the floor.

"I don't suppose you've heard anything from Tom? News about the investigation?"

"Nothing so far," Christopher said, pulling open the wardrobe. "There was no murder, so they aren't likely to be working around the clock."

I supposed not. "Do you expect to see him later?"

He shook his head. "Not tonight. That would mean another raid, and I can't very well hope for that, can I?"

"You could do. Or you could phone in an anonymous tip yourself, on the way there."

If the Metropolitan Police received a tip-off about the drag ball, Tom would most likely be there in advance of any raid to drag Christopher to safety before anything could happen to him.

He shook his head. "I'd never. I don't want to put any of my friends in danger of being arrested."

"Of course not. You just like it when Tom rushes to the rescue."

He didn't say anything to that, although his cheeks turned pink under the blusher. I added, "Have you ever considered that perhaps you ought to give the man a break and not put yourself in harm's way simply so he has to save you?"

"It isn't harm's way," Christopher protested, turning from the wardrobe with a petal pink, tasseled gown in his hands. "I'm perfectly safe."

"As long as Tom gets to you before the other police can," I said.

"Yes, of course. But what are the chances that they'll raid us again?"

"I'd say they're pretty good, actually. Tom yanked you out of harm's way in April. There was no ball in May, because they were regrouping, but then there was another raid in June, that you only missed by the skin of your teeth, and only because Crispin and I interfered. Tom was there looking for you during that one, too."

Christopher made a face, but insisted, "There won't be a raid tonight."

"How can you possibly know that? Did Tom tell you?"

He didn't answer, and I asked, "Would you like me to come with you?"

"Under no circumstances," Christopher said and tugged the pink frock over his head. When his head came out of the other side, he added, as he shimmied the gown down the rest of the way, "Mum and Dad would kill me if they knew that I had taken you to a drag ball. They wouldn't be happy about me going, either—"

Certainly not.

"—but they'd be even less happy about my debauching you."

I rolled my eyes. "It's hardly debauching, Christopher. I went to the ball at Rectors in June, remember? If just being there is enough to debauch one, I'm debauched already. And don't forget that I'm older than you, too."

"Only by four months or so," Christopher said. "Not enough to matter."

Perhaps not. The fact that I was a young woman and not a man weighed heavier than that I was older in this case.

"At any rate," Christopher said, smoothing the dress over his (non-existent) hips before walking to the toilet table and the wig waiting there. I watched as he dropped it on top of his head and adjusted it.

"At any rate, what?"

He met my eyes in the mirror. "If there is another raid, and if Tom isn't there to rescue me, and I do get arrested, I need someone here I can ring up to bail me out. I can't involve Tom, not at that point—if he came to bail me out, his career would be over—and I don't want them to phone Beckwith Place, or, God forbid, Sutherland House."

I shuddered delicately at the thought. "Decidedly not. We don't want your parents to know anything about it, and if the police rang up Sutherland House, even if it were to talk to Crispin, it would get back to His Grace, wouldn't it?"

"I'm afraid it would," Christopher said, leaning into the mirror and doing the final adjustments to his face and hair. "That's why I need you to stay here. If I get arrested, I'll have them notify Evans, and then Evans will knock you up, and you'll come to the police station with enough cash to take me home. And Mum and Dad and Uncle Harold need never know that anything happened."

That all made sense. However— "Wouldn't it be simpler if you just stayed home? There'd be no danger of being arrested then."

"It would," Christopher said with a grin, "but it's been some time since I had fun, Pippa, and I'm looking forward to it."

"Well, thank you very much for that," I sniffed, faux offended. "Am I no fun, then?"

"You're plenty of fun, my darling." He dropped a kiss on my cheek before snagging his evening cloak from the wardrobe and wrapping it around himself. "But you know what I mean. Now, how do I look?"

He struck a pose.

"Too much like Laetitia for comfort," I said sourly.

"Other than that?"

"You're stunning. As you well know." And so was she, not that that needed mentioning. "Are you certain you won't tell me where you're going to be?"

"Not a chance," Christopher said, and click-clacked his way through the door and down the hall and across the foyer. "Be good, Pippa. Don't wait up."

I hadn't planned to. If he got himself arrested, Evans buzzing from downstairs would wake me, and I would deal with it then. And that was if Tom didn't already have any raid well in hand. I certainly wasn't going to lose sleep over it.

So I waved Christopher off, and locked the door behind him, and went about changing out of the afternoon frock I had worn to tea with Wolfgang, and into pyjamas. It was still early, of course, but I had no plans to go out again, and I was alone in the flat—not that Christopher's presence prevented me from lounging about in my sleepwear. But no one else was here, nor did I expect anyone to turn up, so I might as well make myself comfortable for the rest of the evening.

I curled up on the Chesterfield with a book, enjoying the peace and quiet. Tea with Wolfgang had taken care of my hunger pangs for the time being, so it was several hours later that I meandered into the kitchen and put together a supper of toast and paté and cucumbers. That done, I headed back to the

Chesterfield, but before I got there, the buzzer in the foyer rang.

I headed for it, with my heart knocking against my ribs. It seemed a bit early for a raid—barely gone eight—but stranger things have happened. "Yes, Evans?"

"Visitor for Mr. Astley, Miss Darling."

"Mr. Astley isn't here," I said, and thought better of it. "Who is it, Evans?"

If it was Crispin, perhaps Wolfgang had been right and he truly had seen him in the Savoy lobby earlier.

"Mr. Gardiner, Miss Darling," Evans said.

Uh-oh. Tom wouldn't be happy when he got up here and I told him where Christopher had gone—or rather, when I told him that Christopher had departed to another drag ball, since I didn't actually know his precise whereabouts.

On the other hand, he wouldn't be happy about my sending him away without seeing him, either, now that he knew I was at home.

I sighed. "Send him up, Evans."

"Yes, Miss Darling."

Evans disappeared, and I put down the food so I could unlock the door and wait for Tom.

"Drink?" I inquired when he appeared a minute later. "Tea? Toast?"

"No, thank you, Pippa." He gave me a distracted sort of look that didn't seem to take in the fact that I was standing in front of him in my jim-jams. Instead, he scanned the sitting room and its total lack of Christopher. "Kit not here?"

"He's gone out."

I said it very blandly, with no inflection whatsoever. His eyes narrowed anyway. "Don't tell me he went to a ball?"

"Why ask if you already know?"

He muttered something. It was undoubtedly a bad word, so I didn't ask him to repeat it. "Where?" he asked.

"I have no idea. He doesn't tell me these things, you know. Afraid I'm going to follow him there, no doubt."

Tom didn't answer, and I added, "You would know if there was going to be another raid tonight, wouldn't you?"

"I do try to keep up. Although I've been busy today."

He hesitated a moment before he added, "I thought Kit had stopped frequenting those."

"Not at all," I said. "He missed September's ball because we were at Marsden Manor that weekend, but other than that, I don't think he has ever made a decision that he wasn't going to go back."

Tom muttered something else, his jaw—very nice and strong—tight.

"Have a seat," I added, when he kept standing in front of the Chesterfield. "Are you certain I can't get you anything to drink?"

"No, thank you, Pippa." Although he did sit down, and put the Homburg on the small table next to him.

"You're not on duty, are you?"

He shook his head. "Just not hungry. I grabbed a bite with Finch before we parted ways for the night."

"At least you don't have to work through the night on this one."

He leaned back. "No, this is one of the cases we work between the urgent ones. Until someone dies in a more sinister manner than Lady Latimer's butler, anyway."

"Do you think that's going to happen?"

"That depends," Tom said, making himself comfortable. "Sooner or later, he's going to burgle a house where someone is awake and sees him—"

"Someone was awake and saw him at Marsden House," I pointed out.

"Someone who doesn't hide under the blankets and hope he goes away. Someone who goes after him instead."

He sighed. "I thought better of Lady Laetitia, to be honest. I thought she would have been the type to shriek and send him packing."

I would have thought the same. There's one thing to see a burglar and actively attack him. I don't know if I would expect any woman to do that, although had it been my bedchamber he had invaded, I would certainly have been tempted. But it's quite another to hide under the blankets and hope the danger goes away. Laetitia wasn't a shrinking violet in any other aspect of her life, and I was surprised that she hadn't shown more gumption on this occasion.

"She's lucky he was more interested in getting away than in her," Tom added ominously, and I shivered.

"Indeed."

"But sooner or later, someone will see him who won't pull the counterpane up over their head. And at that point, depending on the situation, the only way he can get away might be to attack first. And if he does..."

I nodded. If he did, it could very easily turn fatal. A pistol, a knife, or even just a push from the top of a staircase if the burglar didn't carry a weapon. Any and all of those could result in someone's death.

"Is there any way to determine who might be targeted next, and warn them?"

"It's high society," Tom said. "The Bright Young Set and their families. So no, no real reason to suspect that anyone in particular is next. I'm sure word is getting around by now, but other than that, there's not much we can do to put anyone on alert."

"Laetitia and Lady Violet Cummings were both at Marsden Manor last month," I said.

Tom nodded. "But Lady Latimer was not, nor were the Wickstroms. Or the Harrimans."

No, they hadn't been. I wasn't sure I even knew the Wickstroms or Harrimans, and while I had come face to face with the elderly Lady Latimer at some point, it hadn't been at Marsden Manor.

"Besides," Tom added, "surely you're not suggesting that this character was present in Dorset for Lord St George's engagement party? That would make him one of the aristocracy."

A gentleman thief. That creature of myth and bad penny dreadfuls. Popular in fiction but not in real life, where gentlemen generally have means of support other than stealing.

"Of course not," I said. "If Dominic Rivers had still been alive, perhaps I would have considered him. He was dealing dope, so he might not have been above a bit of thievery, too. But he's dead, so it's a moot point. Almost everyone else at the Manor that weekend was a friend or a relative of mine. Christopher, Francis, Crispin... even Geoffrey, I suppose. He'll become a family member once St George and Laetitia tie the knot."

Tom nodded. "But Lord Geoffrey Marsden has been waiting for trial since then, so it couldn't have been him last night."

No, it couldn't have been. "The only ones of the gentlemen I didn't know before I got there, were Bilge Fortescue and Reginald Fish. I'm sure Lady Serena alibies Bilge..."

"I haven't looked into Bilge Fortescue," Tom said, "but yes, if there was a question about that, I'm sure she would do."

Precisely.

"Not that I think Bilge had anything to do with it. I knew

the bloke at Eton, and if there's anyone who lacks the personality to be a gentleman thief, it's Bilge Fortescue."

No doubt. "The Honorable Reggie didn't strike me as being the type, either," I agreed. "So the whole thing is most likely just a coincidence, and Marsden Manor has nothing to do with it."

Tom nodded. "Likely not."

"Do you have any idea…?"

He shook his head. "London is a big place, and so far, he hasn't left us much to go on."

"No fingerprints? You're checking the pawn brokers, I assume?"

"Yes, Pippa." His lips twitched. "I don't need you to tell me how to do my job."

"Of course not. I was merely curious. Do you have no idea who might be behind it? Is there only one person, do you think, or several? A gang?"

"So far," Tom said, "there seems to be just one. But unless he has a different existence during daylight hours, and runs his own jewelry store, he has to take the spoils to someone to deal with for him. So far, we haven't been able to identify that person, or persons, either."

"I don't suppose it's likely that he just wants to keep what he steals so he can gloat over it?"

Tom smirked. "No, Pippa, I don't imagine so. There's quite a bit of risk involved in this, as I'm sure you've realized. He'll go to prison for a long time when he's caught. The people he has stolen from are well-connected and powerful, and they will want to see justice served. I don't think it's something someone would do without a hefty payday."

"He must be selling the jewelry to benefit from stealing it, then."

"Maybe so," Tom said. "But there are other ways to benefit.

Selling the jewelry as is could be difficult. There are some well-known pieces in the spoils, things that someone might recognize—"

Like the Sutherland parure, or the parts of it that had gotten away.

"I wouldn't put it past Uncle Harold," I said. "I'm frankly surprised that he agreed to part with the earrings before the wedding ceremony. Everything except the ring is usually kept as a carrot to make certain the bride makes it to the altar for the nuptials."

Tom lifted a shoulder and reached for his hat. "I should go. Before it gets too late."

"I don't mind the company," I told him. "Although..." I tilted my head to contemplate him, "perhaps you plan to go in search of Christopher?"

"I plan to find out whether any raids are scheduled for tonight that may affect Kit," Tom said, which sounded like the same thing.

"And if you find out that a raid is scheduled?"

"Then I'll go there and find Kit and bring him to you before anything can happen to him."

His jaw looked quite heroic.

"That's lovely," I said. "Would you mind if I accompanied you?"

He squinted at me, and I added, "You're off the clock, aren't you? Doing this on your own time? Just two friends looking for a mutual friend who went out to a party? And I would be with you, so it's not likely that I would run into any trouble."

He sighed. "I suppose I can't stop you. Although if Kit has a hissy fit when he sees you, don't blame it on me."

As if I would. "Five minutes," I told him, as I pushed to my feet and headed for the hallway and the door to my room.

CHAPTER EIGHT

THE LAST TIME I had crashed one of Christopher's drag balls, I had been wearing black tie evening kit complete with topper, and I had been accompanied by Crispin, in one of Christopher's gowns and makeup. This time, I didn't bother with any of that, just pulled on a skirt and blouse, jacket and brogues—for easy movement in the event that we'd end up having to evade pursuit—and yanked a cloche hat over my brown bob. I hoped that we wouldn't have to do any running— my scabbed knees were still stiff—but if the worst came to the worst, at least I would be prepared for it.

"Ready." I walked out into the foyer. Part of me had been concerned that perhaps Tom would take the opportunity to make himself scarce while I was in the other room—Christopher would have thought nothing of sneaking off by himself, had he decided I was better off staying home alone—so I was pleased to see Tom still waiting.

He gave me a quick up-and-down. "You don't want to wear something more appropriate to the occasion?"

"I'd rather wear something that will allow me to run, should the need arise," I told him, and headed for the door. "Where shall we go first?"

The answer was Scotland Yard, where Tom disappeared inside the building whilst I made myself comfortable in the passenger seat of the Crossley Tender, watching as police constables and blokes in mufti came and went—there was even one fellow being taken inside in handcuffs—and then Tom came back out and I straightened. "Well?"

It was impossible to tell from his face or body language whether we were going to have to save Christopher from a raid, or whether he'd be taking me home to the flat for the rest of the evening.

He twisted the key in the ignition and the Tender rolled across the cobbles. He had to raise his voice to be heard over the twin sounds of the motor and the tires on the uneven surface. "They're in the cellar on Heddon Street."

"You mean Christopher and company? In a cellar on Heddon Street?"

Heddon was a small street, practically an alley, that ran parallel to Regent Street and Savile Row just on the edge of the Mayfair neighborhood. It missed being in Soho only by virtue of being on the west side of Regent Street instead of on the east side. I was familiar with it, although if you didn't know that it was there, you could be excused for not noticing it.

"*The* cellar," Tom said, with emphasis. "The old Cave of the Golden Calf."

It took me a moment to place the reference, and then a few more to dredge up what I knew about the old nightclub that had gone by that name. By then, we were circling Trafalgar Square.

"I didn't realize that it was still open," I said. "Or that it was open again."

"As far as I know," Tom answered, "it's not."

"Another case like Rectors, then? A private arrangement?"

"Most likely." The yellow street lamps of Cockspur Street illuminated his face in flickers as we made our way up towards Haymarket. "Just like Rectors, the Cave went bankrupt, although a decade sooner. It only lasted two years, from 1912 to 1914. The war killed it."

"And it's been sitting empty since then?"

Tom shrugged. "It hasn't come to my attention in the time I've worked for the Yard. That doesn't mean something hasn't been going on there, but whatever it is, it hasn't drawn the attention of the police."

"Until now."

"Yes," Tom agreed. "Until now."

"If we're on our way there, can I assume that a raid is scheduled?"

"I didn't want to be too obvious," Tom said, maneuvering the Tender onto Haymarket Street from Cockspur. "I can only ask about this so many times before someone starts to suspect that I have a personal reason for inquiring."

Yes, of course. "In other words, you aren't certain?"

"I know where tonight's event is taking place," Tom said. "Someone took the trouble to dig that information up. From that, I can assume that there's at least a fifty percent chance that there's another raid scheduled."

That made sense. "So we're going to rescue Christopher?"

"We're going to take a look at the situation," Tom said. He glanced at me, up and down for a second. "Neither of us is exactly dressed for crashing a drag ball."

No. He was dressed in tweed and a Homburg, and so was I, more or less. There wasn't a stitch of evening wear between us.

"We'll just have to do the best we can," I said. "Besides, the first time you rescued Christopher—or the first time I knew about it; when I heard the two of you arguing in the foyer of the flat, the day before the old Duke of Sutherland died—you were wearing the same thing you are now. A lack of evening attire didn't stop you then."

"And it won't stop me now," Tom said, and turned the Tender into Piccadilly Circus, where I had scurried across the street just last night, "but it won't make it any easier."

No, I didn't expect it would.

The Tender passed the entrance to the underground, where I had tumbled down the infamous staircase, and turned onto Regent Street. I peered out the window. "It's right up here, isn't it?"

"On the left," Tom nodded. "The entrance to what looks like an alley."

He indicated. I nodded. It did look very much like the entrance to an alley, or at least it looked more like one of the narrow, medieval London streets than the wide boulevards that were *de rigeur* in this part of town. Regent Street was at least twice, if not three times wider, than Heddon Street.

Tom pulled the Crossley Tender to a stop by the pavement, and cut the motor. Silence descended, or as silent as it ever is in London at any time of day or night. There were people walking, many of them in evening wear, most of them headed in the direction of Piccadilly and the nightlife. And there were plenty of motorcars, Hackney cabs as well as private conveyances. I could see no police vehicles other than the one we were in, so forces had not started amassing for the raid yet, if there was to be one.

"It's still early," Tom said when I commented on it, and opened his door. "Ready to go?"

"Please." I opened my own door and hopped onto the pavement, forgetting for a moment that I had hurt myself yesterday. My knees twinged, and I grimaced.

"All right?" Tom came around the motorcar and gave me a look.

I nodded. "Forgot for a moment that I'm wounded. It's fine."

His lips twitched, but he didn't say anything else, just presented his elbow. "Shall we, then?"

I put my fingers on it. "By all means."

We crossed the pavement and ducked onto Heddon Street.

It's a small stub of a street, narrow and enclosed by tall buildings in red and pale brick. The building to our right was broken up by several arched openings on the ground floor, outlined in white cement, or perhaps limestone. One opening was a door, the other windows. The windows were dark, and so was everything else. The cobbles under our feet were uneven, and I clung to Tom's arm as my ankle twisted.

"Do you hear that?" he asked.

I had been too busy trying to keep my balance to do anything that required effort beyond staying on my feet. But as the traffic noise from Regent Street faded, I picked up what his sharper ears had already noticed: the dull thump of music from somewhere down the narrow street.

"I can feel it," I said, through the soles of my brogues and up my spine, "but I can't tell where it's coming from."

"Down there." He nodded to the brick building at the end of the street, dead-ending into another brick wall. "That's the old Cave of the Golden Calf."

I eyed it dubiously. "It doesn't look like a nightclub."

"That's because it isn't," Tom said. "The nightclub is in the cellar. Always has been."

He indicated an unassuming door set into the wall beside the much wider and more ostentatious main entrance. "There's the way in."

"When I went with St George to Rectors," I said, eyeing it, "there was a nun in a habit guarding the door."

Or a man dressed in a nun's habit; he hadn't been an actual nun, nor had I ever supposed him to be.

"There might be someone inside, guarding this one," Tom said, nudging me towards it.

I flicked a look up at him, even as I allowed it. "Do you know the password, if there is someone?"

"Do you?" He looked down at me.

"It depends," I said.

He nodded. "Well, if it comes to it, I have a badge."

"I'm sure you do. Although flashing that might do more harm than good."

He didn't respond to that. When I looked up at him, it was dark enough in the shadow of the building that I could barely make out the lower half of his face, the chin and mouth and the tip of the nose below the brim of the Homburg.

"Are you certain we should both go inside?"

"I'm certain *I* should go inside," Tom said, "and I'm equally certain that you won't agree to stay here while I do."

He was right about that.

"Nor," he added, "do I particularly want to leave you up here alone. Kit would have my hide if anything happened to you, and he isn't the only one."

No, he wasn't. The entire Astley clan, with the exception of Uncle Harold, would have something to say about it if I died from being left alone in a dark alley at night. Nor did I particularly want to be left alone, of course. Not because I was worried —the alley was deserted, and besides, I can take care of myself —but because I was curious. We were here: there was no way I would consent to being left outside while he ventured in.

"Come along," Tom said. He reached for the door. I waited for him to pass through before I followed.

I had expected some sort of lobby, I suppose. Instead, we walked directly onto a dark and narrow landing with a stairwell going down into blackness. The music was louder in here, but still muted, as if there were a door or two between us and the musicians.

Tom took my arm as we advanced the couple of steps towards the staircase. "Don't want you to fall again."

No, that wouldn't be good. Unlike last night, there was no one in front of me to break my fall, so if I tumbled face-first down the staircase, I would surely break my neck, or if not that, at least both my arms.

There were seventeen steps down, and at the bottom, we found ourselves standing in front of a heavy door. In front of the door stood a man in a deerstalker hat.

"I know about this," I told Tom delightedly. "May I?"

He nodded, hazel eyes amused, and I turned to the gentleman in the hat. "Hello, Sherlock Holmes. We're here to see Watson."

The gentleman's face didn't change, but he stepped aside, pulling the door open at the same time. A wave of jazz music poured through and filled up the stairwell. When I stepped across the threshold with Tom right behind, the doorman winked, albeit not at me, but at Tom.

"How did you learn the password?" Tom wanted to know when the door was shut at our back, sealing the noise back into the club. He had to lean in to speak directly into my ear.

I leaned in the other direction to speak into his. "St George told me. The password to the nun at Rectors was 'sister.' He said if the doorman was dressed up as Sherlock Holmes, the password was 'Watson.' Apparently there's a place in Spitalfields where you have to tell them that you're there to get lucky, although I've never been."

His lips twitched. "Lucky, or to Spitalfields?"

"Both," I said, looking around. "You knew all this already, I assume?"

"I knew the passwords, yes. Those are common knowledge, at least at the office. I don't think I know the place in Spitalfields."

"How about the one in Marylebone?"

"Not that one either," Tom said. "I suppose I shall have to ask Lord St George for elucidation."

He turned his attention to the rest of the club and the reason we were here. "Do you see him?"

The old Cave of the Golden Calf was an oppressively low-ceilinged room with brightly-colored but faded murals along three walls. As best I could see through the heavy layer of cigarette smoke, they depicted oceans and jungles and other types of landscapes, in quite a primitive style. One wall showed an array of what were surely natives—naked and brown—frolicking with... were they horses? In some sort of mud-puddle, it seemed, or perhaps just dirty water. There were bare behinds on display—on the wall, I mean, not on the dancefloor—although the figures facing the room were at least decently covered, by what looked like palm fronds or the horses' heads.

A few divans sat along the walls, and an array of tables had been moved aside to make an open area for dancing in the middle of the floor. What looked like perhaps seventy to a hundred people moved to the sounds of the jazz band playing on the small stage.

Just like the last time I had crashed one of Christopher's drag balls, it took a moment or two to realize that most of the dancers, even the ones with the high heels in the sparkling gowns, were men. And of course I knew that already, having watched Christopher put on his face and wig and pink frock in front of my makeup mirror a few hours ago. But it was one thing to know it intellectually, and another thing for my eyes to see it. We see what we expect to see, what we're used to seeing, and at first glance, I saw men dancing with women, the way they do all over London. It was only after the first second that my brain caught up with what I was actually looking at, which were men dancing with other men.

"There," I said, pointing. Christopher's petal pink dress was fairly easy to pick out among all the evening suits and darker gowns. "Dancing with the bloke with the carnation in his lapel. Next to the redhead in the seafoam green."

The red bob was certainly a wig, just like the person in the seafoam was of the male persuasion. It was quite a nice frock he had on, however.

Tom nodded. He started forward, and I grabbed him by the sleeve. "You can't just grab him and haul him off."

"I've done it before," Tom said, eyes on Christopher and his jaw tight.

"He's not doing anything to him." The bloke with the carnation wasn't doing anything to Christopher, was what I meant. No one was doing anything to Christopher. He was here of his own free will, and seemed to be enjoying it. His poppy-red lips were curved in a smile, and his eyes sparkled.

And perhaps that was exactly what Tom objected to.

"Why don't we simply dance our way over there?" I suggested. "Christopher will see us, he'll understand why we're here, and he'll come quietly. There's no need to cause a scene."

"There's every need," Tom growled. "That... that... *chap* is feeling him up."

The emphasis he put on the word made it clear that the word he would prefer to use was one altogether less restrained.

"He's not."

Admittedly, the gentleman's hand was roving over Christopher's back in a way more suitable to a secluded alcove than the middle of a dancefloor, but it looked no different than what was going on all over the rest of the club.

"Any lower," Tom said, "and that hand palms Kit's arse."

That was rather a crude assessment, if entirely accurate, and for a moment I couldn't get my voice to cooperate. Tom, meanwhile, didn't take his eyes off the pair, and I could feel the tension build up around him, like Mount Vesuvius about to blow.

"Let's dance," I said brightly when I had my breath back, and held my hands out. Tom's eyes lingered on the dancefloor for a second before he transferred his attention to me. It was another second before he processed my position and what he was expected to do. Then he nodded sharply, took my hand in his, snaked his other arm around my waist, and pulled me into a quickstep.

I sincerely hoped he did a better job of subterfuge if he ever had to go undercover during work, because there was none here. No slow circling of the floor, to make us look like we belonged. No attention on his dance partner—me—at all. Just a straight line into the middle of the floor, where we ended up next to Christopher and the latter's dance partner. I elbowed Christopher discreetly in the ribs, and he moved out of the way, courteously, without looking at me.

"Cut in," I told Tom, and he gave me a look.

"Do you want me to dance with Kit or the other bloke?"

"Christopher," I said, "of course."

"And how does the other bloke react to losing Kit and ending up with you?"

I didn't know, but now that he mentioned it, perhaps I didn't want to find out. I couldn't imagine that the other bloke would be happy. I wouldn't at all be what he wanted.

But needs must. I took my hand off Tom's shoulder to poke a finger into the bare skin of Christopher's upper arm.

"Ow!"

He jerked and turned towards me, mouth already open to remonstrate, and then his eyes widened with recognition. "Pippa? What are you doing here? And..." His eyes moved left, or right for him. "Tom? What's wrong?"

He glanced around the room, having already—of course—guessed what might be coming.

"Nothing," I said. "We've come to take you home."

Christopher's eyes narrowed and his jaw set stubbornly. But before he could inform us that he didn't want to go home—because that opinion was absolutely coming—his dance partner got involved.

"What's all this, then?" He squared his shoulders. Tom gave him a narrow look—it's a classic question for any constable to ask, after all, so perhaps Tom wanted to ascertain that the chap wasn't a policeman here undercover—but they must not know one another, because other than a perfectly natural few seconds of mutual glaring, nothing indicated previous acquaintance.

Having made his dislike plain, Tom turned his attention back to Christopher. "Time to go, Kit."

"What if I don't want to go?" Christopher asked. He folded his arms across his front and stuck his bottom lip out, sulkily.

"Yes," his dance partner nodded, and shoved his shoulder between Christopher and Tom. "What if he doesn't want to go?"

Tom's eyes narrowed, and so did the other bloke's. By now, other people had started to notice the four of us standing stock still in the middle of the dancefloor, and we were getting a bit of an audience.

I rolled my eyes and leaned closer to Christopher. "Do you really want him—either one of them—to prove his devotion with a fistfight in the middle of an illicit club full of boys in makeup and dresses? You know what will happen if the police show up."

He didn't answer, just watched Tom and the other chap squaring up, and I added, "Everyone in the room gets hauled off to jail, Christopher. Including you and me. We'll have to apply to your father for bail money. And what do you imagine happens to Tom if Pendennis learns that he got into a bloody boxing match in a place like this? Over you?"

Christopher's lips parted for a moment—perhaps he contemplated the idea and decided he liked it; something like that would certainly allay whatever concerns he had about Tom's feelings, wouldn't it?—but after a moment he glanced over at me. "We'd have to say that he did it for you, I suppose."

"So we'd lie, is what you're saying. You, I, and Tom get arrested for indecent behavior in an illicit establishment operating without a license—I see liquor, Christopher; I'm sure there's no license for that—and we lie about what Tom's doing here? And you think that's fair to him?"

He didn't answer, and I gave him a push. "Just agree to leave. I don't want to say the word out loud for fear of causing a panic, but it starts with an R and ends with a D, and there have been several of them already."

Christopher's eyes widened, and I continued, "It isn't certain that there'll be another tonight, but Tom was able to dig up this location, so it's likely that someone is keeping an eye on it. If tonight passes without any trouble, and Lady Austin decides it's safe to come back next time, I'm sure it won't be equally safe then."

Christopher nodded. His eyes flickered over the room once before they returned to me. "Very well, then. I suppose if I don't come along quietly, Tom will manhandle me out of here?"

"Don't be silly," I said. "He would never lay a hand on you, and you know it."

"You didn't see what happened in April," Christopher retorted. "He threw me over his shoulder and hauled me out, kicking and screaming."

My lips twitched. There had been an equal amount annoyance and shivery delight in his voice when he said it, which made me want to smile. Instead of doing so, I told him, "We ought perhaps to try to avoid that this time. The less attention on us, the better."

Christopher nodded. "If there's going to be a..." He hesitated, "a you-know-what later, I don't feel good about leaving everyone else here to be swept up in it, Pippa."

No, of course not. "But if you start yelling about it, you'll start a riot, and we definitely don't want that."

"Definitely not," Tom agreed. He wrapped a hand around Christopher's wrist. "Come along, Kit."

I waited for the chap Christopher had been dancing with to object, but Tom must have cowed him sufficiently, because when I glanced over my shoulder to where he had been standing, there was no sign of him.

"You too, Pippa," Tom added, as he tugged Christopher towards the door. "Chop-chop."

I gave one last look to where the other bloke had been standing before I scurried after them.

"Coming."

WE GOT a few stares on our way out—more because of me than either Tom or Christopher, I thought; I suppose my type wasn't usually seen here—but no one tried to stop us. Tom shoved the door open and pulled Christopher through, and I caught it on the backswing and followed. The chap in the deerstalker arched a brow when he saw Tom— "Back so soon?"—

and then lowered both when he saw Christopher. "Problem, Kitty?"

"Not for me," Christopher said calmly, but with a flirtatious flick of his wig. "He's ever so masterful, don't you know?"

The tops of Tom's cheekbones darkened, and I giggled. Christopher smirked and added, "Although you may want to close down early tonight."

"Is that so?" The eyebrows rose again, and the doorman examined Tom a bit more closely. "Know something we don't, do you?"

"We don't know anything for certain," I said, to take some of the pressure off Tom. He was caught between a rock and a hard place, poor chap: on the one hand, he wanted Christopher (and to give him the benefit of the doubt, me) safely out of the Cave of the Golden Calf before anything happened, but on the other hand, he didn't want to totally botch a police operation, either, or so I assumed. Every other time this had happened, I supposed he had simply lain in wait so he could remove Christopher from the line of fire at an opportune moment. Here, we were practically forcing him to out himself as a police officer, as well as to give the potential arrestees advance warning of an upcoming raid, and it couldn't have been easy. "Just forget we were here, please."

I nudged Christopher, who nudged Tom, who started up the staircase to the street. Behind us, the music and voices became louder for a second as I assumed the doorman opened the door to the nightclub to start evacuating the guests.

CHAPTER NINE

PART of me half expected to walk through the door into Heddon Street and come face to face with a police cordon. That wasn't likely to have happened in the time we had been in the cellar, of course, not when Heddon Street had been deserted when we went inside. But my guilty conscience, or whatever you want to call it, nonetheless conjured an imaginary battalion of police officers ready to arrest Christopher and myself, and subject Tom to the law enforcement equivalent of a court martial, as soon as we walked out.

None of that happened. Heddon was just as peaceful and quiet as when we had left it. There was the faint sound of music from below, and the buzz of traffic from Regent Street and Piccadilly, but other than that, everything was silent.

Not that that seemed to calm Tom at all. He gave a quick but comprehensive look around the deserted street before heading for Regent at a good clip. "Come along. Move it."

This was addressed to Christopher, who traipsed behind, tethered to Tom by the latter's fingers wrapped around his wrist. As I had seen for myself earlier, the cobbles were uneven and a person was likely to court a twisted ankle if he or she wasn't careful. Christopher kept up, but he also kept swearing under his breath about the treatment he was receiving.

"Slow down, dammit. I can't walk as fast as you can in these shoes."

"Should have thought of that before you came here," Tom told him, although he did slow down a little. The only reason I noticed was because it made it a little easier for me to navigate the cobblestones, too.

"If I had realized that I'd be required to run for my life," Christopher said tartly, "perhaps I wouldn't have done."

Tom shot him a look over his shoulder. "Don't you think you ought to have prepared yourself for that, Kit? After the last raid, and the raid before that, and—"

"He's got you there, Christopher," I said, as I minced along behind the two of them.

Christopher sniffed. "I'm well aware, Pippa." He gave an exaggerated shudder, and added, "Wouldn't even let me pick up my evening wrap. Now I shall probably get a cold on top of everything else. Not to mention that I shall have to spend the money for a new one."

Tom muttered something, but by then we were out of the alley and standing on the pavement on Regent Street.

"I can go back for it," I offered, but Tom shook his head.

"Under no circumstances will either of you set foot in that place again. I'll buy you a new wrap myself if I have to, Kit."

The Crossley Tender was parked a few yards away, and Tom tugged Christopher towards it. I followed. Before Tom opened the passenger door, however, he shrugged out of his tweed coat and draped it over Christopher's bare shoulders. "There."

Christopher blinked. "Well," he said after a moment, "it isn't velvet and ermine, but I suppose it'll do."

"Glad to hear it. You'd best go into the back where you're less visible."

Tom pulled the door open and moved the front seat forward. Christopher made a moue—I'm sure he would prefer to sit next to Tom—but he didn't complain, just made his way into the rear of the motorcar.

I ambled over and, as soon as Christopher was situated in the back, fitted myself into the front passenger seat. Tom made certain my skirt had made it all the way into the motorcar and made to close the door. And just as he did, a gentleman in evening kit—one I had noticed out of the corner of my eye, but to whom I had paid no attention beyond that—slowed to a stop as he reached us. "Philippa? Is that you, *mein Schatz?*"

"Wolfgang." I smiled brightly, even as I felt Christopher's consternation from behind me. "What are you doing here?"

He was dressed for an evening out, in a handsome, black overcoat and topper, with a silk scarf around his neck, so the question was mostly rhetorical. He was on his way to a restaurant, or the theatre, or somewhere like that. Perhaps he had a date.

He smiled. "That should be my question, should it not?"

Should it? While I contemplated that, and also how I felt about him possibly going on a date with someone who wasn't me—was this evening what the note had been about?—Wolfgang nodded to Tom. "Detective Sergeant Gardiner." He flicked a glance into the back of the motorcar. "And... Lady Laetitia? How lovely to see you again."

He clicked his heels together and inclined his head. Christopher muttered something non-committal in a breathy, higher-pitched voice than usual, and shrank as far back into the dark of the backseat as he could. His voice sounded nothing like Laetitia's, and I could see Wolfgang's eyebrows begin to draw together. Tom must have seen it, too, because he jumped into the fray. "*Graf* von Natterdorff. Out on the town?"

Wolfgang took his eyes off Christopher to focus on Tom. "I'm on my way to Piccadilly."

"I'd offer you a lift," Tom said, "but as you can see, we're going in the opposite direction."

He indicated the nose of the Tender, which was, indeed, facing away from Piccadilly.

Not that I wanted Wolfgang to get into the Tender with us. He didn't know about Christopher's habits—or if he had picked up on the fact that Christopher was queer, he didn't know that my cousin had a penchant for women's frocks and drag balls— and it was probably best that he didn't find out. The fewer people who knew about that, the better.

And yes, I do recognize the hypocrisy. Considering that Wolfgang was someone I contemplated marrying. I shouldn't be keeping secrets from him, even if they were Christopher's secrets and not my own.

Wolfgang waved the offer, or rather the lack of offer, away. "No matter. It's a pleasant evening for a walk. You're headed back to the flat, I presume?"

He looked at me. I nodded. We hadn't discussed it, but I was sure that's where Tom was planning to take us.

"Just the three of you?" Wolfgang glanced into the backseat again, and I knew without looking that Christopher was pressing his back against the upholstery to get as far into the darkness as he could. "Where is Lord St George this evening?"

There was a beat of silence. It went on a second too long, or perhaps that was simply my guilty conscience. "Coming," I said eventually. "He and Christopher. By the way, Wolfgang, I don't know who you saw at the Savoy earlier, but I don't think it was either of them. Christopher said he hadn't left the flat during the time I was gone, and—"

Wolfgang waved it away. "Likely just a chance resemblance." He took a step back from the car. "I shan't keep you any longer. May I contact you tomorrow, Philippa?"

"Of course," I told him. "I'm looking forward to it."

He nodded. "Until then, *mein Schatz.* Detective Sergeant. Lady Laetitia."

He clicked his heels together again, and bowed to each of them. Christopher murmured something suitable, while Tom nodded back. "Good to see you, Natterdorff. Until next time."

He turned the key in the ignition as Wolfgang walked away. I resisted the temptation to turn and peer after him. "Do you think he suspected?"

Tom waited until he had cranked the motor before he answered. "Suspected what? That Lady Laetitia isn't Lady Laetitia but Kit?"

"He seemed to suspect something," Christopher said, leaning forward to put his chin on the back of my seat. "Although it might simply be that he was surprised that the two of you and Laetitia would go anywhere together."

We rolled away from the curb.

"He definitely knows that Laetitia and I don't get along," I said as we proceeded up Regent Street towards Oxford Circus and home. "And of course he knows that Laetitia and Crispin are engaged. I wonder what he thought Tom and I were doing together?"

Tom slanted me a look. "Aren't you and Natterdorff engaged, as well?"

"It's open to interpretation," I said, and Christopher added, "Pippa doesn't want to move to Germany."

"I can't blame you there," Tom said.

I slanted a look back at him. "Why is that? Have you been to Germany?"

"Once, a few years ago," Tom said, "and it was fine. But this is home, isn't it?"

"Not for Pippa," Christopher told him, and I shot him a look over my shoulder.

"Of course it is, Christopher. Why else wouldn't I want to go?"

"You were born there."

I scowled at him. "I'm well aware of that, thank you. And I suppose I mightn't mind a trip to see it again, perhaps. But I wouldn't want to live there. I'm English now."

"I can't imagine Natterdorff agreeing to stay here forever," Tom commented, and I turned back to him.

"I have no idea whether he would do or not. The question hasn't come up."

"He didn't suggest staying," Christopher ventured, "did he?"

"It's likely he couldn't," Tom answered, before I had the opportunity to say that no, Wolfgang hadn't suggested it. "He must have business here, something that allows his presence in England, a decade after the war, as a German. But there's likely to be a limit to the government's largesse. I doubt he'd be allowed to stay indefinitely."

"If he married me?" Or I married him, rather.

"Perhaps," Tom allowed, "although it's possible that that would affect your own situation instead."

"My situation?"

"If you're half German, and you're choosing to marry a German, the British authorities might decide that you're putting Germany above England, and send you there."

"Can they do that?"

"I imagine they could if they wanted to," Tom said. "I'm not with the diplomatic corps, so I'm not the right person to ask. But it wouldn't surprise me."

Nor would it surprise me, really, now that he had pointed it out. I sat back against the seat and drew my bottom lip into my mouth, gnawing anxiously.

"Surely not?" Christopher said from the backseat.

Tom flicked him a look in the mirror. "I don't know, Kit. But I don't think it's a risk I would want to take."

No, I didn't think I wanted to risk it either, now that the hazards had been pointed out to me. "That's going to be an awkward conversation."

"You've already laid the basis for it," Christopher told me, "by saying you'd prefer to stay here. It's just one step further to break things off completely."

I supposed he was right about that. The question was, did I want to break things off completely?

On the one hand, there was Germany and not wanting to go there. There was the possibility that I was, perhaps, risking my life here in England simply by associating with Wolfgang.

On the other hand, there was the fact that I liked him well enough, and that by marrying him, I'd become a *Gräfin*. Not that I particularly wanted to be a *Gräfin*, but it was the sort of thing a young woman of our class aspired to. And there was a part of me that wanted to see Heidelberg again, even if I didn't want to live there permanently.

But I could always take myself to Heidelberg on holiday. I wouldn't have to marry Wolfgang for that. I could talk Christopher into going with me, or perhaps Aunt Roz. Or both. Christopher's mother might want to see the place where her sister had lived and died. My father had died on the Front, I didn't know exactly where, and had been laid to rest in a hurried ceremony in a field somewhere on the Continent. But my mother had a proper grave in a proper graveyard, and her sister might want to see it.

"St George would be devastated," Tom said and brought me out of myself and back to the interior of the motorcar. We had passed Oxford Circus and were on our way towards Tottenham Court Road.

"Excuse me?"

"St George. He would be devastated if you ran off to the Continent."

I snorted. "Hardly. He's marrying Laetitia, and I think they'd both be happier if I made myself scarce."

"I don't think Crispin would agree with that," Christopher said from the backseat. "He rather enjoys his pining, I think."

Tom chuckled. I glared at him, and he added, "Come now, Pippa. This can't have come as a surprise. We've all been telling you to stop flirting for months."

"I haven't been flirting," I said mulishly. I liked bantering with Crispin—he's clever and quick-witted and has a wicked sense of humor when he's not being deliberately cruel, or at least when he isn't being deliberately cruel to me—and I'll also admit, under pressure, that I have enjoyed the occasions upon which our banter had made Laetitia (and sometimes her mother) squirm with discomfort. But that didn't mean I'd been *flirting*. Certainly not. Just because I enjoyed the bickering, didn't mean there was anything romantic afoot.

"Here we are," Tom said. He turned the Tender onto Essex and we could see the Essex House Mansions looming at the end of the street.

"Are you coming up for a drink?"

Tom slanted Christopher a look in the mirror. "I don't think I'd better, Kit. It's been a very long day."

Yes, of course it had been. He had been working since four o'clock this morning, hadn't he?

"Any news on the investigation?" Christopher wanted to know.

"I updated Pippa." He glanced at me as he slid up to the curb on the opposite side of the street from our front door. "She can tell you. But the short answer is no. We still don't know who the bloke is or how he picks his victims, just that he sticks to a certain sphere of society."

"The ones with money," I said, as I fumbled for my door handle. "Just stay where you are, Tom. I'm perfectly capable of letting myself out of the motorcar. And letting Christopher out, too. You stay there, where no one can run you over, and let us get out on the pavement."

Tom nodded. "Under normal circumstances, I'd do a better job of convincing you I'm a gentleman, but at the moment—"

"No worries," I told him as I moved the seat aside and reached into the backseat for Christopher. "We can manage."

"Will you let us know how the investigation fares?" Christopher stepped onto the pavement and shrugged the tweed coat from his shoulders. He took a moment to fold it gently before placing it on the seat next to Tom. "Thank you for the loan. Not a gentleman, you said?"

"I suppose I did that part well enough." Tom smirked up at him across the passenger seat. "As for the rest, I imagine I'll be in touch in a day or two. In the meantime, try to be good."

"I'm always good," Christopher said, to which both Tom and I rolled our eyes.

"Off you go," I flapped my hand at Tom. "You know where to find us."

He nodded, before putting the motorcar into gear and rolling off. We stood on the pavement and waited for the Crossley Tender to move out of the way, before we looked right and left and right again. "Need a hand?" I asked Christopher.

He smirked. "No, Pippa. I'm perfectly capable of walking in heels."

He stepped from the pavement down into the street and turned to me. "In fact, you look like you're having a bigger problem than I am."

I was, in fact, teetering on the edge of the pavement and not looking forward to bending my knees to make the step down. It's amazing how such a little thing as scabs can make it difficult to navigate daily life.

"I'll be all right," I said, and Christopher snorted.

"Of course you'd say that. Take my arm, Pippa. There's no shame in needing help."

I sniffed, but did it. "I made it home on my own last night, you'll recall."

He braced himself as I leaned on his arm, and then relaxed again when I was safely off the pavement. "I recall. With blood running down both your legs and hands. Come along."

He put a hand against my lower back and headed across the street.

"Vehicle coming," I said.

He nodded. "I see it. We'll be all right."

"It's not slowing down."

"The driver sees us," Christopher said, and he—or perhaps she—must do, because the light from the headlamps had hit us by now, and while I didn't stand out particularly well in my dark skirt and jacket, Christopher—in his pale pink frock and bare white arms and shoulders—ought to be as visible as a lamp himself. Nonetheless, the motorcar didn't slow down, but instead seemed to speed up as it approached us.

"Something's wrong," I said, as I hobbled as fast as I could across the street.

"We'll be all right," Christopher repeated, although this time there was a tense undertone to his voice that hadn't been there before. His hand on my back had gone from being a supportive guide to actively pushing me forward as I crossed the street. "Come on."

"I'm coming." I put on a burst of speed, ignoring the protests from my knees. We reached the opposite side of the street with room to spare, and climbed the curb onto the pavement while the motorcar was still a couple of car-lengths away. At that point, I assumed it was safe to stop and breathe... and that was when the vehicle shot forward, jumped the curb, and came straight for us.

CHAPTER TEN

FOR A SECOND, all I saw was headlamps. I'm fairly certain I saw my life flash before my eyes, too. Then Christopher gave me a yank and a push, both at the same time, and I tumbled into a heap on the pavement. So did he, with a thud and a grunt. The tires passed us both with inches to spare, and a cloud of exhaust enveloped us as the motorcar jumped back down into the roadway and sped off. From somewhere nearby, but not too near, I could hear a wordless bellow of consternation, and then rapid footsteps. Evans, I assumed, finally noticing what was going on outside the lobby.

My hands were bleeding again, and so, I was sure, were my knees. Christopher, too, was rather the worse for wear. His pretty pink gown was dirty and torn, although his elbow-length opera gloves had spared his hands from getting torn up too badly. The gloves were a lost cause, of course, the palms shredded. The fact that he had escaped mostly unscathed, didn't stop him from sitting up and spitting out a string of words that would have been more at home in Francis's mouth.

"Christopher!" I said, shocked.

He turned to me. "We're lucky to be alive, Pippa."

I supposed we were, at that. A head-on collision with the front of a motorcar would have sent us both flying. We could have broken our necks, or our skulls. We would certainly have broken other bones. We were indeed lucky.

And then Evans was there, puffing, and the conversation between us was over for now.

"Miss Darling." He stared at me, eyes wide. "Mr.... um."

"We're all right, Evans," I said and extended a hand. "A bit of help, if you don't mind?"

"Of course, Miss Darling." He took my hand and hoisted me to my feet. We both ended up staring at our bloody palms in consternation for a moment while Christopher got up.

"Pippa is right, Evans. We're all right. A few scratches, is all."

He swept the wig off his head, exposing his usual sunny blond hair, slicked back against his skull.

Evans nodded. "Yes, sir." It wasn't the first time he had seen Christopher dressed up as Kitty—it couldn't possibly have been —but it was obvious that he didn't know how to address him.

Christopher didn't let it bother him. "Did you get a look at the motorcar, Evans? All we saw were the headlamps."

"A Hackney," Evans said promptly.

"Was it really?"

"It looked like one," Evans said. "Can't say whether it was a for-hire car or not."

No, that isn't always easy to do, especially when it goes by at such speed.

"We'd better get inside," Christopher said with a glance up and down the now quiet street. "Don't want them to come back."

We certainly didn't. He presented his arm—rather incongruous in his pink tasseled gown—but I took it and limped towards the entrance to the Essex House. Evans held the door, and we made our slow way across the lobby.

"Any other news, Evans?" Christopher wanted to know as we approached the lift.

The doorman shook his head. "No, sir."

"No messages or anything?"

"No, sir."

"I've been gone less than two hours," I reminded him. And then, when the doorman opened the lift door, "Thank you, Evans. We'll see you tomorrow."

"Yes, Miss Darling." He closed the grille and door carefully behind us, and we ascended to the second floor.

"You go wash up first," Christopher told me when we were inside the flat. "I'm not hurt. The gloves protected my hands. But you've torn open the scabs on your knees again. Go put some plasters on, and then meet me in the sitting room. We'll talk."

I nodded and headed for the washroom while he disappeared into my bedchamber to take off his makeup and put away Kitty.

Fifteen minutes later we were sitting on opposite sides of the Chesterfield with a cup of tea each—each with a drop of something extra in it, for nerves—and I was shaking a little bit. Yesterday's incident had been easy to dismiss as accidental. This one was harder to reject.

"No," Christopher agreed when I brought it up, "that was certainly no accident. The motorcar jumped up on the curb to get to us. Until then it might have been a coincidence…"

"Until then," I agreed, "I thought it was simply a vehicle traveling a bit too fast. Inconsiderate, certainly, not to slow down for two people crossing the street. But some people are inconsiderate, and Hackney cabs are known for driving fast. You don't think—?"

"No," Christopher said. He was cradling the cup between two hands—saucer be damned—and might have been shaking a bit, too, now that I looked at him. "Until the pavement, yes. I thought the same thing you did, that someone was just being a bit of a bastard. But if that had been the case, they would have tooted the horn, don't you think? And anyway, jumping the curb was a definite attempt to hit us."

"It seemed to be." I took a sip of brandy-laced tea and coughed. "Who would do that?"

"It depends on whether we think the target was you or me or both of us," Christopher said. I opened my mouth and closed it again when he added, "For a simple explanation with no additional implications, it might have been a cabbie who was in a hurry and who thought he'd teach us to get out of the way faster next time."

I suppose it might have been. Some people have anger issues. Although it was quite the risk to take. What if we hadn't moved out of the way quite as thoroughly as we had done? The motorcar might have clipped one of us. Was that worth teaching someone a lesson about crossing the street at too slow a pace?

"Unlikely," I said, "but I suppose it isn't impossible. What else?"

"It might have been the same person who pushed you down the stairs yesterday."

It might have been. Except—

"I'm fairly certain yesterday was an accident, Christopher. Why would anybody want to push me down the stairs, or for that matter run me over?"

"If we knew that," Christopher said, "we'd know who it was."

"Yesterday you thought it was Wolfgang."

"I wasn't serious," Christopher said. "Or not serious enough to worry about you going to tea with him today. He just seemed like the most likely suspect. You had just left him, so we know he was in the area. You had just told him you didn't want to move to Germany—"

"That's hardly reason enough to push someone down the stairs. Besides, we know he wasn't in the area today. We saw him just twenty minutes ago on Regent Street."

"That's enough time to find a Hackney and get here," Christopher said. "We managed."

I supposed we had. "And what would be his reason for wanting to kill me today? We made up about Germany. He spent half of lunch telling me about *Schloss* Natterdorff."

"Jealousy?" Christopher suggested. "Perhaps he thought you and Tom were out together?"

"Surely he can't have missed how Tom dotes on you?"

"I wasn't there," Christopher said. When I opened my mouth to protest, because he certainly had been there, he added, "As myself, I mean. Your fiancé called me Lady Laetitia."

"You do look quite a lot like her when you're dressed up as Kitty. It's the hair, I suppose—same Dutch Boy cut, even if yours is a wig—and you both have blue eyes. You're a bit taller, an inch or two, perhaps..."

"But I was sitting down," Christopher said, "and in the back of the motorcar, in the dark."

I nodded. "He did seem to think you were she." Although there had been a double-take at one point, a moment's doubt, perhaps when Christopher spoke. He didn't sound like a woman, no matter how much he could make himself look like one.

"Or if he didn't," I added, "at least he didn't look at you closely enough to actually recognize you."

"He had opportunity, at any rate," Christopher said. "He

could have flagged down a Hackney and followed us here, and made it by the time we were crossing the street. Anyone else—as long as it wasn't simply a homicidal cabbie—would have had to lie in wait for us to come home."

"That seems like a lot of trouble to go to for no reason. But I suppose it's possible. Who else do you suspect?"

"Laetitia?" Christopher suggested. "She was near Piccadilly yesterday, as well."

She had been. But— "I think Crispin would have noticed had she up and left the table to run across the street to push me down the steps to the underground, don't you? He said she hadn't done. Besides, aren't they back in Dorset by now?"

Christopher shrugged. "I assume so. I don't actually know where they are. I haven't phoned to make certain that's where they went."

"Well, it certainly wasn't Crispin's H6 that ran us down," I said.

He shook his head. "Of course not. Crispin would never."

"If he took her to Dorset, she wouldn't have had time to get back to London."

"Perhaps they didn't leave," Christopher said. "Perhaps they simply dropped us off here this morning, and went to Sutherland House, and now Laetitia is there or back in Marsden House."

Perhaps. It hadn't been Christopher at the Savoy during tea, but it might have been Crispin.

"Anything's possible," Christopher agreed. "Although I didn't ring him up to tell him you were seeing Wolfgang today. I assumed he was in Dorset, or perhaps Wiltshire, and at this point it's really only rubbing salt in the wound, isn't it, when there's nothing he can do about it. But I suppose it might have been him."

Laetitia stayed on the list, then, if they were both in London. Although—

"Why would Laetitia want to be rid of me? Even if he is in love with me—ugh—she's the one who's marrying him. Why does it matter how he feels, or whether I'm still alive?"

Christopher looked at me. "Would you want to marry someone who was in love with someone else?"

"Of course not. But she knew that when she accepted him. She has known it for a while, I think."

Some of the things I had overheard back in May, during a conversation at the Dower House, made a lot more sense in that light.

"Be that as it may," Christopher said, "I'm sure she'd like it better if he loved her more and you less. And one way to accomplish that is to get rid of you."

I suppose. But— "Killing me seems needlessly risky. Marrying me off to Wolfgang and sending me to Germany would probably be enough to accomplish the same thing. Besides, it's not as if she won't have to deal with other women after they're married. If he doesn't love her, there's no chance he'll remain faithful."

"Her problem," Christopher said with a shrug, "not ours."

I tilted my head to contemplate him. "That's rather callous, isn't it?"

"If she pushed you down the stairs and tried to run you over with a Hackney cab? And we still don't know who took that potshot at you from the woods during the hunt last month, either, remember? It might have been her. She was out there in the woods with a rifle. So no, I don't think it's particularly callous at all."

When he put it like that, perhaps I didn't, either.

"Any other ideas?" I inquired. "If Wolfgang doesn't have a

motive for killing me, and Laetitia doesn't have the means because she's in Dorset, who else is on the list?"

"Might be someone who doesn't like men in evening gowns," Christopher said lightly, as if it was in any way all right to run someone down because you don't like how they're dressed.

"Do people do that?"

"I haven't had it happen to me. But I think most people look at Kitty and think she's a girl."

Yes, I could see that. He isn't the most masculine-looking bloke even when he's dressed like one—he's tallish for a girl, but not much taller than Lady Laetitia, and slender, with narrow shoulders and a pretty face, big eyes, and a soft cupid's-bow mouth—so he doesn't look too different from the rest of us girls in our drop waist dresses and cropped hair.

"That's awful," I said, and Christopher nodded, "but I'd be very surprised if that were the case. If most people look at Kitty and think she—you—is a girl, then it's not likely that a random cabbie can tell the difference from a distance."

Christopher lifted a shoulder. "Might have been someone who followed us from the Cave of the Golden Calf."

"Someone other than Wolfgang, do you mean? Like the bloke you were dancing with? He'd be more likely to try to take out Tom, don't you think?"

I saw a flash of worry cross Christopher's face at the idea of that, that the Hackney cab might have followed Tom after it tried to run us down, but then he shook his head. "Only until he noticed that Tom was driving a police-issue Tender, surely. You don't run down a copper in front of Scotland Yard and live to tell the tale."

Likely not. "Do you know him well? The chap at the nightclub?"

"Not to say well," Christopher said. "I've seen him around. We've danced before."

"Does he have enough of an emotional attachment to you that he'd want to hurt you—or Tom—for leaving the nightclub the way you did?"

Christopher snorted. "I'd hardly think so. Nothing's ever happened between us."

"Nothing's ever happened between me and St George, either," I pointed out, "and apparently that hasn't stopped him from developing an emotional attachment."

He stared at me, incredulously. "You and Crispin grew up together, Pippa. How can you say that nothing ever happened between you?"

"Nothing romantic. Nothing that would make him think falling in love with me," my face puckered, "was a good idea."

"I'm sure he knew when it happened that it wasn't a good idea." Christopher shook his head. "No, I doubt the chap from the nightclub came after me with a murderous Hackney. Any other bright ideas?"

I thought about it for a moment while I took a sip of my now-cool tea. "Someone who thought you were Laetitia and saw an opportunity to get rid of her?"

"And who might that be?" Christopher took a sip of his own genial beverage before putting the cup on the table the better to use his fingers to check off suspects. "It wasn't you. It wasn't Crispin."

I opened my mouth to protest—it could certainly have been Crispin; he had the best motive of anyone, since no one else was looking at a lifetime of being married to Laetitia—but I closed it again when Christopher continued.

"He's either in Dorset or Wiltshire, and if he isn't, he's probably with her. And if he isn't with her, he would still know that it wasn't

Laetitia crossing the street with you. He knows you well enough to know that the two of you would never be here together, and he knows me well enough to recognize me, even in a gown and wig."

"Fine," I conceded. "Not Crispin. I don't think anyone else in the family is in London this weekend. Who else is there?"

"I imagine the people who dislike Laetitia Marsden are legion," Christopher said, "but in this case I was thinking specifically of the gentleman who burgled Marsden House last night."

The gentleman burglar? "Why would he want to kill her?"

"Because she saw him," Christopher said triumphantly. "And he knows that she saw him."

"But she didn't recognize him. Or she would have told the police who he was."

"But he doesn't know that," Christopher said. "Or perhaps he's afraid that if she thinks about it further, she'll remember something that might incriminate him. Or if she doesn't know who he is now, if she sees him again, she'll recognize him."

"That seems like a rather paltry excuse for murder. Besides, if he wanted her dead, why not simply kill her last night before he left?"

"Trying to make it look like an accident?" Christopher suggested. "As for paltry... do you have any idea what the Sutherland parure is worth?"

"A lot?" I shook my head. "All he got was the ring and the earrings. Surely the tiara and necklace are worth more."

"Of course they are. But just those few diamonds are worth plenty. And now the parure is incomplete. Uncle Harold must be having a fit."

"Enough of one to drive up to London and try to mow down Laetitia? Or who he thinks is Laetitia?" Because he certainly wouldn't recognize his own nephew under the gown and wig.

"I wouldn't think so," Christopher said judiciously. "Uncle Harold is too invested in getting Crispin settled before he can lose his mind and elope with you, I think. Although I don't think he's happy about the loss. Or will be, once he finds out about it, if he doesn't know already."

Certainly not. "You don't think he'll take it out on St George, do you?"

Uncle Harold has a tendency to take his displeasure out on his only son and heir. Admittedly, it's usually when Crispin has done something Uncle Harold doesn't like—such as giving vent to his sarcasm when it would be healthier to keep his mouth shut, for instance, or simply talking back to his father when Uncle Harold would prefer blind obedience—but I wouldn't put it past my courtesy-uncle to lose his temper over this, too.

"I don't see how he can," Christopher said, "when it isn't Crispin's fault."

"That hasn't stopped him in the past."

"Hasn't it?" He shook his head. "I don't think so, Pippa. But it's nice of you to worry."

I opened my mouth to object to the terminology—I certainly wasn't *worried* about St George—and then closed it again when I couldn't make even myself believe it.

Christopher, kindly, didn't comment. "I suppose we'd better turn in," he said instead, lifting both arms up above his head and stretching. "This wasn't how I expected to end the day, I'll admit."

"I'm sorry," I said, as I scooted towards the edge of the Chesterfield preparatory to talking my abused knees into supporting me. "Tom came to see you, and when I told him that you'd gone out, he went immediately into rescue mode."

"I didn't need rescuing," Christopher grumbled.

"Well, you don't know that," I pointed out, reasonably, "do

you? There could be a raid on the Cave of the Golden Calf right now."

"I'm grown," Christopher said, "and I can take responsibility for myself."

"I don't think he thinks that you can't. He's not stopping you from being yourself, Christopher. He's simply trying to stop you from ending up in the workhouse because of it."

"I wouldn't—"

"You might. And what's more, if you were arrested, the tabloids might find out. And then Aunt Roz and Uncle Herbert would find out, and so would Uncle Harold. And while your father wouldn't disown you, and your mother only wants you to be happy, His Grace, the Duke of Sutherland, would likely cut you out of the succession."

He opened his mouth, most likely to tell me that he couldn't care less about the succession, but I kept talking. "All Tom is doing is trying to keep you safe. You could make it a bit easier for him."

"How am I not making it easy?" Christopher wanted to know. "I came away with you two, didn't I?"

"You could have told him where you were going, and when. Then he could have told you whether there was a raid scheduled or not. And if there was, you could have stayed home. And he could have gotten a good night's sleep instead of having to rush off to save you."

Christopher made a face. "I suppose so."

"So you'll let us know in advance next time?"

"I'll think about it," Christopher said and pushed to his feet. "Come on, old girl."

He extended a hand. I took it and let him pull me up.

CHAPTER ELEVEN

"YOU LOOK WELL," I told Violet Cummings the next afternoon.

We had slept in, in deference to our aches and pains and the interrupted slumber from the night before, and then we had spent the time over elevenses wondering how to spend the rest of the day. It was Christopher who had suggested a visit to Lady Violet. Not only had she, or her family home, been burgled by who we assumed to be the same person as had made off with the Sutherland diamonds, but the last time I had seen her, at Marsden Manor in Dorset in September, I had been absolutely certain that she was as good as dead. It couldn't hurt to stop by and congratulate her on coming through the ordeal alive, and while we were at it, make a few discreet inquiries into the burglary.

And if we had to throw Lady Laetitia's business under the bus to do it, well, I wasn't going to worry about that.

"Thank you." She smiled graciously, although I got the impression that she didn't one hundred percent believe me.

Nor should she. She did, in fact, look all right, but 'well' might be overstating the fact. I knew that it had taken several weeks before she had been able to get out of bed at all, weeks during which everyone who knew her had believed that she would never wake up again, and if by some miracle she did, she wouldn't be the girl she had been.

She had been as slim as a snake even before the incident. Now she was downright bony, her eyes were enormous over too-prominent cheekbones, and her skin had an unhealthy pallor. She hadn't taken the time to take care of her hair during the time she'd been bedbound, because there was a quarter inch of visible roots at the bottom of her pale blond hair. But she was dressed in a pretty afternoon frock, with her face on, and sitting upright at a table in the parlor, receiving guests, and that couldn't be overstated.

"I'm sure someone has told you what happened in the aftermath...?" I added.

She had missed Cecily's funeral, of course, as well as Dominic Rivers's ditto.

She nodded. "The girl's in prison. Geoffrey is waiting for the next Assizes."

Precisely. "And you? How do you feel?"

"Better," Violet said decisively. "Still weak and I tire easily, but better every day."

"That's wonderful." I glanced at Christopher across the table. He glanced back at me, deadpan. I guessed it was up to me to carry on.

I turned back to Violet. "I don't know whether you've heard from Lady Laetitia lately...?"

"She stopped by," Violet said, and put a red-painted nail to her red-painted lips as she looked up at the ceiling, "perhaps a week ago?"

"Then you haven't heard the news."

"What news?" She smiled, just a bit wickedly, and her tired

eyes sparkled. "Don't tell me. She's decided to throw Crispin over and take vows?"

I snorted. "Hardly." The day Laetitia Marsden entered a convent was the day pigs flew over Nottingham. "No, they're still together. Dining at the Criterion Restaurant just the other night."

"Then I'm afraid I simply can't imagine." She raised her teacup, pinky extended delicately.

"The Sutherland diamonds are gone," I said. "A burglary early yesterday morning."

Her eyes widened and the tea must have gone down the wrong way, because she choked and began coughing. After a moment of watching, Christopher got up and thumped her on the back. Carefully, of course, since she appeared as if a gentle breeze could knock her down. When she had stopped gasping, he conjured a handkerchief from his pocket and held it out to her so she could mop at her streaming eyes.

"Thank you."

She dabbed them dry. Christopher stuffed the pocket square back into his trousers, but we both knew it was a lost cause; the mascara would have transferred to the silk square, and we would have to throw it away once we left Cummings House. There's simply no way to get petroleum jelly and coal dust out of raw silk.

Christopher took his seat again and picked up his teacup, and I turned back to Violet. "She told me that you too had had a burglary."

Violet nodded. She was still dabbing at her pale cheeks, but with her fingertips now. "A few weeks ago. I was alone in the house. Mother and Father had gone out."

"There were servants, surely."

"Of course." The look she gave me said, as clearly as words, that I ought to know that the servants don't count.

It's the way she has always looked at me, so I moved past it. "Did you see the burglar?"

She shook her head. "I was asleep. I didn't know that anything had happened until the next morning, when Father found the safe in the library empty."

"He got into your safe?"

She nodded. "Didn't he rob the Marsdens' safe?"

"I don't imagine there was anything in the Marsden safe that was worth taking," I said. "The Marsdens don't spend much time in London, do they?"

She didn't respond, and I added, "Laetitia was only up for the weekend. And the maid had gone to bed, so the jewelry was on the dressing table."

"How careless of dear Laetitia." Violet sniggered. "She's been after the Sutherland diamonds ever since Crispin came down from Cambridge two years ago. It seems like poetic justice that she'd get her hands on them and a month later, leave them on the dressing table to be stolen."

Perhaps it did. Unfortunately, the loss of the ring did nothing to actually release him from the engagement, more was the pity.

I didn't say so, of course—I had said so before, *ad nauseam*, and saying it again would not make any difference—but Violet must have read my mind, or at least my expression, because she added, perhaps in an effort to be sympathetic, "It could be worse, you know."

"Could it?"

"She loves him. At least she has that going for her."

I supposed she did, now that I thought about it. I had always discouraged Crispin from proposing to Laetitia because he didn't love her, and I still stood by that, even if I had had to reconsider my stance on him throwing caution to the wind and proposing to the girl he really loved. If that girl was me, as

Christopher assured me she was, I could only be glad that Crispin hadn't gone down on one knee and declared his love, because I wouldn't have responded well.

But now that Violet had pointed it out (and I had had a moment to consider), I supposed she was actually right and it could have been worse. He could have ended up engaged to someone he didn't love, who also didn't love him.

"His father might have set him up with someone like me," Violet said, as if she had, indeed, read my mind and not just my expression. "I wouldn't have put it past Duke Harold."

She looked from Christopher to me and back. "Don't get me wrong. I enjoy Crispin's company. But I don't love him, and I don't want to marry him. We wouldn't get on well together in the long term."

"He can be a bit of a pill," I agreed, blandly, while Christopher ventured, "But if his father and yours had insisted—"

Violet confirmed, "I would have considered it. So just be grateful that it didn't happen that way."

Indeed.

"But you don't know anything about the burglary?" I pressed. "No idea who the burglar was, for instance?"

She shook her head. "How would I possibly know that? I don't associate with the types of people who break the law."

"Dominic Rivers broke the law," I pointed out, and I was absolutely certain that she had associated with him.

Her eyes turned cold and flinty. "Dom is dead. He certainly didn't take my mother's emerald and sapphire brooch."

I hadn't suggested that he had done. But before I could say so, Christopher asked, "Your mother lost an emerald and sapphire brooch?"

He gave me a significant look, as if this ought to mean something to me.

Violet nodded. "Emeralds, sapphires, and diamonds in the shape of a peacock. Lovely piece, if a bit old-fashioned."

"Valuable, I suppose?" She didn't answer—I'm sure the answer was self-evident—and Christopher added, "How many emeralds? And sapphires and diamonds?"

"Oh, God." Violet flapped a hand. "Who knows? Ten? Fifteen?"

"You wouldn't recognize them if you saw them again?"

She stared at him as if suspecting he had lost his mind, and Christopher clarified, "Not the brooch. I'm certain you would recognize that. But the individual stones."

Violet shook her head. "One diamond is very much like another, isn't it? Just like one emerald is like another, and one sapphire—"

"Yes, of course." But he did give me another significant glance, even if he didn't ask any more questions.

"Coincidence," I told him thirty minutes later, as we made our way along Curzon Street towards Hyde Park Corner and the nearest tube stop.

"Mmm," Christopher responded. The murmur had a distinct disbelieving quality to it, something not easy to do with a single letter.

"There's no evidence whatsoever that Wolfgang has anything to do with the jewelry thefts."

He flicked me a look. "You thought of it, too."

I opened my mouth to argue that I hadn't. Before I could do, he went on, "You must have, because I haven't mentioned his name. All I did was look at you."

"Thought transference," I told him sullenly. "We're soulmates, Christopher. Platonic soulmates. Capable of mindreading."

His lips quirked. "Is that what we are?"

"Something like that." I shrugged irritably. "I'll admit that the thought crossed my mind, and before you looked at me. But simply because a brooch made of sapphires and emeralds went missing from the Cummingses, doesn't mean that the ring that Wolfgang offered me was made from those same sapphires and emeralds."

"Of course not," Christopher agreed. "But it's significant, don't you think?"

"I don't know that I do," I said. "There are plenty of sapphires and emeralds in the world. Plenty of rings, too. And besides, Wolfgang wouldn't resort to thievery."

"How do you know?"

"Well, why would he? He's the *Graf* von Natterdorff with a *Schloss* in Baden-Württemberg. He has no need to steal other people's heirlooms. I'm sure he has plenty of his own."

"We have only his word for that," Christopher pointed out, and when I turned to stare—or glare—at him, he added, "Be reasonable, Pippa. How do you know that he is what he says he is, other than that he says it?"

I opened my mouth, and then closed it again. I had taken for granted that he was telling the truth, because why wouldn't I?

"He went to university," I said eventually. "The Mensur scar, remember? Mensur dueling is something that the German students do at university. His family had enough money to get him an education."

"That doesn't prove that he's the *Graf von und zu* Natterdorff," Christopher answered. "He could be someone else, with enough money to go to uni. Like you and me. We don't have titles, but we went to university. Besides, did you not tell me that your father had a Mensur scar?"

I blinked, surprised that I had never caught this anomaly on my own. "He did do."

"And he was a craftsman, didn't you say?"

"He was." My father made furniture. Lovely, hand-crafted, expensive furniture.

"And if he had a Mensur scar," Christopher continued, "then it's not only the children of the wealthy who have them."

Perhaps not. "Wolfgang had the money to stay at the Savoy, though."

"But not forever," Christopher said.

"Does anyone have enough money to stay at the Savoy forever? Does even Uncle Harold have enough money for that?"

"Of course he does," Christopher said.

"Well, lots of people don't." Christopher and I certainly didn't. For a few days, yes. For weeks at a time, no. "If Wolfgang were poor, don't you think he would have stayed somewhere else from the start? Why waste money on the Savoy if you're on a budget?"

"He may have had his own reasons for choosing it," Christopher said.

"Such as?"

He gave a half-shrug. "Access to people with money? I wonder whether there were thefts at the Savoy during the time he stayed there?"

"We can ask," I said, "although I can't imagine that they'll tell us."

"The doorman told you that Natterdorff isn't a guest anymore. He might tell you this, as well."

I supposed he might. "Are we going to the Savoy, then?"

"No," Christopher said. "But the next time you're invited for tea or supper there, I plan to lurk in the lobby and follow Natterdorff home after he leaves you. And while we wait for that to happen, I shall ring up Tom and ask him whether there have been reports of thefts at the Savoy."

"That will make for a handy excuse to contact him," I agreed. "Home, then?"

"Home," Christopher agreed, and took my arm for the descent into the underground.

THE OPPORTUNITY CAME SOONER than either of us had anticipated. That same evening, a note arrived from Wolfgang asking me to share luncheon with him the next day. Not at the Savoy this time, but at Sweetings on Queen Victoria Street in Blackfriars.

"A bit out of the way, that," Christopher commented as we huddled over the note. "I wonder whether he lives out that way now?"

He might well do. It was certainly away from our usual haunts, which stretched from the Savoy on the Strand west to Piccadilly and Mayfair. Venturing east towards the Tower of London was unusual, to say the least.

"There's no lobby at Sweetings," I pointed out, "so if you plan to lurk, you'll have to find somewhere else to do so."

"Across the street ought to do." He squinted at me. "You're going, then?"

I snorted. "Of course I'm going. It's not every day a woman gets invited to Sweetings for luncheon."

It's the premier oyster bar in the city, that has been around since Victoria was on the throne. Christopher and I are more likely to snack on a serving of beans on toast at home than to venture out to Sweetings on an average Monday.

As a result, I was practically giddy by the time we came up out of the underground at the corner of Cannon and Queen Victoria Streets the next afternoon. I was wearing my favorite blue and white afternoon frock, and a matching blue cloche, while Christopher had on his own cloche hat with a little clutch of violets on it, and one of my skirts and jackets.

Other than the cloche, which had caught his eye at Style & Gerrish in Salisbury in April, Kitty's wardrobe tends to run to evening wear. When Christopher needs something for daytime, he usually raids my wardrobe.

The skirt was a bit shorter on him than on me, seeing as he's a couple of inches taller than I am. It's a good thing that I'm not one of those terribly daring Bright Young People who hem everything to a practically indecent length, because had I been, Christopher wouldn't have looked decent at all. As it was, the bottom of the skirt covered his kneecaps, but just barely, and I'm certain the couple of gentlemen who gave his nicely-turned calves admiring glances on their way past, would have been appalled to realize that they were, indeed, ogling a man.

"I'll wait here, shall I?" Christopher inquired after we had made our way across Cannon Street and halfway down Queen Victoria. The restaurant sat on the pointed corner of Queen Victoria and Queen, a half block away, across from Bow Lane and Watling Street, and the gothic St Mary Aldermary Church.

I eyed the doorway he indicated, and then looked across the street. "Are you certain you wouldn't prefer to go inside the church for a bit? You'll get cold, waiting out here, and I'm sure we'll be inside a while."

Not to mention that he had come down from Oxford with a first in history, and he rather likes old churches. St Mary Aldermary was close to a thousand years old—or at least the first St Mary Aldermary had been. This new version—not new at all—was from the mid-1600s, so quite old enough in its own right to interest my cousin.

Under normal circumstances, he would likely have taken me up on the suggestion. Under these, he scoffed. "Looking like this? No, thank you. I'm sure I would be struck dead as soon as I crossed the threshold."

"I don't think God cares that you're wearing a skirt," I said. "Weren't skirts *de rigeur* in Jerusalem back in the day?"

He smirked. "I was more worried about the vicar coming after me with a hymnal than God striking me down with a bolt of lightning."

Ah. "I suppose I can't argue with that. But do you have to lurk in doorways?"

"I hardly think anyone's going to look at me and think I'm for hire," Christopher said coolly. "Unless you're telling me I look cheap, Pippa?"

"Of course not." There was nothing cheap about him, not the clothes he wore—mine—nor the face he had painted on himself. He looked like an elegant young lady of the upper echelon, not tawdry at all. Certainly not someone who was available for the right price.

"It's just not common for nice women to loiter in doorways for hours at a time," I added. "And it's cold, and likely to get colder..."

"I doubt it'll be hours," Christopher said. "And if it is, I'll manage. At least it isn't raining today."

No, it wasn't. October had started off nice and warm, but then we'd had a few days of thunder and lightning about a week in, and that had brought in gray skies and lower temperatures. It was not so cold that we couldn't be outside comfortably, at least as long as we were walking around, but I rather thought Christopher might freeze had he to stand in a doorway for an hour or more waiting for Wolfgang and I to appear again.

"Perhaps you could simply lunch at Sweetings yourself?" I suggested. "There's nothing wrong with a young lady lunching on her own."

"I'm sure there's not. However, I rather think your beau will recognize your clothes, don't you?"

I eyed him. "Perhaps he would." He had seen them all before, as a matter of fact, so perhaps Christopher was right and it wasn't a risk we wanted to run.

He patted my arm. "Don't worry about me, Pippa. Just go meet Natterdorff. See if he'll tell you where he lives now. And if he does, drop a glove on your way down the street, so I'll know not to follow him."

I promised I would do, and then I continued up the street towards the entrance to Sweetings. By the time I turned around, he had melted into the doorway and was nowhere to be seen.

CHAPTER TWELVE

I EXPECTED the meal to be somewhat awkward, and I wasn't surprised.

"I wasn't certain you would want to join me," were the first words out of Wolfgang's mouth after the obligatory greetings. He pulled out the chair of a table by the window overlooking Queen Street and waited for me to sit before he pushed it in behind me.

"Whyever would you think that?" I inquired as he took the couple of steps around the small table and seated himself with his back to the view.

"The last few times I have seen you haven't exactly gone my way." He gave me a rueful smile.

"Nonsense," I said briskly. "We had a nice time at tea the other day. I'm just sorry you had to leave early."

He didn't say anything, and I added, "I hope everything progressed all right with your business matter?"

"Of course. Merely a bagatelle." He waved it away.

"I don't think I've ever asked," I said. "What is your business here?"

"Top secret," Wolfgang said. I stared at him—truly?—and after a moment, he looked up and winked. "Diplomatic relations, *mein Schatz*. I go around London and make myself agreeable."

"Do you really?"

"Of course." He grinned. "I'm agreeable to you, am I not? And to your cousin? And his friend, the policeman? And Lord St George and his fiancée?"

Well, yes. Of course he was. With the exception of Crispin, of course, who didn't find him agreeable at all. Or vice versa.

"The diplomatic corps?" I said uncertainly, and he chuckled.

"Nothing so exalted, I'm afraid. I'm just here as my lowly self, making connections with the British. To do my little bit to mend relations after the war."

I nodded, even though his explanation explained very little. Then again, he was the *Graf* von Natterdorff, so it wasn't as if he had to have a job. The rest of us didn't, either. I had tried for a while, right after we landed in London, but finding a position hadn't been easy, and I had given up fairly quickly. Christopher had worked hard to talk me out of it—he'd rather have me at home where he could natter at me and I could take care of him, and if he had to support me financially to achieve that, then he was happy to do it—and I hadn't had the heart to keep insisting.

On the other hand, it didn't really explain what sort of business associate had communicated with Wolfgang the other day. If he had no official business interests, why would he have a business associate?

But before I could circle back to the question—or even ponder it further inside my own head—the waiter had arrived at the table, and it was time to order food. I ended up with an order of crab bisque followed by a prawn cocktail, while Wolfgang ordered a cup of soup of his own and then the wild turbot with mustard sauce. It was the most expensive item on the menu, and he didn't even blink. Clearly money was no object, whether he was gainfully employed or not.

The waiter withdrew along with the menu cards, and Wolfgang smiled at me. "Where were we?"

I smiled back. "Regent Street, I suppose. Was that where your note took you after tea yesterday?"

Something flickered in his eyes, as if he didn't like my harping on the note, but his voice was still pleasant when he told me, "Not at all. I was simply on my way out to dinner. I assume you and your friends were doing the same?"

"We were actually headed home," I said, since that had been after Tom and I had extricated Christopher—or Kitty—from the Cave of the Golden Calf.

"And where was the Viscount St George? I don't think you said."

I hadn't, in fact. I had said that he was coming, and so was Christopher, and then we had left without waiting for them. I wondered whether Wolfgang had looked back and noticed, or whether he was simply responding to my awkwardness about the whole thing.

When I didn't answer, he added, "I didn't think his fiancée went anywhere without him."

"That—" It was on the tip of my tongue to blurt out that she didn't, and that it hadn't been Laetitia in the backseat of the Tender, but I bit back the impulse. "That's mostly true, actually. She had mislaid him, and required our help to find him again. That's why Tom and I were in our day-clothes and she was dressed for the evening."

"Dear me," Wolfgang said, "no one had taken him, I hope?"

"The way they took Flossie Schlomsky, do you mean? No, not at all. He had merely taken himself off to a place where she wouldn't be welcome."

He smirked. "A house of ill repute?"

I snorted. "Some people would say so, certainly. But it was simply an old nightclub down at the end of Heddon Street, and a private party. Christopher fetched him."

"Your cousin? I didn't see him there."

"If you had stayed around another few minutes, you would have seen them both."

He nodded, quite as if he believed it, although there was something in his tone, or perhaps his eyes, that indicated that he might not. He turned his spoon over in his hands for a moment, eyeing it, before he looked up at me. "May I be honest, Philippa?"

"Of course," I said, even as my heart started to beat faster. It's rarely good news when someone leads off with a question like that.

"For as long as I have known you, I have had the impression that your emotions have been engaged elsewhere."

My... what?

"Until he got engaged, I assumed it was the young popinjay—"

"Crispin and I are not involved," I said automatically.

Wolfgang nodded. "Of course not. If that had been the case, I presume he wouldn't have proposed to someone else."

Yes, you'd think so, wouldn't you?

"I thought it was possible that you still harbored feelings for him," Wolfgang continued, and I endeavored not to gag.

"I assure you, I don't." Or no romantic feelings, anyway. Feelings of wanting to wrap my hands around his throat and squeeze, certainly.

"Is it the young policeman, then?" Wolfgang inquired. "Detective Sergeant Gardiner? Or perhaps your cousin?"

"My..." There were so many things wrong with both of

those questions that they quite took my breath away. There was, however, no question about where to start.

"Christopher? You think I'm in love with *Christopher?*"

My voice had risen into a range only discernable by bats and dogs. Wolfgang sat back in shock, but I think it was simply the level of noise coming out of my mouth that affected him, and not what I was saying. He looked nonplussed at my reaction, as if he couldn't fathom why such an idea would be off-putting.

"Christopher," I said, doing my level best to sound calm, "is my best friend. He's the next thing to my brother. We grew up together. His parents consider me the daughter they never had. While other people may suspect that we live in sin," the Earl and Countess Marsden came to mind, which was funny, actually, since at least Laetitia's mother also suspected that I had been trying to deprive her daughter of her rightful claim to Crispin before the engagement, "I can assure you that I do not feel that way about Christopher, nor does he feel that way about me."

Or about any girl, but there was no need to share that, not even to prove to him how appallingly far off the target his suggestion had been.

I took a breath and began again. "As for Tom—"

"Who?"

"Detective Sergeant Gardiner. I assume he is who you're talking about, and not, for instance, his colleague, Detective Sergeant Finchley?"

Wolfgang nodded, looking reluctantly fascinated in spite of himself, and I continued, "Just as you suspect that my emotions are engaged elsewhere, I'm fairly certain Tom's fond of someone. Someone who isn't me, although that hardly needs saying."

He looked intrigued, and I added, "I'm not going to go into details about that. I don't know whether he has even admitted it to himself. And I could be wrong about those feelings, anyway."

Tom might simply be fond of Christopher because the latter was Robbie's little brother and Cousin Robbie had been Tom's best friend. Tom's feelings for Christopher might not be romantic at all. But however it all played out, it was no one else's business but theirs, and certainly none of Wolfgang's.

"All you need to know," I told him, "is that there's nothing going on between me and anyone else. I abhor Crispin. Christopher is my brother. And Tom is a friend. And that's all."

Wolfgang nodded, although his lips twitched. "I don't suppose there are any news about the burglary?"

"I haven't spoken to Tom since that night," I said, as the waiter stopped by to place our drinks on the table. When he had withdrawn, I added, "He didn't know much then, although I suppose he might have discovered something in the couple of days since."

"But you haven't heard about it if he has done?"

I shook my head. "Is there a particular reason you're interested?"

"Not aside from the fact that it concerns someone you care about," Wolfgang said smoothly.

I wanted to tell him that I didn't care about Lady Laetitia (nor about Lady Violet, nor for that matter about the aged Lady Latimer), but I suppose it also concerned Crispin, and I suppose I did care (marginally) about the Sutherland diamonds. They were ugly, of course, but they were still Sutherland property, and no one had the right to steal them. So instead of protesting, I merely made a sort of acquiescent noise and said, "No, I haven't heard anything new. It's a shame about the Sutherland ring and earrings, of course. They're ostentatious and gaudy, and I wouldn't have them as a gift—"

"There's no chance of that now, surely."

"None at all," I agreed. Nor had there ever been, but there was less of one now, when they were in someone else's hands and not Crispin's. "But it's a shame that the parure is no longer complete. There's a great, big, monstrous tiara in addition to the ring and earrings, and a necklace and a couple of bracelets, I think. I'm not certain I've ever seen the whole thing in use. My late aunt was a dainty woman, and the stones dwarfed her. She didn't wear them much."

Wolfgang made a humming noise.

"Such wouldn't be the case with Laetitia," I said, "of course, but if I remember correctly, the betrothed gets the ring upon the acceptance of the proposal, and it looks like Crispin threw in the earrings, too, but she won't get the rest of the parure until after the wedding. In case she needs incentive to go through with it, I suppose..."

I would have needed incentive to get through a wedding to Crispin, although the parure wouldn't have done it for me. Laetitia probably didn't need any incentive, since she wanted to marry him.

"The ring you showed me," I said to Wolfgang. He met my eyes across the table, startled. "Was that a Natterdorff heirloom?"

He smirked. "No, *mein Schatz*. I didn't come to London thinking I would find a bride, so the Natterdorff engagement ring is still in Germany."

"There's no one there who could have mailed it to you?"

He tilted his head to contemplate me. "Would it have made a difference if I had offered you the Natterdorff engagement ring?"

"Not at all," I said. "My answer would have been the same no matter what. I wouldn't accept or deny a man because of a ring."

He nodded. "To answer your question, there's my grandfather. But he would hardly risk sending one of our heirlooms in an envelope across half of Europe and the English channel when I could just go to Hatton Garden and look for something there."

Of course. "I just wondered if it was an heirloom," I explained, "because I have nothing from my father's side of the family. Aunt Roz has everything from her family, or if my mother had anything, it's gone now. But I don't think, in 1914, when my parents sent me to England for my safety, that they thought it would be the last time they saw me, or I them."

Wolfgang reached out and placed a hand over mine on the table. "Likely not. I'm sorry, my dear."

"Me, too," I said with a sniff. "I don't think about it most of the time. But I know next to nothing about my father. In fact, it was just the other day that I was talking to Christopher, and he reminded me that my father had a Mensur scar on his cheek—"

My eyes lingered on the one across the table from me, and a muscle in Wolfgang's jaw jumped. I looked away. "—and I wondered how that came about."

He didn't speak, and I added, "I always thought Mensur duels was something the students did at university. But my father was a craftsman. He made furniture. He wasn't likely to have attended university. So how did he get it?"

"There are other ways to get a facial scar than fencing for sport," Wolfgang said.

"Yes, of course there are. Perhaps he grew up in rough circumstances, and someone brought a knife to a fistfight at some point, or perhaps one of his tools slipped while he was working, and he cut himself..."

"Perhaps," Wolfgang agreed.

"But it seemed like something I ought to know about my own father. Do you know, I don't even have a photograph of him?

There's a portrait of my mother at Beckwith Place, from when she and Aunt Roz were young, but every day—or every year, at least—I'm less and less able to bring my father's face to mind."

They were more just flickers of memories now, of sitting on my father's lap while he read to me, of holding my mother's hand while we walked, of talking at the table in our flat while eating *Sourbraten* and *Spätzle* with butter and herbs. My father's hands, full of cuts and scrapes from the shop, holding a knife and fork, while my mother's upper-crust British voice asked how work had been...

But as for bringing his face to mind, no. I couldn't do it.

Wolfgang nodded sympathetically. "For what it's worth, and from what I remember, you look like your mother but with your father's eyes."

Indeed I did. My mother at fourteen or so, in the portrait at Beckwith Place, looked very much like I had done at that age, except for the eyes and a few other small differences. It was difficult to say what, if anything, other than my green eyes, I had inherited from my father's side of the family.

The waiter rescued us from becoming too maudlin. As he appeared beside the table with two cups of crab bisque, Wolfgang withdrew his hand, and I did the same. And if I had to surreptitiously touch the napkin to my eyes, it's no one's business but my own. The cups descended and the waiter stepped back, waiting for approval.

"It looks lovely," I told him, a bit stuffily, "thank you."

He clicked his heels and withdrew. I picked up my spoon and dipped it into the bisque.

THE SOUP WAS EXCELLENT, and so was the prawn cocktail. So was Wolfgang's turbot. When he offered me a bite,

I took it off the end of his fork and tried not to wince at the gesture.

It's not that I hadn't taken bites of food off the tines of Christopher's fork before, because of course I had done. But that was different. This felt... overly familiar. Something one might do with a romantic interest, such as a fiancé or husband—or, of course, a cousin and brother. I could imagine Laetitia opening her mouth, birdlike, so Crispin could deposit a tempting morsel therein. Or perhaps the opposite would be more likely to happen. Laetitia waving a piece of food in his face, wanting him to be sweet and romantic. He'd probably feel about it the way I did. I could practically see his sneer in my head as he'd fight back whatever sarcastic remark came to mind.

But never mind all that. I took the piece of turbot between my teeth and pulled it off the fork without actually touching the silver. "Delicious," I told him once I had munched it down, and if my smile was a touch strained, it was the best I could do.

He smiled, pleased, and went back to his fish. I picked up another prawn and bit into it with a snap.

We ended the meal with a joint serving of spotted dick—it came with two spoons, so there was no need to share any more flatware—and then Wolfgang pulled out my chair and helped me into my coat before he placed his hand on the small of my back for the trip across the floor.

"Let me get you a Hackney," he told me as we stepped outside on Queen Victoria Street. As he looked around for a vacant cab, I did the same in an effort to spot Christopher. There was no sign of him, although I couldn't see into the alcove he had tucked himself into earlier, so he might still be there and watching.

"Don't be silly," I answered. "It's broad daylight, and ten minutes on the underground. Just walk me to the entrance. Unless you're taking the tube back to the Savoy, too?"

It was a perfect opportunity for him to tell me that he was no longer living at the hotel, and I held my breath—hopefully not too conspicuously—while I waited to see what he would say.

"I have some business to take care of in the area," he told me, neatly sidestepping both the bait and the opportunity to tell me something more. Not a direct admittance that he was no longer at the Savoy, but also nothing that directly said that he was.

I filed the omission away in the back of my head and smiled. "Would you like some company?"

The alcove where Christopher had taken refuge earlier was empty. I flicked a glance into it, and then around to see whether I could spot him anywhere else. When I couldn't, I turned my attention back to Wolfgang, who seemed to be contemplating my offer with all the seriousness it deserved.

I admit it, I was interested to hear what he decided. If he was telling the truth about having business in the area, it might be interesting to see where he was going. And if he had lied... well, it would be good to know that, as well.

Eventually, he shook his head. "That won't be necessary. I'm sure you have better things to do with your afternoon."

I didn't, actually. I was just going to go home and wait there for Christopher to turn up. But I didn't want to push too hard and give Wolfgang the idea that I suspected something. So I smiled graciously and let it go. "Nothing much. Although I'm certain Christopher and I can find something to occupy our time."

"Give your cousin my best," Wolfgang said and steered me towards the stairs to the underground. The tunnel gaped like an open maw, and I fought back a shiver. Between the memory of tumbling headfirst down the stairs the other night, and Wolfgang's hand on the small of my back, all it would take was one push and I'd pitch forward...

"Cold?" He rubbed gently, circularly, and I pulled in a breath.

"A little. It got cold quickly. The weather was so nice just a few days ago..."

"Time to dig the winter wardrobe out of mothballs," Wolfgang said cheerfully and dropped his hand. "Be careful going home, Philippa. Perhaps we can see one another again tomorrow?"

"I wouldn't be surprised," I said. "Just send me a note, unless you want to arrange something now?"

"I shall send you a note with particulars for supper. Would seven o'clock suit?"

I told him it would suit admirably, and he told me to expect a missive with the name of a restaurant and that he'd look forward to seeing me. And then I watched him walk away—at least for a few feet—before I turned and descended the stairs into the underground.

CHAPTER THIRTEEN

I SPENT the next couple of hours—after I made it back to the flat—trying to get warm. The weather really had turned quite cold in the past few days, and the temperatures felt as if they had dropped another few degrees just in the time I had been inside Sweetings. I really hoped that Christopher was dressed warmly enough while he was trailing after Wolfgang all over City and Holborn and wherever else the *Graf* von Natterdorff decided to go.

He must have been busy, at any rate, because teatime came and went with no sign of Christopher. I had my cup of Darjeeling and a bun, and finally warm, settled in to reread *The Secret of Chimneys* by the wonderful Mrs. Agatha Christie. The book was more than a year old by now, and *The Murder of Roger Ackroyd* had been released since, but I had enjoyed *The Secret of Chimneys* better. It had romantic intrigue and missing diamonds and a dashing prince masquerading as an adventurer, and while *The Murder of Roger Ackroyd* was a masterpiece of literary homicide, *The Secret of Chimneys* was just good fun, and also bore some charming parallels to my own situation.

There were murders in the book, of course. A villainous waiter, as well as His Highness, Prince Michael of Herzoslovakia, ended up dead, whilst there were no corpses in my own life at this moment. But there were the missing Sutherland diamonds—not quite the Koh-i-Noor, but an acceptable substitute—and a dashing jewel thief, and an attempt on Laetitia's life—unless it had been an attempt on Christopher's or mine. There was even, if I stretched credulity, a foreign-born adventurer, even though Wolfgang was a mere *Graf*—the equivalent of a British count or earl—and no prince. Still, beggars can't be choosers, and we take our entertainment where we find it.

Suffice it to say that I devoured the book eagerly, and didn't come up for air until the windows had turned dark and it was time to prepare supper. And it was at that point that I began to worry about Christopher and why he wasn't home yet. It had been hours since Wolfgang and I parted ways. Surely whatever business Wolfgang had had in the vicinity of Sweetings was concluded by now, and he had headed back to wherever he laid his head these days?

And even if he hadn't done, even if he were still out there walking around, surely Christopher wasn't still tagging along behind him? There's a limit to how long one can trail a suspect, even in a busy place like London. Sooner or later, the target is bound to notice that the same person has been behind them, or in front of them, or on the other side of the street, for five or six hours straight. Christopher isn't stupid; he would have known that.

He hadn't been arrested, had he?

For the first time I considered that perhaps it hadn't been the best idea to let Christopher go out as Kitty in broad daylight in the middle of London. The buggery laws are in full effect, and that includes coppers going after pretty boys with powder compacts in their trouser pockets. Christopher didn't just have a compact, he had a full chemist's shop of makeup on his face, and he was wearing high heeled shoes and sheer stockings and women's unmentionables under his—or my—skirt. If a powder compact was enough to get someone arrested, Christopher didn't stand a chance.

And I had let him do it anyway—hadn't even considered warning him against it, honestly—because I didn't think there was much of a chance that anyone would look at the pretty girl with the big eyes and dainty features and see a man. He's prettier than I am, especially with his face made up. Someone would have to look pretty closely to pick up on the fact that he's a bloke and not a bird.

Although it wasn't impossible that someone had done just that.

If that was the case, there were two options. Or perhaps three, depending on who had caught on. If Wolfgang had realized that the young lady who had been following him was none other than Christopher Astley in drag, he would certainly have had something to say about it. But Christopher could also, fairly legitimately, claim to want to know more about the man who was wooing his cousin, and there wouldn't be much Wolfgang could say to that.

If a stranger had noticed... well, if the stranger had been wearing a uniform, Christopher might be sitting in a jail cell right now. But if so, wouldn't he have phoned me to arrange for his bail? That was the agreement that we had.

And if the stranger hadn't been a copper, but instead had been someone who had a problem with pretty boys in frocks, Christopher might be in hospital, or could even be lying in an alley somewhere.

I pushed away the mental pictures that that idea conjured,

because they made it difficult to breathe, and instead focused on what my options were.

There weren't many. I didn't know where he had ended up, so I couldn't go out to look for him. He had started on Queen Victoria Street, but he could be anywhere by now. That had been hours ago.

I could stay where I was and wait for him to come home. It was just possible that nothing had gone wrong, that Christopher was still on the trail, or that Wolfgang had noticed him and they were bonding over drinks in a pub somewhere.

Or Christopher might have contacted Tom at some point, or met another friend, one I didn't know. The chap he had been dancing with at the Cave of the Golden Calf the other night, for instance. And now they were off somewhere doing something I ought perhaps not think too deeply about, and Christopher had forgotten to contact me, or simply hadn't thought he needed to.

I could contact Tom myself, and ask him whether he'd seen or heard from Christopher. If he had done, then I could stop worrying. If he hadn't, I'd have someone who would worry along with me—because Tom would definitely be worried. He was also someone who had access to resources I didn't, such as information on whether Christopher really was sitting in a jail cell right now, or even if he—God forbid—was lying on a slab in the morgue.

The motorcar from the other night flashed quickly through my mind, and I realized that there might be another reason why Christopher hadn't come home. It amounted to the same thing —he was lying in a hospital bed or an alley or the morgue—but not because of a random bloke who didn't like boys in frocks, but rather because someone had deliberately tried to run him over just a few days ago and that someone had come back today to finish the job.

Or he might have been kidnapped. Why hadn't I thought of that before? Christopher was the nephew of the Duke of Sutherland, the son of Lord Herbert Astley. There would be money in holding him for ransom. His father would certainly pay any amount to get him back. Uncle Harold might not, but Uncle Herbert wouldn't quibble over draining the coffers for his youngest son.

There was no reason to think anything like that had happened, though, I told myself. It was much more likely that Christopher had run into someone he knew, or had contacted someone he knew from a call box somewhere—perhaps he had found himself in need of a place to take refuge for a while, perhaps while Wolfgang was inside an establishment of some sort, and a call box is great for that sort of thing—and he had taken the time to ring up someone while he was in there. It would certainly add verisimilitude.

Tom's flat wasn't on the exchange, although of course Scotland Yard was. Beckwith Place was, too, in the event that Christopher had decided to phone home to say hello to his parents and his brother. We hadn't been in Wiltshire in over a month, and then it had only been an overnight stay before driving to Marsden Manor with Francis and Constance the next morning. Christopher might have decided he would like to hear his mother's voice.

Sutherland Hall was on the exchange, too, of course, if Christopher had wanted to update Crispin on whatever was going on. And that wasn't an improbability at all: he might feel bad about having spilled the beans about Crispin's supposed attachment to me, and had thought it only fair to let Crispin know that he, Christopher, had blabbed.

That meant ringing up both Sutherland Hall and Marsden Manor, most likely, in case Crispin was snugged up there with his fiancée.

There wasn't much I could do about Tom, I decided. I didn't want to leave the Essex House Mansions long enough to go to Chelsea and back. There was a chance that Christopher might come home while I was out, and I didn't want to miss him. But I could run down the street to the call box on the corner, and ring up Scotland Yard to see whether Tom was still at work. And while I was at it, I could phone both Beckwith Place and Sutherland Hall, too. Maybe even Marsden Manor. And if none of that bore any fruit, then I would track Tom down. Tomorrow morning, latest.

But for now, the call box. I put my jacket and brogues on, hoping all the while that I would hear Christopher's key in the door and see him come into the foyer. When neither of those things happened, I dragged a cloche over my bob and headed down to the lobby.

"You haven't seen Mr. Astley, have you, Evans?"

Evans blinked up at me from behind the counter. He was reading Agatha Christie too, I saw. He tried to hide the book from my sight, but I caught a glimpse of the black and read cover with its big question-mark, and recognized it.

"Mr. Astley, Miss Darling?"

"Christopher," I said. "My flat-mate."

He shook his head. "No, Miss Darling. Not since the two of you left together before noon."

"And no messages from anyone?"

"No, Miss Darling."

"I'm going down to the call box on the corner," I said. "If anyone comes for me, keep them here until I get back, will you, Evans?"

"Yes, Miss Darling."

"Happy reading," I told him, and headed out the door before he could get up to open it for me. "Good choice, Evans."

"Thank you, Miss Darling," floated after me as the door

slowly shut. By then, I was several steps down the pavement towards the call box.

My first call was to Scotland Yard, where I was told that Tom had left for the evening and would be back tomorrow. When I asked if I could leave a message, the desk sergeant took down my name and said that he would pass it along, but of course the morning was a good twelve hours away, and I didn't know whether I could wait that long. Nonetheless, I thanked him, and dialed Beckwith Place.

"Pippa!" Aunt Roz said delightedly when she recognized my voice. "We haven't heard from you in forever."

"We saw you just last month, Aunt Roz."

"Not for long enough," Aunt Roz said. "How are you, my dear?"

"I'm fine," I said, not entirely honestly.

"And your young man?" There was a subtle change in her voice that I might not have noticed had I not been listening for it.

"Wolfgang? He's fine, as well. Or was the last time I saw him."

"And when was that?"

"Luncheon," I said. "He took me to Sweetings. We had crab bisque and prawn cocktail and turbot."

"Sounds lovely," Aunt Roz said, and sounded somewhat envious.

"It *was* lovely. Listen, Aunt Roz..."

"Yes?" my aunt said brightly.

"Christopher—"

But I couldn't bring myself to say that he was missing. It would only upset Aunt Roz, when there was nothing she could do about it, and besides, I didn't actually know that he was missing. He might turn up on his own, full of apologies for having worried me. He might have sent a note that went astray before reaching me before he went off to spend the night with a friend. I might be overreacting.

"Christopher?" Aunt Roz prompted.

I waited for inspiration, but then, before I could actually, consciously come up with something to say, my brain took over, and I blurted, "Christopher told me that Crispin—"

"Ah," Aunt Roz said when I faltered. "I wondered how long he would be able to keep quiet about it."

"Do you mean to say that it's true?"

"Of course it's true," Aunt Roz said. "Dear me, Pippa, the boy could hardly be more obvious about it."

"It wasn't obvious to me," I grumbled.

"Well, it ought to have been." Aunt Roz's voice was brisk. "He could barely look at you without getting starry-eyed at first."

Starry-eyed, was it? "I don't remember that."

"Of course not. You were too busy sniping back at all the sarcasm he employed to cover it up. Really, he's very good at misdirection, isn't he?"

He certainly was. More than five years of it by now. "I have a hard time believing it," I confessed.

"Do you really? I assure you, Pippa, we've all known for years. Why do you suppose my late sister-in-law lost her mind and tried to shoot you at Sutherland Hall in April?"

Um... "Because she knew that I was trying to figure out who had killed Duke Henry and his valet and she was afraid that I would succeed?"

"I'm sure that was part of it," Aunt Roz admitted, "but he was also so delighted about you being there that weekend that he had a hard time containing himself, and I'm sure his mother noticed. I'm equally sure that Harold had quite a lot to say about it."

Yes, indeed. I had heard some of what he'd had to say, and it had been blistering.

"But surely shooting me is a step too far?" I said.

"She had already shot Grimsby by then," Aunt Roz answered blandly, "so I suppose it mightn't have been that much of a stretch."

Perhaps not. "Be that as it may, what I actually rang up to talk to you about, was Christopher."

"Is that so?"

"He hasn't come home," I said. "I went to lunch with Wolfgang at one, and I haven't seen Christopher since. There's been no note and no message left with Evans. He wouldn't happen to have phoned home, would he?"

"Phoned here, do you mean? I rather think your flat is his home now, Pippa."

Yes, of course it was. "Phoned you," I corrected. "Or Uncle Herbert or Francis."

"I don't believe so, my dear. But wait a moment while I ask."

I heard the ear piece click against the surface when she put it down, and then her voice faded as she walked away. "Herbert? Francis? Has either of you heard from Kit today?"

There was an exchange of voices in the background, too far away for me to make out individual words, and then the click-clacking of my aunt's heels as she came back to the telephone. "Pippa? No, he hasn't rung up here today."

"Thank you," I said. "I assumed he hadn't done, but I thought I would ask."

"Should we be worried, dear?"

She sounded worried, and of course I was past concern into anxiety myself. Nonetheless I told her, as calmly as I could, that, "I'm sure he's just fine. He probably went off with a friend and didn't even consider that I might worry."

"Would you like us to motor up?"

"No, don't be silly," I said. "By the time you made it here, he'd most likely be home. It's much too soon to do anything like that."

"Then will you phone us again in the morning and let us know whether he's there or not?"

I promised her I would, and on that note we hung up. I deposited further coins into the device and asked the operator to put me through to Sutherland Hall in Wiltshire.

There was clicking and whirring on the line, and then ringing. After a few seconds, the phone was answered. "You have reached Sutherland Hall."

"Tidwell," I said. "This is—"

"Miss Darling."

"Precisely, Tidwell. Tell me, has Mr. Astley phoned this afternoon?"

"Mr. Astley?"

"Christopher," I said. "Has Christopher rung up to talk to St George? Is St George even at Sutherland Hall, or is he in Dorset with Laetitia?"

"His lordship is presently at home," Tidwell said smoothly, and I wondered whether I imagined the hint of intrigue in his voice, or whether it truly was there. Christopher had said that everyone knew about Crispin's feelings for me, including the servants. Did that mean that Tidwell knew? Was he thinking about it right now?

Tidwell rather liked me, I thought. I liked him back. Certainly a lot better than I did Uncle Harold, or for that matter Crispin himself a lot of the time.

"Would you like for me to fetch his lordship?" Tidwell prodded, and I shook myself free of my musings.

"That won't be necessary, Tidwell. I simply wanted to ask—"

"It's no problem, Miss Darling. His lordship is standing right here."

I definitely didn't imagine that undertone. Tidwell was, unless I missed my guess, gloating.

"Tidwell," I cried, "I don't want—" but of course by then it was too late.

"You don't want me?" Crispin's voice said. "Yes, Darling. I'm well aware of it."

"It's not that I don't want you," I said crossly, because of course he would lead off with that, and while before my talk with Christopher I wouldn't have thought twice about it, now I wondered how I could have been so stupid as to not recognize the many double entendres he often utilized. "I simply don't have a need to talk to you. Tidwell could have told me what I wanted to know."

And, in fact, already had done.

"I've always suspected that you like Tidwell better than you do me," Crispin said.

"Of course I like Tidwell better," I answered. "Tidwell's the best thing about Sutherland Hall. I've often said so."

"Of course you have, Darling." He sounded indulgent, and I couldn't believe I had never noticed that before, either. When I didn't respond, he added, "To what do I owe the pleasure?"

"I wanted to know if you had heard from Christopher," I said, although I already knew the answer. Not only had Tidwell assured me that Christopher hadn't rung up, but Crispin was talking to me the way he always did. If he knew that Christopher had spilled the beans on his feelings, that wasn't likely to be the case. He's plenty brazen, and could undoubtedly have carried it off in style had he been forced to, but he had picked up the receiver from Tidwell by choice, and I didn't think he would have volunteered to speak to me had he known. He would undoubtedly be afraid of me taking the mickey.

That was clearly not a concern today, because he smirked. I could hear it all the way from Wiltshire. "Why? Is he missing?"

When I didn't answer the question, he repeated it, but this time without the smirk and with a lot more consternation. "Wait, Kit's missing?"

"I don't know that he's missing," I said. "I'm sure he's just fine somewhere. I just don't know where he is. We parted ways in front of Sweetings at one—are you familiar with Sweetings, St George?"

"Everyone's familiar with Sweetings," Crispin said. "Where was he headed?"

"Nowhere. I was going inside—"

"Let me guess. Luncheon with Wolfie?"

"What else? Don't distract me, St George. I went in, Christopher stayed out, and when we came back outside after the meal, I didn't see him anywhere."

"No, why would you?" Crispin asked reasonably. "He wouldn't stand outside Sweetings and wait for you to finish eating."

"Of course he wouldn't. Not under normal circumstances. Today, however, he was supposed to wait for Wolfgang, and then follow him home—"

"Oho!" He sounded gleeful. "Trouble in paradise, is it?"

"There's no need to sound so pleased," I grumbled, although of course I knew—now—why such a thing might make him happy. "He moved out of the Savoy, all right? Several weeks ago, according to the doorman. But he still sends me notes on Savoy letterhead. Almost as if he wants me to believe—"

"—that he's still staying there. How very unusual, indeed. I would be intrigued, too."

Yes, of course he would be. So would anyone with an ounce of curiosity in them. "He was dressed as Kitty," I said. "Christopher, I mean. He didn't think Wolfgang would be likely to recognize him. I didn't, either. But he didn't come home for tea, and then he didn't come home for supper, and now it's late, and..."

"And you're alone and worried."

"If you want to put it like that," I said.

"How would you put it?"

"Fine. I'm alone, and yes, I'm worried. Not enough to do anything about it—"

"What do you call ringing me up?"

"I call it making inquiries," I said. "I suppose you haven't heard from him at any point today?"

"Should I have done?"

A loaded question, that one. I decided it would be better if I refrained from answering it.

"I don't know what happened," I said instead. "Perhaps nothing. But I thought, if he followed Wolfgang around City, that there might have been a point where he would have wanted or needed to take shelter. Call boxes are handy for that. And if he was inside one, pretending to use the telephone, I thought it just possible that he might have actually rung someone up."

"And you thought that would be me?"

"Well, he couldn't phone me," I pointed out. "The flat is not on the exchange. Tom isn't either. I don't think he'd ring up Scotland Yard to pass the time, not unless something was wrong. I already checked with Aunt Roz. So I thought he might have phoned you. You are his best friend, after all."

"Aside from you," Crispin muttered. "And Gardiner, I suppose."

"Tom and Christopher are..." I hesitated. "I wouldn't call

them best friends. And if they're together and he simply forgot to inform me of that fact, no one will be happier than me—"

"Except Tom," Crispin said, and this time I absolutely could not miss the innuendo.

"I wish you wouldn't say things like that," I complained. "Besides, I don't know whether they're at that point yet. I don't even know if Tom knows—"

"—that Kit likes him? He'd have to be stupid not to, and he isn't."

"It isn't always easy to tell," I said sourly. "Some people are good at hiding their feelings."

There was a beat. I wondered whether he had heard something in my voice, or whether the hint of accusation was only audible to me.

"Kit isn't," he said after a moment. "He makes no secret of the fact that he can't keep his eyes off Gardiner. And the way he came rushing down to Dorset last month, after Kit rang him up, I don't think it's only him."

No, I didn't think so, either. "It's a big step, though. Especially for a Scotland Yard detective. There are situations where he would be expected to arrest Christopher, not drag him off home to protect him."

Crispin didn't say anything to that. "What do you plan to do now?" he asked after a moment.

I took a breath while I thought about it. "I don't know that there's much I can do. I don't know where Wolfgang lives, so I can't go there and ask him whether he's seen Christopher..."

"Do you think that he might have done something to Kit?"

"I don't know what I think," I said. "All I know is that Christopher was supposed to follow Wolfgang this afternoon. That's what we planned. Although I didn't see him after I stepped into Sweetings. Something might have happened while

I was inside the restaurant, and he might have left by the time we came out again. Perhaps he met a friend and went with him instead of waiting around."

Given our plans and his own curiosity about Wolfgang, it didn't seem likely, but again, it wasn't impossible.

Crispin hummed. "What else?"

"I left a message for Tom at Scotland Yard. He has access to resources I don't. Like the morgue and today's arrest records."

"Do you think someone arrested Kit?"

"I don't know what to think," I said again, "but he was a young man dressed in women's clothes walking through London in broad daylight. It's possible."

"Is there anything I can do?"

I couldn't think of anything. "If you were in London I'd ask you to come by and distract me, but since you're not..."

"I could be in London in a couple of hours."

"Not on my account," I said. "I'm going to bed and hopefully forgetting about all of this until tomorrow."

The smirk returned to his voice. "I could go to bed, too."

And there it was again. One of those innuendos that I had never taken seriously and that I now had to wonder how he meant.

"Not with me," I said. "You're engaged to Laetitia, remember? No fooling around for you."

"What Laetitia doesn't know—"

"She'd know," I said. "And then she'd kill you." Or more likely me.

"Why, Darling, I didn't know you cared!"

I sighed. "Go to bed, St George. I'll have Christopher ring you up when he gets home. That way you won't have to worry."

"And if he's not home by tomorrow morning?"

"Then I'll ring you up again myself," I said.

"Good enough. Sleep well, Darling."

"You too," I told him, and headed back up the pavement towards home.

CHAPTER FOURTEEN

I DIDN'T SLEEP WELL, of course. Not only because I was on the Chesterfield, for the second time in a week—I didn't want to be too far from the front door in case someone/Christopher arrived in the middle of the night—but also because I kept being visited by bad dreams. I was running through the fog—it's always foggy in such dreams, and Britain is so often foggy in life, too—and I could see Christopher ahead of me, but I couldn't catch up to him. Or I caught up and reached out, but the blond that I had thought was my cousin turned out to be Crispin or Wolfgang instead. Or someone else, someone entirely unrelated to the current situation. Once, he was Ronnie Blanton, a blond chap whom Crispin knew, whom I hadn't seen since early June. Once, 'he' was even Lady Violet Cummings, wearing her mother's sapphire and emerald peacock brooch.

But the point is that I didn't sleep well. I kept starting awake every hour or so. By the time the knock on the door finally came, in the wee hours of the morning just before dawn, I dragged myself off the sofa and staggered, half-awake, across the foyer, where I fumbled the locks open and pulled on the door. Outside stood a familiar figure in tweed, blond hair gleaming under the electric lights in the hallway, and I pulled him inside the flat with a sob and flung myself into his arms.

It was only once I was there, rubbing my cheek against itchy tweed—tweed that was slowly turning moist from the tears leaking out of my eyes—that I realized I had made a mistake. Christopher had left the house wearing my clothes yesterday afternoon; he wouldn't return in a well-cut tweed suit that looked like it had been made for him. He owned a tweed suit that had been made for him, but it was still hanging in the wardrobe in his room. And aside from that, Christopher doesn't smell like fresh starch and expensive tobacco and petrol. His scent is lighter and fruitier, especially when he's dressed as Kitty.

By then, a pair of arms had gone around me too, and I was being held tightly against a lean body. Tightly enough that he had no problem feeling my reaction once I caught on to the fact that this wasn't Christopher's shoulder I was sobbing on.

A second passed while his grip tightened, and then he dropped his arms and stepped back. "Good morning, Darling."

I did the same, flushing to the tips of my ears. "St George. I'm sorry, I was half asleep and I thought—"

"I know what you thought. No reason to spell it out." He glanced around. "He isn't home, then?"

I shook my head. "Come in. Close the door behind you. Did you drive all night to get here?"

"Only half of it." He shut the door behind him and followed me into the sitting room. "There are very few cars on the road at night, so I don't have to worry about the speed limit."

"How many times were you stopped and ticketed?" I

wanted to know as I gathered my blanket and pillow from the sofa.

His lips curved. "None. But I did have to outrun a copper somewhere near Basingstoke."

"Of course you did. And purely for the sport of it, too, I'm sure. He probably knew it was you, you know. Getting away from him won't change that."

Every copper in every town between here and Little Sutherland was familiar with Crispin's Hispano-Suiza, not to mention Crispin's penchant for taking his life in his hands.

"He'll have to prove it was me to give me a fine," Crispin said with a shrug and turned his attention from the sofa to me. "What are you doing, lounging around in your pyjamas? Why aren't you ready to go?"

Go where? And aside from that— "Has it escaped your attention that it's five o'clock in the morning, and that I didn't know you were going to be here?"

"Oh, so when you rang me up last night, it wasn't a cry for help?" He smirked, as if he knew the answer to that question already.

"Of course not," I said steadily. "I merely wanted to know if Christopher had contacted you. I didn't think you would spend half the night getting here so you could help me look for him."

"Well, I had to wait for Father to fall asleep before I could get away. He would have told me not to bother."

Yes, most likely he would have done.

"Well, it's too early to do much," I said, "and too dark to see anything, as well. Everyone else is asleep. Why don't you get a couple of hours' sleep yourself, and then we can get started. Perhaps we can catch Tom at home before he heads out for the day."

"Knock me up at seven, then." He headed for the Chesterfield, snagging the pillow out of my arms on his way past, before dropping down on the leather.

"You can nap in Christopher's room," I said, turning on the spot to follow his progress. "It doesn't have to be in the middle of the flat."

"I don't want to get too comfortable," Crispin answered, untying his shoes and shrugging out of his jacket and waistcoat before tugging off his tie. "This way, I won't bother you while you get ready."

He wouldn't bother me if he were in Christopher's room either, preferably with the door shut, but as I had chosen to spend my own night on the sofa instead of tucked up in bed, I had no room to tell him to do otherwise. Instead, I just waited until he had made himself comfortable, curled up on his side on the Chesterfield with one hand tucked under my bed pillow, before I shook out the blanket I was holding and draped it over him.

"Thank you, Darling," came from underneath the folds. I could see the tip of his nose and his eyes, and they didn't open.

"No problem at all," I told him, and then I turned out the light and left him there in favor of scurrying into the hallway and my own room.

I had no pillow and blanket, of course, without which there was no point in trying to go back to bed. I was awake now anyway, so I changed into a skirt and jumper, as it had been cold yesterday, and I didn't imagine that it would be any better today, especially if we were to spend most of the day tooling around in Crispin's motorcar. I brushed my teeth, fluffed my hair, put on makeup, and finally, with nothing else to do but with another hour to go before I could wake Crispin, I wandered into Christopher's room and sank down on the edge of the bed and folded my hands in my lap.

I don't know what I thought I was doing. The only time we

were able to do mind-reading, was when we were in the same room, partaking in the same conversation, and someone said something that we both thought was funny or interesting. At that point our eyes would meet, and I'd know that Christopher was thinking what I was thinking. But the rest of the time, no. He's the closest thing I have to a soulmate, and I love him to pieces, but I could not reach out mentally and get any kind of response back. Nor would I have expected to, had I been reasonable about it, because that sort of thing just doesn't happen in the real world. But I was worried, and short on sleep, and a bit taken aback that Crispin had motored here in the middle of the night from Wiltshire and was currently snuggled up on my couch... and I suppose I wasn't thinking clearly. So I spent a few minutes reaching out, trying to find Christopher, and of course I had nothing to show for it. I couldn't tell whether he was happy or sad, comfortable or suffering some great fate. I couldn't even tell whether he was alive. I would like to think that if he were dead, I would know it, but I certainly couldn't feel it that morning. Although that meant that I could tell myself that he was alive, of course, so that's what I did. With gusto.

Because there was no real reason to believe he wasn't. The most likely explanation for his absence was that he had gone off somewhere willingly, with someone he knew, and had either forgotten to let me know, or the message had gone astray on its way to me.

The second most likely explanation was that something had happened to him—he had been hit by a motorcar, for instance—and was currently in a hospital bed somewhere, unconscious, unable to let me know what had transpired.

Down the list from that, was that someone had taken him against his will, and was keeping him hostage. But who would want Christopher? He's from a wealthy family, yes, but Crispin is worth quite a lot more. And while they do look alike, there was no way that anyone would look at Kitty and think that she —that he?—was Crispin. It wasn't even likely that anyone would look at Kitty and think that she was Christopher, not unless they had come across him—as her—before.

So no, Christopher was alive somewhere, where he had gone hopefully of his own free will, and once Crispin was awake, we would get started on looking for him.

With a few minutes to spare, I wandered past the Chesterfield into the kitchenette and started boiling water for coffee. I'm normally a tea drinker, but after the night I had had—after the night we had both had—I figured the extra dose of caffeine would help us both to wake up.

Crispin was out for the count, eyelashes fluttering and lids twitching as he dreamt. He didn't even stir when I brushed past him on my way to take a seat on the coffee table with a cup of coffee in each hand. "Rise and shine, Goldilocks."

He muttered something indistinguishable at that, but didn't open his eyes. Not until I put one cup down and poked him in the cheek. "Up and at'em, St George. It's just gone seven and there's coffee."

His nose twitched at that, and his eyes fluttered open. For a moment or two they were cloudy and confused, and then they fastened on me and cleared. "Darling." His cheekbones darkened, and he cleared his throat and sat up, dropping his gaze from my face to the cup in my hands. "Did you say coffee?"

I shoved it at him and lifted the other cup from the table for myself. "I normally take it light and sweet, but black as tar seems indicated today. The better to wake us up."

"Indeed." He took a sip and winced. "You weren't joking, were you?"

Not at all. "Neither of us got much sleep. I thought it might help."

"I won't need it." Crispin smirked. "You always keep me on my toes."

And there it was, another of those comments that, before this weekend, I would have taken at face value—a joke about our usual animosity and constant bickering—but which I now heard as yet one more misdirection.

When I didn't say anything, just stared at him, he flushed. "What now?"

I looked away. "Nothing. Never mind."

"Are you certain?"

"Positive," I nodded. There was no need for us to talk about this. He hadn't brought it up in the past five years, and nothing had changed since the last time I saw him. Nothing aside from the fact that now I knew how he felt—or ostensibly felt.

But he was still engaged to Laetitia, and I was still not interested in any kind of relationship with him—not that we could have had one at this point, considering Laetitia. So what this really came down to, was me wanting to grab him by the shoulders and shake him, and shriek, "What were you thinking? You can't be in love with me!" But since nothing good would come of that, especially on a day when we would be spending hours and hours together, it was just as well if I didn't make the situation any more awkward than it already was. No matter how curious and/or appalled I was.

He pushed to his feet, and then shoved the coffee cup into my hand. "Let me visit the loo, and then we can head out."

"There's no rush," I began, although of course there was. Not enough of a rush that we had to leave right this minute, though. "You can take the time to finish the coffee."

"That's all right, Darling." He shot me a smirk over his shoulder on his way to the hall doorway. "As I said, your presence is abrasive enough to keep me alert."

"Ditto," I told him, as I picked myself up and headed for the kitchenette with the two cups.

Five minutes later we were in the Hispano-Suiza, making our way along the still-dark streets towards Chelsea. Christopher and I had left a message at Tom's flat once, and I was able to direct Crispin to it. By the time we pulled up across the street, the sun had risen east of London, and the street lamps were off. Tom's building, all four stories of it, sat silent.

"There's no doorman," I told Crispin. "We can ring the bell and see if he's at home. If not, I suppose we can leave another message."

"You left one at Scotland Yard last night?"

"When I rang up," I confirmed, "yes."

"Let's go, then." He pushed his door open. I did the same, and hurried around the motorcar. He was eyeing the building. "Which flat is his, do you know?"

"I've never been inside," I said, "so I'm afraid I have no idea. The only reason I know where it is at all, is that Christopher took me here once. But we only left a note."

He nodded. "No time like the present."

He presented his elbow and I hooked on for the trip across the street.

We found Tom's card—Thomas Gardiner, 3C—beside one of the buzzers, and Crispin put his finger on it. The buzzer, I mean; not the card. Nothing happened—there was no sound— but 3C was probably far enough away that even if it rang inside Tom's flat, we wouldn't hear it. A minute passed—Crispin pressed the buzzer again twice—and then an irate voice called down from above. "What the bloody hell is going on?"

We stepped back out of the doorway and peered up. A window two floors above had opened, and Tom was peering out, his hair in disarray and his face flushed.

"Oh," he said when he saw us, "it's you two. What's wrong?"

And then he must have noticed the Hispano-Suiza parked on the opposite side of the street—it's difficult not to, when the motorcar is bright blue—and some of the angry color faded from his face in favor of a more subdued pallor. One might even say that he paled. "St George?"

"In the flesh," Crispin confirmed. I supposed that, up until then, Tom must have assumed I was with Christopher. It's an easy mistake to make, even for someone who hadn't just been ripped from sound sleep. Crispin was with me, where Christopher was likely to be. It was still a bit dark down here on the street, so visibility was somewhat compromised, and Crispin was wearing a hat, so Tom couldn't see that his hair is a shade lighter and cooler in color than Christopher's. From up above, he might not even be able to see Crispin's face well enough to tell the difference.

It also answered the question of whether Christopher had spent the night with Tom, of course. And obviously he hadn't, if Tom was asking about him.

"Where's Kit?"

"That's what we want to talk to you about," I said, and watched the rest of the color fade from Tom's face.

"Two minutes." He withdrew from the window, and the sash slammed down. We migrated back to the front door—I assumed he would unlock it from upstairs so we could go in and up—but instead a minute passed, and then another, and then Tom appeared in the lobby.

He had clearly dressed in a hurry, because his collar was askew and he was still tying his tie as he came across the floor towards us. After he had pulled the door open and joined us on the top step, he began buttoning up his jacket.

"What happened?" he wanted to know, between one button and the next.

"Christopher didn't come home last night," I explained, "so I rang up Sutherland Hall to ask whether St George had heard from him. I rang up Scotland Yard and Beckwith Place, as well; there will be a message for you when you go in. And then St George drove up to Town—"

Tom shook his head. "Never mind that. What do you mean, Kit didn't come home last night? Where is he?"

"If we knew that, we wouldn't be here," Crispin told him. "He and Philippa went out together in the middle of the day yesterday. He escorted her to Sweetings on Queen Victoria Street, where she was meeting Wolfie—"

"That's not important right now, either," I interrupted. "At least I don't think so. I left Christopher on Queen Victoria Street at one o'clock. I haven't seen him since."

"Where was he going from there?" Tom asked.

"That's the thing," I answered, and I'll admit that I squirmed somewhat guiltily as I said it, "he wasn't going anywhere. Or nowhere I know. He planned to stick around and then follow Wolfgang home after he and I parted ways."

Tom's eyebrows rose. "And why would he do that?"

I explained again about Wolfgang and the Savoy, and ended with, "We were curious, that's all."

"Of course you were." The tone indicated a distinct lack of sympathy with our curiosity.

"Don't *you* find it curious?" Crispin wanted to know. When Tom didn't answer, he continued, "There can only be one logical reason why the man would leave the Savoy but continue to use Savoy letterhead in his correspondence with Philippa, and that's to make her believe he was still staying there."

"Perhaps he's merely being frugal," Tom suggested, a bit

dryly, "and he didn't want to spend the money on extra notepaper if he didn't have to?"

Crispin scowled at him. "When was the last time you left a hotel after a stay and took their stationary with you so you could continue to use it after you left?"

"Never," Tom admitted cheerfully. "Simmer down, St George. Just because it's unusual doesn't mean it's criminal."

"We didn't say it was criminal," I pointed out. "Just that it seemed a funny thing to do. And can you think of any reason anyone would do it, other than to give the impression that he's still a guest?"

"I can think of a few fraudulent ways that it could be used," Tom said, "although there have been no reports of anything like that from the Savoy."

"That reminds me," I said. "I wanted to ask you—or rather, I think Christopher did—whether there had been any reports of thefts at the Savoy during the last few months."

"Thefts?" Tom repeated. "I'm sure there must have been a few, although I can't think of an instance off the top of my head. But those things do happen, especially to tourists. And of course the Schlomskys stayed at the Savoy while they were in London. That was kidnapping for profit, not theft, but it was a criminal act even so."

"I'm not worried about that." I waved it off. "Wolfgang had nothing to do with that."

Tom's brows rose, and so did Crispin's. "Did you just accuse Wolfie of theft, Darling?"

"No," I said crossly. "As I said, this was Christopher's idea."

"Christopher accused Wolfie of theft?" Crispin echoed, at the same time as Tom asked, "That the *Graf* von Natterdorff has something to do with the jewelry thefts we've been investigating?"

"I think," I said, "that he just thought it was interesting that

Wolfgang had moved out but without telling me where he had gone, and that he knew, or at least had met, several of the victims. Lady Violet Cummings was at that weekend party at Marsden Manor a few weeks ago, remember—"

"I'm hardly likely to forget that she was almost murdered right in front of me," Tom nodded.

"And the night that Laetitia's engagement ring was stolen, Wolfgang and I had seen her and St George at the Criterion Restaurant. She was wearing the ring as well as the earrings, and the missing pearl necklace, as well."

"So Natterdorff knew that Lady Laetitia was in London that night, and that the jewelry was with her, and that she was likely to be busy with other things."

"I suppose so," I said, with a glance at Crispin, whose cheekbones were pink along with the tips of his ears.

"I'm not certain I appreciate your insinuation, Gardiner," he muttered.

"I'm quite certain you don't," Tom answered blandly, "but that doesn't change the fact that it was a logical assumption. I don't think anyone thinks that the two of you aren't enjoying your marital privileges ahead of time."

"As it happens—"

Tom raised a hand. "I don't want to hear it. Let's get back to the important bits."

Crispin scowled, but seemed to agree that his relations with Laetitia—whether they were of a carnal nature or not, and it sounded as if he had been trying to claim that they were not, hard as that was to believe—were less important than trying to figure out where Christopher was. "By all means."

Tom turned back to me. "So Kit was supposed to follow Natterdorff when the two of you parted ways."

I nodded. "I didn't see him at that point, however, so he might have been gone already. Or he had simply moved out of the doorway where I left him, and into a shop, or into the church across the street, or for that matter into a Hackney cab."

"But you didn't see him after you came out of the restaurant after lunch?"

I shook my head. "The last time I saw him was at one o'clock precisely, just down Queen Victoria Street from Sweetings. He went into a doorway about halfway between the tube station and the door to the restaurant. The doorway was empty when we came back out. Wolfgang walked me past it to the stairs to the underground."

"And you haven't heard from him since?"

"I haven't heard from either of them. And it isn't like Christopher, Tom. If he could have contacted someone, he would have done. Maybe not me—he might have rung up Sutherland Hall or Beckwith Place, or even Scotland Yard, if he was trying to get a message to someone and wasn't terribly picky about who it was—but he wouldn't have vanished without a trace. Not of his own free will."

Tom nodded. "Not of his own free will, then. What have you done so far?"

I told him what I had done, which in retrospect wasn't much. I had mostly spent the time since lunch yesterday waiting and wringing my hands.

"And now you're here," Tom turned to Crispin.

The latter nodded. "Philippa rang me up last night. I motored up from Wiltshire and got to London early this morning."

"Too early to do much," I added. "I put him to bed for a few hours—he'd motored through the night—and then we came here."

"And no one has heard from Kit?"

"I haven't," I said, and Crispin shook his head. "He didn't

contact Aunt Roz and Uncle Herbert. I assume he didn't contact you?"

Tom shook his head.

"Then no. He either went off somewhere with someone he knew—like the bloke he was dancing with the other night; you recall, I'm sure—"

Tom's expression said as clearly as words that yes, he recalled.

"—or something bad has happened to him."

Tom nodded. "Anything else you haven't told me?"

I grimaced. "He was dressed as Kitty. He thought—we thought—that it was less likely that Wolfgang would recognize him that way."

"He didn't seem to do so the other night," Tom agreed, and I shook my head.

"But that was at night, in the back of the Tender. In broad daylight, it might be different."

He didn't say anything, and I added, a bit diffidently, "Have you... um... spoken to Christopher in the past few days? Since that night?"

Tom shook his head, clearly expecting the worst.

"Do you remember when you dropped us off outside the Essex House Mansions?"

"Of course I remember," Tom said. "It was only a few days ago. Hardly something I'd forget, is it?"

"Do you remember that we waited for you to motor away before we crossed the street?"

He nodded.

"By the time we reached the other side, there was another motorcar coming down the street towards us. A black one. It looked like a Hackney."

"Yes?" Tom said.

I made a face. "It jumped up on the pavement and came within a few inches of hitting us both."

They both stared at me.

"I don't know whether it was an accident," I said, "or if it wasn't, whether it was me or Christopher it was after—"

"Or Laetitia," Tom said. When Crispin arched an incredulous brow, he added, "Come now, St George. You know as well as I do that Kit looks quite a lot like your fiancée when he's dressed as Kitty. It's the black wig more than anything, I suppose..."

"I'm still not sure I like what you're insinuating," Crispin said stiffly and Tom smirked.

"I'm not insinuating anything, St George. It's not as if you're attracted to Kitty, are you?"

"Are you?" Crispin shot back, and then shuddered. "Lord, no. Not that she—that he—isn't quite lovely like that. But unlike some people, I recognize my cousin. Even in drag."

Tom nodded. "I wish you two would have told me this before now, Pippa."

"There was nothing you could have done," I said. "A black Hackney. There are thousands of them in London. And we don't know that it wasn't an accident, anyway."

"It does put a different complexion on this thing, though. If Christopher was the target, and now he's missing."

Yes, of course it did. But I had been the one pushed down the stairs to the underground. And Laetitia was the one who had seen the jewelry thief. It had seemed more likely that either of us two was the target of the person in the Hackney rather than Christopher.

Of course, Christopher was now the one missing, so there was that.

"Let's go," Tom said and nodded towards the Hispano-Suiza. "You drive, St George."

"Are you certain you trust him to do that?" I asked, at the same time as Crispin inquired, "Where to?"

"Scotland Yard," Tom said, with barely a flicker of a glance at me, while Crispin shot me a scowl. "From there I can at least make sure that he wasn't picked up for public indecency and hasn't spent yesterday afternoon and last night in a jail cell. After that, we'll start ringing up hospitals."

"After you, Darling." Crispin opened the car door for me to crawl into the backseat. He flipped the seat back and situated himself behind the wheel. "Ready?"

"As I'll ever be," Tom said, and shut his own door. The Hispano-Suiza started up with a roar, and we took off down the quiet street like a bullet from a gun.

CHAPTER FIFTEEN

I WON'T BORE you with a recounting of the time that
Crispin and I spent sitting in the waiting area at Scotland Yard
while Tom was in his office on the telephone. It was utterly
stultifying, of course, and at the same time nail-biting, sitting
here waiting for news, and we spent the time sniping at one
another in the way we usually do when we're together. The
higher the tension, the more tense the sniping became. It was
familiar enough that I was able to forget, for long seconds of
time, that apparently he was in love with me. There was no sign
of it, or no more sign than there had ever been. He entered into
his usual cutting sarcasm with gusto, and even if I caught the
occasional double entendre that I would have normally let pass
without notice, bickering with him felt no different now than it
had ever done. And it gave both of us something to focus on
other than Christopher's disappearance and what Tom might
be digging up.

Some people gave us curious looks as they went in and out,
and a few even addressed us. Or addressed Crispin, more

specifically. By name, or rather by title, but either way they clearly knew who he was.

"What was that about?" I inquired after one of them, a strapping young specimen in mufti, had walked past and out the door. "Do you have a police record that I don't know about?"

He shook his head. "Grimsby dug up whatever there was to know, Darling. If you read his dossier, you know it all."

Not all, clearly. His feelings for me had not been in the dossier.

"I don't recall there being much in it about you being arrested," I said.

"That's because I can usually talk my way out of being arrested," Crispin answered. "Or bribe my way out of it, if all else fails."

I blinked. "Does Tom know that his colleagues are open to bribery?"

"I have no idea what Gardiner knows or doesn't know," Crispin said. "And perhaps 'bribe' is too strong a word. Let's just say that some people are amenable to looking the other way given the right incentive."

Just as he said it, the door to the street opened, and a WPC walked in. Crispin gave her an appreciative up-and-down look, and when she gave him a stern one in return, he winked at her. I waited for a verbal slap to come his way, but instead she smirked and kept going. I waited until she had disappeared through the door on the other side of the lobby before I said, "You found your female constable, St George? It's just a few months since you were excited to learn that they existed. Did you deliberately go look for one?"

He arched a brow. "Did that look deliberate to you, Darling? I'm just sitting here. I can't control who comes and goes."

"You mean you didn't know her?"

It had certainly looked like a meeting between chums, or at least between two people who had made each other's acquaintance before now.

"I've never seen her until this moment," Crispin said. "I'm irresistible, Darling, and the sooner you learn that, the better."

"I've never had a problem resisting you," I pointed out, and he snorted.

"That's because I've never subjected you to the full force of my charm. If I had done, you would have folded like a cheap suit."

"Would not."

"Would, too."

"I think it's much more likely," I said, before he could prove his assertion, or try to, "that it's simply a matter of whether someone knows you or not. I know very well what a bastard you are—"

"Don't let my father hear you say that, Darling. Or my fiancée, either."

I ignored him, since that wasn't the sort of bastard I was accusing him of being, "—so you don't impress me. But someone who doesn't know anything about you, other than that you're sitting here looking like a good time—"

"You think I look like a good time?" He sounded delighted at the admission.

"Less now than when you're all dolled up in evening kit with a glass of champagne in your hand," I said, "but yes, of course you do. This can't possibly be news to you."

His mouth curved. "It's news that you think so."

I rolled my eyes. "Don't let it go to your head, St George."

The curve turned into a smirk. "Too late, Darling. It's already there."

Of course it was. "That aside," I said, "I've always found

you imminently resistible. Because I know you, your abhorrent personality makes up for any bit of outward appeal that you may have."

The smirk broadened into a grin. "You say the sweetest things to me, Darling. Outward appeal, is it?"

"You're pretty," I said, "and you know it. Sometimes I think you know it all too well."

Such as now, when he was fluttering his eyelashes at me like a flirtatious girl.

"Stop it," I told him sternly. "I'm not falling for it."

"Darling..."

"No. You're not supposed to call me that, remember?" And certainly not in that tone.

He smirked. "Philippa..."

"Not that, either. You know I don't like it."

"What do you like?"

"Not you," I said, and that was when the door to the interior of Scotland Yard opened and Tom stepped through. I breathed a sigh of relief and straightened on my chair. "Tom. What news?"

Beside me, Crispin did the same thing. "You look glum, Gardiner. It isn't bad news, is it?"

"It's no news," Tom said, and I breathed out, relieved, even as I was still worried.

"Nothing at all?"

Tom shook his head. "He wasn't arrested, as himself or as Kitty."

I didn't think it likely that he had been—he would have rung me up had that happened, or so I assumed—but I supposed there had been a chance that he'd been arrested and simply not offered a chance to phone anyone. Now that chance was out the window, it seemed.

"You checked the morgue," Crispin said, his voice carefully controlled, "I presume?"

Tom made a face. "Much as I hated to do it, yes. No one matching Kit's description was brought in last night. Not to the morgue, nor to any of the London hospitals."

The only option left was the dank cellar, then. Or something like it. A bedroom in a cottage in Thornton Heath, like the one where Flossie Schlomsky had been kept.

Something popped into my mind, and then exited, just as quickly, when Tom said, "I also took the time to ring up Germany."

Ring up— "Why?"

"Better get with the program, Darling," Crispin advised. "He wanted to make sure that Wolfie is really Wolfie, I imagine. Is that right, Gardiner?"

Tom nodded. "Got it in one, St George."

"And is he?" I wanted to know.

"He's Wolfgang Ulrich Albrecht *von und zu* Natterdorff," Tom said, "or so it seems. I phoned the local constabulary in Natterdorff—that's a hamlet in the vicinity of where the castle is located—"

I nodded, since Wolfgang had told me as much. Crispin did as well, although this was most likely the first he had heard of it.

"And I described the chap we know. The local bobby recognized him. He's the grandson of the old count, it seems."

"I could have told you that," I said. "He's an orphan, like me, but his grandfather is still living."

Crispin looked at me, brow elevated. "If his grandfather is living, he can't be the *Graf von und zu* Natterdorff, Darling."

"Of course he can," I said. "You have two grandfathers, don't you?" Or did, until Duke Henry died? "Just because he has a grandfather, doesn't mean that that grandfather is the *Graf*. He could have been Wolfgang's mother's father."

Crispin looked as if he had bit into something foul. He doesn't like being wrong. "But he's not," he asked Tom, "is he? The old man, I mean?"

Tom shook his head. "He's the *Graf von und zu* Natterdorff, and Wolfgang's paternal grandfather."

"So if the grandfather is the *Graf*," I asked, "what does that make Wolfgang?"

"Apparently he's the *Graf von und zu* Natterdorff, as well. Don't ask me how it works—" this came with a warning look at Crispin, "—but that's what the bloke at the constabulary called him. The young *Graf*."

"Maybe they call them all *Grafs*, then? The one with the title as well as the one coming into it?"

"Who knows," Tom said. "The important bit seems to be that he is who he says he is. More or less."

There was a moment of silence. "Let me clear it up for you," Crispin offered. When I shot him a look, he added, down the length of his nose, "I was bred for this, you know. Up until the Great War, German nobility was just like any other European nobility: something I was expected to know about and possibly marry into. I spent hours memorizing lines of succession, and woe betide me if I got any of it wrong."

"I'm glad to hear that you were well educated in useless information," I sniped, even as the last part of the sentence imparted a measure of worry. Uncle Harold has never been easy on his son and heir, and I didn't like the idea of what corporal punishment he might have meted out for Crispin not being up to snuff in memorizing foreign noble titles. "Go on."

He held up a finger. "The old *Graf* is the *Graf*." Another. "His wife is the *Gräfin*." A third. "Their eldest son and heir would have been the *Erbgraf*. Younger sons are called *Junkers*. A grandson would also be called a *Graf*, although with his father out of the way, I suppose Wolfie is technically the *Erbgraf* now—"

"But the bottom line," Tom said, "is that he is not calling himself by a title he doesn't own?"

Crispin shook his head. "He's likely not the *Graf von und zu* Natterdorff—that would be his grandfather—but he's a *Graf* in the Albrecht family, heir to the Natterdorff title."

"Like you," I said, and Crispin gave me a disgruntled look.

"Not at all like me, Darling."

"Philippa. And how on earth is it not like you? You'll be inheriting the title from your father and not your grandfather, but other than that..."

Tom waved the budding disagreement aside. "Bicker on your own time. We have more important things to worry about."

Since he was right about that, I dropped my hands off my hips and turned my attention away from Crispin as Tom continued, "The local bobby didn't know what Natterdorff might be doing in London, or so he said. The Natterdorffs are still wealthy, it seems, albeit not as wealthy as they were before the war—"

"Nobody's as wealthy as they were before the war," Crispin muttered.

I shot him a look before asking Tom, "Then it's possible that Wolfgang wouldn't be able to afford the Savoy long term?"

And perhaps even possible that he might have taken up jewelry theft as a sideline?

"Anything's possible," Tom said. "The chap I talked to had no idea how to get in touch with him. He said he would inquire of the staff at the castle—apparently the old *Graf* is infirm and can't be bothered with questions—but there's no reason to think he'll go out of his way to fetch that information for me."

"Why would he?" Crispin agreed. "You're a Brit. You won

the war. He didn't. And not only that, but you're asking questions about one of his own. He has no reason to do anything for you."

"Precisely. But at least we know that the chap we know is who he says he is, more or less, and that he's not some charlatan trying to get close to the Sutherland family through Pippa."

I sniffed, offended. "He has shown no interest in the Sutherlands, I'll have you know. I don't think he's ever exchanged a single word with Uncle Harold, and as for Crispin, they despise one another about equally, I would say."

"I'm quite certain I despise him more," Crispin said. And added, "He doesn't have to be a charlatan to want to get close to us, you know. If the family is in reduced circumstances, he could be the heir to the Natterdorffs and still want to augment the coffers with Sutherland money."

I snorted. "If so, he really doesn't understand the family dynamic. There's no way marriage to me would get him close to any of the Sutherland money. Your father hates me. He wouldn't gift me so much as a fish spade for my nuptials, let alone a shilling of real cash."

"He might pay Wolfie to take you off his hands," Crispin said, which was so blatantly offensive that I quite lost my breath. "Don't look at me like that, Darling. You know very well that my father would do whatever he had to, to see the back of you."

Yes, of course he would do. Crispin's mother had tried to shoot me. His father would certainly not be above bribery—or above paying someone to get me away from his son. I should be glad it would only be to Germany and not out of existence altogether.

"He really hasn't asked any questions about St George or his father?" Tom wanted to know.

I shook my head. "Not beyond the things everyone asks."

The silence was expectant, and I added, reluctantly, "Like everyone else, he has suggested that I might fancy St George. Or that St George might fancy me. Or that we fancy one another and are simply trying to hide it. The usual claptrap, in other words. I can't imagine why everyone thinks the animosity is a cover for liking one another, or why we would bother to hide it if we did."

There was a pause. A very short one, barely a breath. Under other circumstances—pre two days ago—I probably wouldn't have noticed it. Now I did, but I'll hand it to Crispin, he recovered quickly, and sounded perfectly like himself when he told me, "*You* may not have any reason to pretend, Darling. After all, I'm a catch, aren't I? Anyone would be lucky to have me."

I rolled my eyes. "If you say so. And I suppose I'm not?"

He smirked. "I didn't say that. But Father would certainly have something to say about it if I expressed any kind of fondness for you."

Well, yes. Bad enough that he felt the feelings. Acting on them in any way, even just verbally, would no doubt be anathema to His Grace.

"I imagine he would do," I said. "Something like 'common as dirt and a foreigner to boot,' no doubt."

Crispin's brows drew down as if the words were familiar, and of course they would be; I had lifted them more or less directly from Uncle Harold's diatribe back in April.

"Never mind," I added, before he could place the quote. "It's not important. What do we do now?"

We had no way to contact Wolfgang. And if he was who he said he was, and if he was still wealthy, there was no reason to think that he would have done any harm to Christopher even if he had discovered him tagging along behind him yesterday. If

Wolfgang had nothing to hide, it would simply be humorous to him, I thought.

"I hope you're right," Tom said when I expressed as much. "I imagine our next step is to go back to Sweetings, to visit the other establishments in the area, and ask whether anyone noticed Kit yesterday. Someone might have seen what happened."

Someone might have done, and perhaps I should have thought to do that yesterday afternoon, when it was still light out and when someone might have remembered something. But at that point I hadn't known that Christopher was missing —I had thought he was just tucked away in another doorway or storefront, waiting for Wolfgang to leave so he could follow— and by now, it was all water under the bridge. Second-guessing something I hadn't even known at the time was futile, albeit tempting. I pushed it aside and followed the two men out of the lobby into the courtyard.

"Is it all right if we take your motorcar?" Tom inquired of Crispin. "That way, the Tender will be available to the rest of the team, should they need it."

"Of course." Crispin opened the door and shooed me into the backseat again.

"Is it acceptable for you to simply go off on your own today," I asked Tom, as I smoothed my skirt over my knees, "on something that isn't even officially a case yet?"

"It's a case," Tom answered, as he made himself comfortable in the passenger seat while Crispin fired up the motor. "I know Kit, and he wouldn't stay out all night without letting you know where he was. Especially not with what has been going on lately."

"You don't think it's likely that he met someone he knew, and went somewhere with him?"

"No," Tom said. "If he went anywhere with anyone and

didn't come home, something is wrong and we're right to worry. A few hours would have been sufficient for that sort of thing."

His tone indicated clearly how little he liked this idea, and Crispin slanted him a smirk. "How is it that you know what's a sufficient amount of time for that kind of activity, Gardiner?"

Tom slanted a look back, this one a lot less amused. "Do I look like an innocent to you, St George? Besides, you've brought women home before. Plenty of them, from what I hear. Do you usually spend more than a few hours with them?"

"Not if I can help it," Crispin said, with no attempt to make himself sound like a gentleman. "I'm usually gone as soon as I can fasten my flies. But it's not the same thing, is it?"

"It's exactly the same thing. And I would thank you to refrain from trying to make me compromise myself."

Crispin sniggered, but he took one hand from the wheel to perform a locking motion on his lips.

"I don't think he would have gone home with anyone for that purpose," I said. "He had a reason for being there. He was excited about it. And he knew that I counted on him. He wouldn't have wanted to disappoint me."

And that was aside from the fact that he was in love with Tom, and wasn't likely to have accepted anyone else's invitation to engage in that kind of activity.

"The question, then," Tom said, "is whether whoever took him, or talked him into going with them, knew that they were getting Kit, or whether they wanted Kitty."

"I don't think that should be the question," Crispin protested. "I mean, yes. He does look like a pretty girl when he's all dressed up. But if someone wanted a pretty girl and then they got Kit instead... well, they certainly wouldn't keep him, would they?"

Likely not. They would either toss him back where they found him—in which case he would have made his way home by now—or they would have killed him so he couldn't identify them.

I shook off that idea with a shudder. "What should the question be, then, if not that?"

Crispin flicked a look at me in the mirror. "Whether Wolfie is involved or not."

"I thought we agreed that Wolfgang has no reason to wish Christopher harm."

"*You* may have decided that, Darling. I'm quite certain I didn't."

"You just don't like Wolfgang, St George. But—"

"You're damn right I don't, Darling."

"—we already talked about it and decided that he's not doing anything wrong—"

"*I* decided no such thing."

"—and if he has nothing to hide, why on earth would he—"

"He most certainly has something to hide."

I scowled at the back of his head. "And what is that, pray tell?"

"He left the Savoy and is still pretending that he's staying there," Crispin said. Which, I admit, shut me up. For a moment, at least.

"Fine," I said grudgingly. "He did do that."

"And it's suspicious." He appealed to Tom. "Isn't it?"

"It's certainly interesting," Tom agreed. "Although there could be good reasons for it. Or at least reasons."

"Which would be?"

"He doesn't want Pippa to think badly of him," Tom said with a glance at me, "so he's hiding the fact that he's had to move to cheaper accommodations."

"Lying by omission." Crispin's tone dripped with satisfaction.

"You're a fine one to talk," I told him, and he shot me a look in the mirror.

"What was that, Darling?"

"Never mind," I said sullenly. But five years of silence, really? And he had the nerve to criticize other people for keeping things to themselves?

Now was not the time for that conversation, however. "Yes," I said. "Fine. Wolfgang is hiding something from me. Which is the entire reason we are in this situation to begin with, if you'll recall. Let's just focus on Christopher. You and I can have things out later."

"If you say so, Darling." He gave me another dubious look in the mirror, but focused his attention forward again as we followed Fleet Street and Ludgate Hill past Saint Paul's to Cannon. The dome of the great cathedral faded into the heavy grayish background of the sky.

"Looks like snow," Tom commented.

I turned to him, appalled. "Surely not."

It was cold enough for it, certainly, but we were hardly even halfway through October yet.

He shrugged. "Looks like it."

Hmph. I leaned back against the seat and folded my arms across my chest.

It was a few minutes later that Crispin had parked the motorcar in the small stub of Queen Street, and we were standing where Christopher and I had stood yesterday, with the somber façade of St Mary Aldermary looming across the street and the cheerful windows of Sweetings up ahead.

"There's the doorway." I pointed to it. "The last time I saw Christopher, he went into it while I continued up the street and into Sweetings."

It was a wide doorway, filled with heavy, double, wooden doors. It looked like the entrance to a fortress.

Tom eyed it, his head tilted to one side. "Interesting. I didn't realize what this was."

I flicked a glance at Crispin, who looked as non-plussed as I felt. I turned back to Tom. "You didn't realize... what? I'm sorry?"

"This is the Albert Building," Tom explained. He tore his eyes away from the forbidding entrance for a moment to glance up at the four levels of windows above our heads, before turning back to it again. "I thought they would be flats, so I planned to take you both inside so we could all knock on doors. But I don't think that the incumbent government would be happy about that."

"The... what?"

"This is the incumbent government's office building," Tom said. "I doubt they would appreciate the two of you wandering around inside."

"I'm fairly certain they wouldn't appreciate that at all," I agreed. "Can you go inside yourself, and look around? You work for the government, or some periphery of it."

"I work for the Metropolitan Police Department," Tom corrected, "but yes, I could probably go inside. More easily than the two of you could, anyway. Although it's not likely that anyone up there has Kit stashed away in a closet."

No, it wasn't. "Will you do it anyway? Just to make certain?"

"Of course I will." Tom squared his shoulders under the tweed. "Who knows? Perhaps someone up there deals with German relations, and it turns out that Natterdorff chose this restaurant for a reason."

"He did say that he had business in the area," I said. It wasn't impossible that that business had had something to do with British-German relations. He had implied as much, in fact, even if he had denied that it was in any official capacity.

"What will you two do while I canvass the Albert Building?"

"I want to visit the church," I said, gesturing across the street at it, "and we can also stop into all the retail establishments we can see, and ask whether any of them noticed Christopher. It should keep us busy for a while."

I glanced at Crispin, who nodded.

"Very well," Tom said. "Shall we meet at the motorcar after we're done?"

We agreed to do so, and then we watched as he rang the buzzer next to the formidable wooden door, gave his name and occupation to the disembodied voice that answered, and pulled the door open. He gave us one last look before stepping across the threshold. The door shut behind him with the approximate sound of a crypt door. I shuddered.

"None of that, Darling." Crispin put a hand on the small of my back and turned me away. "He'll be all right. And so will we. Shall we visit the church or the tobacconist first?"

I ran my gaze from the line of shops on the first floor of the Albert Building and then across the street and up the wall and the clock tower of the church opposite. If Tom had vanished inside the equivalent of a vault to search for Christopher, how could I do any less?

"Church," I said firmly.

CHAPTER SIXTEEN

ST MARY ALDERMARY looked gray and tired from the outside, the way that most of London does, especially under a heavy October sky. Inside, however, it was bright white, with tall, ornately carved ceilings, and lots of dark wood.

"Geoffrey Chaucer's father was buried here," I told Crispin as we made our way up the middle aisle, glancing into each pew as we passed to make sure Christopher wasn't curled up on top of or underneath one. "Or so the story goes, anyway. I don't think there's any evidence of it anymore. If there was ever a crypt in this spot, I don't think it exists anymore."

"Good," Crispin said.

Yes, indeed. There was no part of me that wanted to descend into the cold and damp of a crypt to look for Christopher's potentially dead body. I fought back a shiver and added, "In a much happier event—or so I assume—John Milton married his second, or perhaps his third, wife in this church, as well."

He nodded. "Lovely place for it."

"Yes, it is. Or it might have been. It was the church before this one. I have no idea what it looked like." I gazed up at the soaring arches of the ceiling, and added, "Probably not like this."

Crispin grunted and turned his head to peer down the next pew.

"How does it feel?" I asked him.

He flicked me a distracted glance. "How does what feel?"

I gestured in a circular motion. "The church experience. It's just about two months, isn't it, until it's your turn?"

He made a face. "Don't remind me."

I smirked. "Second thoughts, St George?"

"It wouldn't matter if I did, would it now, Darling?"

No, of course it wouldn't. Laetitia's regrets might make a difference, but his wouldn't. He'd only be able to escape the marriage if she let him escape.

I twisted the knife another quarter turn. "How is the wedding planning coming?"

"I leave that to Laetitia and her mother," Crispin said.

"You'll just show up when and where they tell you to, and wear what you're told?"

"I'll be wearing a morning suit, Darling, as is appropriate for a daytime wedding." He sent me another look. "You've received an invitation, haven't you?"

I snorted. "Of course I haven't. Neither Laetitia nor her mother is likely to want me there. Nor your father, for that matter."

"But you'll be Christopher's escort, won't you?"

"I have no idea," I said, and mentioned nothing about the fact that for all we knew, Christopher might not be with us two months from now. Christopher might not be with us tomorrow. It was much better, more calming, not to consider that as a possibility. "It depends on whether he asks me, and also whether Wolfgang is going. I don't think Christopher's received an invitation either. He hasn't said anything about it."

And we did get our post from the same place, namely Evans.

Crispin scowled. "They'd better not try to keep my cousin from attending my wedding."

"I'm sure they won't," I said. "It would look very bad if they excluded your closest family. Besides, if I'm not invited to the reception, the church is open to everyone. I remember the notice in the *Times* said so. I'll cheer you on from the spectator section."

"Thanks ever so," Crispin said and came to a stop in front of the altar. "I didn't see anything, did you?"

I had seen plenty of things, but no Christopher. "I'll go left and check the area around the organ and the west gallery," I said. "Will you check the chancel and then go up the right gallery, and we'll meet in the back?"

Crispin nodded and stepped forward. I made a ninety degree turn into the west gallery and over to the pipe organ.

There was no Christopher tucked behind the instrument, of course, nor was there anyone curled up anywhere in the west gallery. I checked the pews again from this angle, just in case I had missed something earlier, and wound up back in the narthex with nothing to show for it. Crispin arrived a few seconds later, hands in his pockets, and shook his head.

"We had to try," I told him as I headed for the door to the outside with him right behind.

"Of course we did. And now we get to try elsewhere."

He opened the door for me and held it while I passed through. I walked into what appeared to be a small squall of icy needles that had blown up while we had been inside. "Brrr!"

"I hope he's somewhere warm and dry," Crispin agreed. "The tobacconist next. Come along."

I latched onto his arm for the walk back across the street.

AN HOUR LATER, when Tom finally emerged from behind the double doors of number 49, we had inquired of clerks in every shopfront up and down the block, from Sweetings to the tube entrance, whether any of them had seen Christopher—or Kitty—the day before. And a few had done, but not in a way that had helped. No one had noticed him leave, or the matter of his leaving. He had been there, and the next time they looked through the window, he'd been gone. In some cases, that had been because he had moved positions: circled the small block or gone into one of the other shopfronts where someone else had seen him. Eventually, no one had seen him anymore, and that was that.

"Seemed a shame," the chap at the confectionary store said. "Pretty girl like that, made to wait around for some bloke who couldn't bother to be on time. If I'd been off the clock, now..."

He shook his head sadly. We smiled and thanked him, and said nothing about the fact that the pretty girl had been a young man, and that the bloke he'd been waiting for had been inside Sweetings lunching with me.

But eventually we ran out of shopfronts and clerks, and we retreated around the corner to Crispin's Hispano-Suiza. And shortly after that, Tom made his way around the corner towards us, as well.

"What news?" I asked him when he had climbed into the passenger seat and had sat back with a heartfelt sigh.

He shook his head without raising it from the headrest.

"Nothing?"

"Not a thing." He turned his head to glance at Crispin. "You?"

"Nothing, either," the latter said. "The church was empty."

"Several of the shop clerks noticed him," I added. "A few even said something to him—greetings mostly, I think—but no one saw him leave. He was there, and then he was gone."

"Same with the upstairs," Tom said. "It took a bit of time to talk my way past security, and then more time to talk to everyone. A few people noticed him outside—they thought he was a woman—but for the most part they were all in their offices during the timeframe. A handful left for lunch or came back during the time Kit was outside, and remembered seeing him. No one saw him with anyone else except for one of the secretaries—"

I caught my breath quickly.

"—who saw him with you."

I sank back against the seat and avoided Crispin's sympathetic look in the mirror.

"What about Wolfie?" he asked. "Did anyone remember seeing him?"

Tom shook his head. "One man in a dark suit is much like another. Not like an eye-catching young woman—or a young man in drag—in a cloche hat with violets on it."

"Even though Wolfgang is exceptionally handsome?" I inquired. "Nobody noticed him?"

"If anyone notices him," Crispin said, "it would probably be because of the scar. He's not *that* handsome."

He certainly was. Not that I was about to get into an argument about it. I had better things to do than try to convince Crispin that Wolfgang was good-looking, especially when I knew that Crispin had every reason to reject the premise.

"Was there a German specialist inside?" I asked instead, and Tom nodded. Instead of commenting on it, though, he said, "Get going, St George, if you please. There's no point in us sitting here."

"I'd be happy to," Crispin said, "if you'll tell me where you want me to go."

"Back to Scotland Yard, I suppose. Perhaps one or more of my inquiries were answered while we were out."

Crispin shrugged and started the motorcar. Tom turned his attention back to me and my question. "Yes, indeed, there was a German liaison upstairs. He didn't know who Natterdorff was, but he was interested in hearing about him."

"Surely they keep track of the foreigners who come here," Crispin said as he maneuvered the motorcar carefully back onto Queen Victoria Street in the direction of the Embankment and Scotland Yard.

"Yes and no," Tom said. "The chap upstairs looked him up at my request, and Natterdorff had the appropriate papers when he arrived here in late July. He also had enough money to support himself, and didn't need to apply for an employment permit from the Labor Secretary."

"Whatever business he's doing doesn't involve a job, then."

Tom shook his head. "Or not a legal one, at any rate. He listed the Savoy as his permanent address on the paperwork, and after someone made certain that he had actually checked into a room there, nothing else happened. He wasn't of particular interest to anyone. Too young to have fought in the war, not on any of the lists of communists that rioted in Hamburg in 1923..."

"And a *Graf*," Crispin supplied dryly from behind the wheel. "That sort of thing matters here, even if the Weimar Republic did away with it half a dozen years ago."

"So we know nothing more than we did this morning," I said.

Tom shook his head. "I'm sorry, Pippa. We know that Wolfgang's business wasn't at the Albert Building. That's one thing. And we know that nobody saw Kit disappear. We can widen the net, I suppose—ask further afield. I can dispatch a constable or two to do that. You don't have a photograph of him, do you?"

"Not as Kitty," I said. "That's not something we want sitting around the flat in case the wrong people notice it. And a photograph of Christopher as himself wouldn't help, I expect."

Tom shook his head. "The constables will have to make do with a description, then. Tell me exactly what he was wearing, if you please?"

I described my clothing and Christopher's hat in detail while Tom took the information down in his little notebook. "The German attaché provided me with a photograph from Natterdorff's file," he added as he slipped the notebook and pencil back into his pocket, "and I suppose it can't hurt to flash that around too, and ask whether anyone saw them together."

"You do suspect Wolfie, then," Crispin commented, and Tom flicked him a look.

"I don't. No more than I suspect the public in general. But it was Natterdorff that Kit was going to follow yesterday, and we do know that if nothing else, there's something a bit dodgy about his living situation. That doesn't seem as if it would be enough motive for kidnapping or, God forbid, something worse, but it has to be considered."

"What do you want us to do?" I asked after a moment, and he turned his attention to me.

"Go home and think, I suppose. Wait for Kit to contact you if he truly is just out there somewhere of his own free will. Perhaps Natterdorff went off to Calais overnight, and Kit went with him."

"Not without his passport," Crispin said.

"Somewhere domestic, then. Cardiff or Edinburgh. Stowe. Somewhere where the telephone exchange is unreliable."

I supposed it was possible. Not likely, perhaps, but possible.

Indeed, if Wolfgang was the jewel thief, perhaps he had

decided to pay the Fletcher family a visit. Their ancestral home was somewhere near the Scottish border, according to Crispin. Northumberland or North Yorkshire or some such place. If Christopher had followed him there, it might be days before he came back.

"You'll let us know if you learn anything new?" I asked when Crispin had pulled the Hispano-Suiza into the courtyard at Scotland Yard and Tom was on his way out of the vehicle.

"You'll be the first," he assured me. "And you'll do the same?"

I promised that we would do, and then Tom went into the building and Crispin put the H6 back into gear, and we rolled off towards home.

"There's nowhere else you want to go?" he asked. "Can I interest you in a spot of tea somewhere?"

"There's tea at home," I answered, "and I'd rather like to know whether there's any post. I also have to ring up Beckwith Place and update them on what's going on. Or rather, on what isn't."

"I had hoped we would be farther along by now," Crispin admitted. "That we'd have made some sort of progress, you know? But instead there's nothing."

"I wouldn't say nothing." It was mostly negative knowledge, admittedly, but it was something. "We know that he wasn't dragged, kicking and screaming, into a Hackney and spirited away. If he had been, someone would have reported it. That isn't the kind of thing that goes unnoticed, especially not on Queen Victoria Street in the middle of the day."

"Especially not with the government offices right there," Crispin agreed.

"And we know that he isn't in jail, or in hospital, or the morgue."

"I suppose that's something. Although at this point, I would almost rather have had him in hospital or jail."

I looked at him—I had moved into Tom's seat now, instead of staying in the back of the motorcar—and he added, "Not the morgue. Obviously not. But at least then we would know something. It's the not knowing that's difficult."

"It's all difficult," I said. "I'm glad he isn't hurt, or hasn't been arrested. But yes, it would be good to know something for certain. I don't know what I'm going to tell Aunt Roz."

"The truth," Crispin said, as he navigated Trafalgar Square and headed north on Charing Cross Road. "Scotland Yard is working on it, and at least he isn't dead, in hospital, or in jail."

He wasn't in jail or hospital, no. But he might still be dead, and we simply hadn't found the body yet. But when I opened my mouth to say so, no words came out.

Crispin glanced over at me and shook his head. "He's not dead, Philippa."

I cleared my throat. "How can you be certain?"

"Because I refuse to believe differently until there's no other choice," Crispin said. After a moment, he sighed. "I suppose I ought to ring up Marsden Manor and let Laetitia know where I am."

"And how is Laetitia going to feel when she hears that you're in London with me?"

I wanted to bite my tongue as soon as the words came out, since they skirted a bit too close to things I wasn't supposed to know, let alone talk about. He didn't seem to think anything of it, though, so perhaps I regularly said things without realizing how they sounded. "She'll have a conniption, most likely. A rather good thing she's in Dorset and I'm in London."

"Or you could simply not tell her," I suggested. "It's not as if something's going on that she needs to know about." Or anything that she would object to, really, if she did know.

He sent me a dubious look. "If I don't tell her and she finds out, there'll be hell to pay."

"What's the worst she can do? Break the engagement? You can't tell me that wouldn't be a relief."

He couldn't, it seemed, or at least he didn't. "I did propose of my own free will, you know," he said instead. "I'm sure you would rather die than tie yourself to Laetitia Marsden for the rest of your life—not that you could do—but it probably won't be so bad."

"How can you say that?" I tried, but he wasn't even listening to me.

"She's beautiful, and blue-blooded, and she loves me, and I like her well enough—"

Hard to imagine how anyone could. However— "You don't love her, though!"

He shot me a look. "I don't have to love her, Darling. I never expected to marry for love. My parents certainly didn't, and I assumed that I would end up hitched to someone they decided on sooner or later."

"That's fine if there's no one else you want to marry," I said, "but—"

"But the girl I want doesn't want me, and isn't likely to ever want me. So I might as well settle for someone I can have."

There wasn't much I could say to that. I certainly couldn't tell him that he was wrong, not when I knew very well—now—who he was talking about, and when there was no part of me that wanted to marry him.

"And as I've told you before," Crispin added, "Father would never approve. We'd have to run away and live in squalor on the Continent—"

"Some women would be happy to live in squalor on the Continent."

He looked pensive. "Laetitia might actually do it, if I asked. She seems inclined to give me whatever else I ask for..."

"Ugh," I said. "That's vile, St George."

"I don't see why." He grinned. "But if it offends you, perhaps we should discuss something else."

Perhaps we should. Although, if nothing else, this topic had taken my mind off Christopher and his plight for a minute or three.

"Do you plan to ring up Laetitia, then?" I asked.

"Perhaps not," Crispin answered. "You're right. With luck, perhaps we'll find Kit before the end of the day, and then I can go back home without anyone being the wiser. What she doesn't know won't hurt her, etcetera."

"If you say so. I still have to ring up Beckwith Place and give Aunt Roz an update. She'll worry more if she doesn't hear from me than if I ring her up and tell her that we know nothing."

"Not nothing," Crispin reminded me. "He's not in hospital, he's not in jail, and he's not in the morgue. That's not nothing. And be certain to mention that Sutherland House stands ready to accept them should they decide to motor up to Town for a few days. We can phone from there if you'd like."

"There's a call box just down the street from the flat," I said. "It seems easier."

He nodded. "I'll take you there, then."

"After you take me home. I want to check with Evans that there's no news before I phone anyone."

"As you wish." We reached Shaftesbury Avenue and veered right towards Bloomsbury.

"NO, MISS DARLING," Evans said ten minutes later. "Mr. Astley is not back, and there's no message from him."

"That's a shame."

Evans nodded. "There is, however, this note for you."

He handed it to me. Crispin craned his neck over my shoulder. "Is that what I think it is?"

"German *Kurrentschrift*," I nodded. "A note from Wolfgang. I forgot that we planned to have supper together tonight. I don't know how I'll let him know that I can't meet him..."

"Stand him up," Crispin said callously, "and he'll get the picture."

He watched as I opened the envelope and removed the single sheet of notepaper from within. I didn't even get to look at the words—very few of them—that were scribbled across the paper before his finger landed on the Savoy Hotel logo in the corner of the sheet.

"Yes," I said impatiently, "I told you that he does that."

"It's different to see it for myself. You're certain he's not staying there?"

"The doorman said he wasn't. Although I suppose he might be mistaken. Perhaps he was thinking of someone else."

"Perhaps I'll swing by and ask," Crispin said.

"It would be easier for me to ring up and ask to leave a message, surely? I have the perfect excuse, after all."

He looked at me, gray eyes serious. "I think you should go."

"To supper tonight? I hardly think I'd be good company, St George."

"If he loves you," Crispin said stubbornly, "he'll want to be with you even when you're not good company. And if he is involved, he'll want to see how you're holding up."

"That's disturbing."

He shrugged. "Think of it this way: if he had something to do with it, he might let something slip. And Gardiner and I can follow him home after the meal. Even if Kit isn't there, at least we'll know where he lives now."

That was a point in favor of putting myself out there. Honestly, sitting across from Wolfgang and making polite conversation when I was afraid of what might have happened to Christopher sounded agonizing, to be honest. Worse than agonizing if I suspected that he had had something to do with it.

I wasn't sure whether I believed it or not. Crispin wanted to believe the worst of Wolfgang, naturally. But he was biased. I wanted to believe the best, or at least I didn't want to believe that someone I knew, someone who claimed to want to marry me, would kidnap and perhaps hurt my best friend.

Especially when there was nothing—or nothing aside from a strange but minor anomaly of stationary—to suggest why he would bother.

But all that aside, I did see Crispin's point, and why it made sense for me to put my feelings aside and go to the Savoy tonight. If Wolfgang wasn't involved, it would exonerate him. If he was involved, at least we'd know. And either way, it would give me something to focus on for an hour or two, that wasn't Christopher and where he was and what he might be going through.

"Very well," I said.

CHAPTER SEVENTEEN

AUNT ROZ MUST HAVE BEEN SITTING beside the telephone, because it was answered almost as soon as it rang.

"Kit?"

"I'm afraid not," I said apologetically.

She breathed out. "Pippa? What news?"

"Very little, I'm afraid. He still isn't home. But we've brought Tom in, and here's what we know so far." I listed all the places that Christopher was not, and could hear her tension dissipate at the same time as it ratcheted up. It was a very strange, if understandable, phenomenon.

"Let me get this straight," she said when I had finished. "So far as we know, he isn't dead, he isn't hurt, and he hasn't been arrested."

"That's correct."

"But we don't know where he is, and he could be dead or hurt somewhere he hasn't been found yet."

I made a face. "That's a possibility, yes."

"We should come up to London."

"Crispin said you might feel that way," I said. "Sutherland House—"

She interrupted me. "Crispin's there?"

"He motored up last night."

"Let me talk to him."

I arched my brows but waved him closer. "Aunt Roz wants to talk to you."

His arched, too, but he took the earpiece and put it to his ear. "Hullo, Aunt Roslyn."

They talked for a minute or two. Crispin's share of it was mostly limited to things like, "Yes, Aunt Roslyn," "No, Aunt Roslyn," "I'm afraid I don't know," and "of course." Of Aunt Roz's part, all I could hear was a faint quacking from the earpiece. He winced once or twice.

"Do you wish to speak to Philippa again?" he asked eventually. My aunt must have said no—my feelings were a bit hurt—because he nodded. "I'll let her know. We'll see you soon, Aunt Roz. Sutherland House is always available to you."

He deposited the earpiece in the cradle and breathed out, closing his eyes.

"They're coming?" I asked.

"I talked her into giving it another day," Crispin answered. "Or she mostly talked herself into it, I suppose."

I supposed so. I certainly hadn't heard him give voice to any kind of persuasion.

After a moment's silence he added, "There's nothing they can do here. We're already doing everything we can. They'd be underfoot."

"Tom probably thinks we are underfoot, too," I pointed out.

"Well, I'm not leaving. But we do need to let him know about tonight."

"Go ahead," I told him, and watched him deposit more coins in the slot and ask the operator to connect him with Scotland Yard. A minute later he was explaining to Tom about the dinner invitation and the plan we—or he—had come up with. "It's the Savoy again, so it ought to be fairly easy to lurk and follow him when he leaves."

"As long as he doesn't go out by one of the entrances we're not watching," Tom's tinny voice came out of the headset. Crispin was holding it, but we both had our ears as close to it as we could manage without bumping heads. I'm fairly certain my hair must have tickled his cheek, although he didn't say anything about it.

"I rang them up," Tom added, "and confirmed that he's no longer a guest there."

"I hope—" Crispin began, and I could practically hear Tom's eyeroll come down the line.

"This isn't my first day on the job, my lord. I rang up from a call box, and I didn't tell them who I was, just that I was trying to reach the *Graf* von Natterdorff and this was the address he had given me. He did not leave a forwarding address with the concierge, although he does sometimes stop by and ask whether any messages have arrived for him since he left."

Theoretically, then, I could send a note saying that I didn't want to have supper, and he would receive it when he got there. But he'd already be there at that point, expecting to find me, which seemed impolite, and besides, we'd lose the opportunity to find out where he actually laid his head.

If he had anything to do with Christopher's disappearance, we might also find Christopher, although I didn't dare allow myself to hope for that. Or at least I did my best to talk myself out of hoping.

I was still talking myself out of hoping when it was time to leave. With Christopher's absence, I had had to put on my own makeup—Crispin was no good at it, or at least he was too heavy-handed for me. The theatrical makeup he had learned to do at Cambridge made me look like a trollop, and I had to remove it and start over.

My lovely ivory gown was dirty and torn from my tumble down the Piccadilly Circus tube stop stairs last week, but of course I had worn it to dinner that night, so I couldn't have worn it again tonight even had it been in perfect condition. You don't want to give an eligible gentleman the impression that you only have one serviceable gown. Instead, I found myself having to decide between the apple green frock Crispin had told me made me look like a Bramley, the butter yellow gown he had once likened to the marvelous Josephine Baker's banana skirt, and the salmon pink I had worn the night we had found Flossie Schlomsky's dead body.

That particular gown had also prompted the comparison of my humble self to a stalk of rhubarb—Crispin seemed to have a strange fixation on fruits when it came to describing my attire—but truly, that last part paled in comparison to the memory of Flossie.

And that part ought to have disqualified the salmon forever. I had, in fact, not worn it since that night. I had bought the ivory to replace it. But now, looking at them all, I found my eyes drawn to it.

"Apple, banana, or rhubarb?" I asked Crispin.

"Pardon me?"

He was not changing his clothes, of course, but was sitting on the Chesterfield flipping through a gossip magazine. It had his face on the cover, and was from several months ago, back when he spent most of his time drunk and carousing with the Society for Bright Young Persons. Laetitia, or perhaps his father, seemed to have mostly cured him of that, at any rate. The few times he had been up to London lately, there had been precious little carousing going on.

"Apple, banana, or rhubarb?" I repeated. "Color-wise."

"Has he seen them all already?"

He had.

"Does he have a favorite?"

Not as far as I knew. He usually told me I looked good no matter what I wore.

Crispin muttered something uncomplimentary when I said as much, and told me, "Wear the green."

"You want me to look round, I suppose." Like the apple he had likened me to.

"It doesn't make you look round, Darling. There's no dress in existence that would make you look round. You're as skinny as a blade of grass"

"Lovely," I said.

"The green brings out your eyes. Wear it."

He turned back to the magazine. I stared at him for a moment—he looked up once, blandly, and met my eyes—before I turned on my heel with a muttered expletive, and ventured back into my bedroom to finish my toilette. Behind me, I heard a magazine page turn over.

When I came back out, Bramley frock on, face in place, hair fluffed and held back with a sparkly barrette to match the diamanté accents on the gown, he spared me a single up-and-down look before he got to his feet. "Ready?"

"You tell me," I said sourly, as I swung my evening wrap around myself. He might have offered to help me with it, having been brought up to be a gentleman, but I supposed I wasn't worth the trouble.

Either that, or he simply didn't want to get too close to me. He rarely touched me, now that I thought about it. For someone who took every chance he could to get a verbal reaction, you'd think he would take the opportunity to get close to me without causing suspicion, too. But he mostly kept his hands to himself, other than the occasional support under my elbow to help me rise or an offered arm to cross the street; something he really couldn't avoid if he wanted to keep his reputation as a gentleman. But beyond that, no gratuitous touching whatsoever.

"You know, St George," I told him as we approached the door to the lift, a spot where we'd have to stand close together whether we wanted to or not, or at least a place where it would appear strange if we stood an inordinate distance apart, "it's all right for you to admit that you think I'm pretty."

The corners of his mouth quirked up. "Is that what you think I think?"

"I certainly hope so," I said. "I didn't go to all this trouble for people to look at me and think I'm plain."

He looked amused. "You're not plain, Darling. And I'm certain Wolfie will appreciate the trouble."

I smirked. "So you do think I'm pretty."

He gave me a quick up-and-down, there and then gone. "Of course you're pretty, Darling. Whatever gave you the idea that I didn't?"

"The fact that you don't look at me much," I said. "Or only as much as you have to, to be polite."

"That's because I'm engaged, Darling. It's really not appropriate for me to admire other women, is it? Especially not in the absence of my fiancée."

Ugh. I took a step back. "No, of course not. Forget I mentioned it."

The lift arrived, and the door opened. Crispin slid the grille to the side and nodded to me to enter. He stood in one corner of the lift, and I kept to the other. After that salutary reminder, the last thing I wanted to do was crowd him.

"Any news, Evans?" I inquired on our way across the lobby.

The doorman shook his head. "No, Miss Darling. I would have rung upstairs if anything occurred."

"Of course you would," I said. "We're going out for a bit. To the Savoy, should you have a need to get in touch."

"Of course, Miss Darling." He touched the brim of his cap and accepted the coin Crispin handed him on our way through the door. "Thank you, my lord."

"Don't mention it, Evans," Crispin said and headed for the Hispano-Suiza. "In you go, Darling."

In I went, and a minute later we were headed down Essex Street towards the Strand.

"You and Tom are certain you have things worked out?" I wanted to know. We had been over this already, but I wanted to hear it again. "You'll drop me off around the corner from the Savoy..."

"So that he won't realize that I'm in London," Crispin nodded. "I'll park the H6 somewhere out of the way so he won't see it—"

Yes, it wasn't a well-designed motorcar for covert surveillance. Too distinctive by half.

"I still can't believe we're doing this," I said. "It doesn't make any sense, St George. Wolfgang has no reason to want Christopher out of the way. Something else must have happened to him."

"If so," Crispin said, his hands easy on the wheel as he steered us through traffic towards Charing Cross station, "we'll find out where Wolfie lives, and that'll be all. And you can't tell me you wouldn't like that information."

I supposed I couldn't. "I'm not saying it isn't strange. Or that he hasn't behaved strangely. It's just difficult to say that it equates to him harming Christopher."

"And perhaps he hasn't done," Crispin said. "Perhaps something else happened there. But he has something to hide, and even if we don't find Kit as a result of tonight's adventure, it would be nice to know what his reason is."

Yes, of course it would. "So you park the Hispano-Suiza out of the way somewhere and join Tom..."

"And we wait for you and Wolfie to finish supper," Crispin nodded. "You let him put you into a Hackney bound for home, and Gardiner and I follow Wolfie to his lair."

Lair, was it? "That wasn't part of the deal," I said.

"What wasn't?"

"I don't want to go home and sit there and wait while you two big, strong men chase down Wolfgang and look for Christopher. That's not fair. He's my best friend. I shouldn't be made to miss out."

"He's my best friend, too," Crispin said. "And if you can figure out a way to get to the police-issue Hackney before Wolfie leaves the Savoy, you're welcome to accompany us. But I don't see how you'd be able to accomplish that."

I didn't either. It would be late by the time supper was over, and it was already dark, so Wolfgang would insist on putting me in a cab for the trip home. And while I could do what I had done last time, and perhaps convince the driver to set me down further up the street, I might not make it back to the Savoy before Wolfgang—and Crispin and Tom—left.

"Perhaps I could simply get into the Hackney the two of you will be occupying? You said that there's a police-issue Hackney, correct? I assume it will be parked out front? Why don't I just get into it, and I'll be with the two of you."

"I won't be in the Hackney," Crispin said. "I'll be in the lobby. That way, if he goes back into the hotel and out through another door, I can follow."

"So you'll be driving the H6."

"There'll be three of us," Crispin said. "Tom is driving a Hackney. It's the most common motorcar in London, and the least likely to be noticed."

I nodded.

"Detective Sergeant Finchley will be driving a police issue Crossley Tender."

I opened my mouth, and he continued before I could express my thought, "Not the Flying Bedstead. This is a Tender without any markings. It looks just like any other motorcar."

"Just like any other police issue Crossley Tender, you mean."

"Without the police department logo," Crispin said.

"Yes, obviously. But it's still a police issue Crossley Tender."

"It can't be helped," Crispin said. "I'll have the H6—"

"So there will be three of you with three different motorcars. You'll practically be driving in a queue behind him. And yet you're sending me home? Why can't I go in the Hackney with Tom, or in the Tender with Finch, or in the H6 with you? You'll be the farthest behind him, right? You have the most easily recognizable motorcar. So why—"

"Because we're trying to keep you safe, Darling. Kit will kill me if he comes back and something has happened to you."

I folded my arms across my chest, sullenly. "Christopher would not send me home like an ornamental object while he had all the fun. No more than he would have agreed to go home to wait if I were the one who was missing."

He didn't answer, and I added, "You can't do this to me, St George. You can't send me home while you follow my fiancé to see whether he has my best friend bound and gagged in his wardrobe. I won't stand for it."

"You won't have much of a choice," Crispin pointed out, and I narrowed my eyes.

"I'm not sure you want to go there, St George. I can assure you, you won't like it."

He smirked, the bastard. "And why is that, Darling?"

"Because," I said darkly, "I'm the one who shall be spending the next hour and a half with Wolfgang, and there's nothing you can do to keep me from saying something to him. Something that will blow up your entire plan and leave you all with egg on your faces."

He shot me a look. "While I admire your creativity, Darling, are you certain you want to do that to Kit? Following Wolfie might be the best chance we have of finding him."

He had a point, unfortunately. A point that he further emphasized when he added, "The longer it is until we find him, the worse the results could be."

Yes, of course. Christopher might be starving to death right now, while I was worrying about being excluded from the excitement.

I sagged back against the upholstery, disappointment along with disgust (at myself) swirling acidly in my stomach. "Damn you. You would bring that up."

"It's the most important aspect of this whole operation, Darling. The entire reason we're doing it."

Yes, of course it was. "Fine," I said. Not graciously, but I got the word out. "I'll go home and wait." Like a useless decorative object.

"Thank you, Darling." After a second he added, "One less thing for me to worry about, you know."

Yes, I knew. I was worried, too.

"So you'll come back afterwards and tell me what happened?"

"As soon as I can," Crispin said. "The very moment I know whether or not Christopher is there."

"Do you swear?"

He flicked me a look before licking the back of his thumb and holding it out.

"Eww," I said, eyeing it.

He rolled his eyes. "Just do it, Philippa. Binding agreement."

"Fine." I licked my own thumb and pressed it against his. "Swear."

"I swear I will leave where I am and come find you the moment I know whether Wolfgang has Kit or not."

"Good enough." I looked around for somewhere to wipe the wetness off my thumb, somewhere that wasn't my evening gown. Crispin dragged his thumb down the front of his jacket, and after a second's thought, I did the same.

He looked at me, brow raised.

"Your spit, your jacket," I said.

"I suppose that's fair." He moved the gearshift and the Hispano-Suiza rolled to a stop at the curb on Garrick Street, just around the corner from the Strand. "Out you go. You're walking from here."

I nodded and fumbled for the door handle. "Be careful, St George. God willing, we'll find Christopher and all will be well. But the last thing we want is for something to happen to you, too. The family couldn't handle losing both of you."

I couldn't, either. Not to mention that I would probably be blamed for it.

"I'll do my best, Darling. You do the same."

I promised I would do, and then I shut the car door behind me and squared my shoulders and set off around the corner and down the Strand towards the Savoy and supper.

CHAPTER EIGHTEEN

WOLFGANG HAD ARRIVED BEFORE ME, and was already in the restaurant when I stepped up to the maître d's podium. The gentleman—different from the other day—escorted me to the table, where Wolfgang jumped up from his chair to pull out mine. The maître d' withdrew and Wolfgang sat back down.

"New chap today," I commented, with a glance at the retreating back of the maître d'. Wolfgang, too, shot a look in that direction and made a vague sort of noise. "Something wrong?" I added.

He shook his head and turned his attention back to me. "Not at all. I can't say that I noticed."

"That the maître d' is someone different from last time? They look totally different from one another."

"Two men with black hair in evening kit?" Wolfgang said, so at least he had noticed that much.

"This one is ten years older, and several inches taller, and swarthier, and has bigger ears. The other chap had a noticeable overbite."

He stared at me.

"Sorry," I said. "I can't help it that I'm observant."

He nodded, but his eyes on me were concerned. "Is everything all right, *mein Schatz?*"

"No," I said, getting right to it. "Christopher didn't come home last night, and I'm worried."

There was no reason to hold back, after all. The sooner I could get it out in the open, the sooner I would see his reaction, and if he wasn't involved, well... it was topmost of mind and if he had been anyone else, it would still have been the first thing I would have wanted to talk about.

"Dear me," Wolfgang said. His lips gave a twitch, which might have been a sign of guilt, if he knew more than I did and he thought my reaction was funny. Or it might simply be that I was behaving like a madwoman and he didn't want to express what had originally occurred to him. I probably didn't sound like someone who wanted to listen to reason.

"He escorted me to Sweetings," I added. "I walked inside to meet you, and he went off on his own. And now he hasn't been home in more than twenty-four hours. I don't know what to do."

My voice was becoming increasingly uneven. The waiter, who had been on his way towards our table, veered off in the other direction at the sound of it, and who could blame him? He probably assumed I was about to break down in tears at any moment.

"I'm sorry to hear it," Wolfgang said. "I like your cousin."

"So do I." He used present tense, and I wondered whether that meant anything. It might, if he knew something I didn't. Then again, it might not.

"But he's a man grown, Philippa," Wolfgang added. "Are you certain he didn't simply meet a friend and go home with him?"

He said 'him,' which might indicate that he knew in which direction Christopher's interests lay. If he had seen Christopher dressed up as Kitty yesterday, he might have drawn that conclusion from it. Then again, I didn't think it proved anything. I might have said something about Christopher's proclivities at some point. It isn't something I tend to blab indiscriminately about, but Wolfgang had been around both of us for long enough that I might have let something slip.

"That's what I thought when he didn't come home last night," I said, without commenting on the pronoun. It might simply have meant a friend of the same gender and platonic variety, after all. "But he wouldn't have stayed out all night without letting me know where he was. And he certainly would have been home this morning."

"Perhaps the police...?"

The waiter made his approach again, and Wolfgang waved him off.

I snorted. Not in response to the waiter veering off for the second time, but to the idea that the police—the regular police, not Tom—might be of any use in this situation. And not only because they'd be honor-bound to arrest Christopher if they found him wandering around London in my skirt and high heels.

"Do you suppose the police would take me seriously if I told them that my flat-mate—my twenty-three year old, male flat-mate, who is cousin to the notorious playboy Crispin St George—didn't come home last night?"

Wolfgang didn't answer, and I continued, "In the best case scenario, they would laugh me out the door. In the worst, they would think it was entirely deserved and that he brought it on himself. Either way, they would do nothing to look for him."

At this point, the waiter was back, and was hovering

anxiously. Wolfgang beckoned him closer. We ordered a drink and an appetizer, and the waiter withdrew.

"So you haven't involved the police," Wolfgang said.

It sounded more like a statement than a question, but I shook my head anyway. It probably wasn't indicative of anything at all that he seemingly wanted to make sure of this point. "No."

"Not even your friend, Detective Sergeant Gardiner?"

"I contacted Tom last night," I said, "to see whether he knew where Christopher was. He didn't."

"And he's not investigating?"

"He's a homicide detective with Scotland Yard. Until Christopher turns up dead—" I grimaced, "—it's not his job."

"So it's just you looking for him, then?"

"I talked his parents into staying in Wiltshire another day," I said. "I had to tell them what had happened, of course. Just in case he had phoned them or they had heard something I hadn't."

"But they hadn't?"

I shook my head. "I tried to make it sound less serious than it is, because I didn't want them to worry."

He nodded, sympathetically.

"And I won't say that I'm looking, precisely. I wouldn't know where to start. But yes, it's just me."

I had already disavowed Tom, and there was no reason, none at all, to mention Crispin.

"I'll take care of you, *mein Schatz*," Wolfgang said, and reached out to cover my hand with his. It was much larger than mine, and swallowed it completely. I tried not to feel suffocated. "I'll help you," he added. "And if the worst comes to the worst—"

I winced, since the worst would definitely be Christopher

not coming home, and I didn't want to imagine that. Wolfgang, however, seemed to have something else in mind.

"—and your family turns their backs on you, you will always have a home with me."

I opened my mouth to say that Aunt Roz and Uncle Herbert would never turn their backs on me, any more than Cousin Francis and Constance would do, but then I imagined how Christopher might not come back, and I saw my aunt's tearful look of blame because I was older than Christopher and should have kept him safe, and I shouldn't have let him go off on his own to be kidnapped or murdered or God knows what else. And suddenly I couldn't force the words out. Laetitia would keep Crispin away from me, and Uncle Harold already hated me, and while Aunt Roz and Uncle Herbert loved me, I wasn't their daughter, not the way that Christopher was their son, and if it came down to a choice between us—if it came down to me having facilitated Christopher's death, because I hadn't taken seriously enough the responsibility they implicitly gave me when I moved to London with him—my aunt and uncle might well turn their backs on me in their grief over losing yet another son. Robbie was a decade gone, lost in the war, and if they lost Christopher too, I wasn't sure how they would survive.

So instead of telling Wolfgang that my family would never cast me off, and would hold on to me all the harder for having lost Christopher—because I simply couldn't be certain that they would do—I swallowed the words, and blinked back the tears, and faced him across the table.

"Thank you."

He patted my hand. "Of course, my dear." And then the waiter approached with our cocktails, and Wolfgang withdrew his hand to his own side of the table.

"Tell me about your grandfather," I said when the waiter had retreated again and it was just the two of us once more. I couldn't talk about Christopher anymore, and I needed something to distract myself from the thought that my family—the only family I had left—might disown me if he didn't return.

Wolfgang looked non-plussed. "My grandfather?"

"You mentioned once that he is still alive. We are both orphans, but you told me that your grandfather is living."

He nodded. "So he is."

"Is that your Natterdorff grandfather, or your mother's father?"

Of course I already knew the answer to that, but Wolfgang didn't know that I knew, and just in case this came up again at a later date, I wanted him to have told me the information himself.

"It's the *Graf von und zu* Natterdorff," Wolfgang said. "My father's father."

"I thought you were the *Graf von und zu* Natterdorff. That's what you said when we first met you."

"We are both *Grafen*," Wolfgang said. "He is the *Graf*. My father was the *Erbgraf* until his death, and now I am the *Erbgraf*."

So the same thing Crispin had explained to me and Tom.

"That sounds confusing," I said. "Before the old Duke of Sutherland died in April, Uncle Harold was the Viscount St George, and Crispin was the Honorable Crispin Astley. Now Uncle Harold is the duke, and Crispin is the viscount. It's easier when they all have different titles."

Wolfgang nodded, but he also asked, "And your cousin Christopher? He is also the grandson of the former duke, yes?"

"He is. But his father, my Uncle Herbert—Lord Herbert— was Duke Henry's younger son. Uncle Harold is older. So

Harold gets the title, and his son becomes the Viscount St George. Uncle Herbert is a Lord, but his children don't have titles."

Wolfgang nodded. "And if something happens to the current duke?"

"Crispin gets the title," I said, "and his son, if he ever has one, grows up as the Viscount St George. But Uncle Harold isn't sixty yet. And he's too ornery to die young."

The late Duke Henry had been almost ninety when he passed, and it hadn't been from natural causes. He might have gone on for another decade if not for that.

"Did your grandfather only have the one son?" I asked, and watched Wolfgang hesitate. "In this country, an heir and a spare is the general rule."

With an occasional girl when the genetic lottery doesn't turn out in the parents' favor. Really, it's as if they don't realize that for the succession to continue to the next generation, they need an equal number of women.

Wolfgang nodded. "In Germany, too."

"It doesn't always work out, of course. Aunt Roz and Uncle Herbert had three boys, and I'm sure they probably hoped that Christopher would be a girl—"

Wolfgang's lips twitched, but he didn't say anything. And because he might have found the idea funny even without the knowledge that Christopher has a penchant for pretty gowns and makeup, I couldn't even draw the conclusion that he knew more about Christopher's disappearance than he let on. It was frustrating.

I ignored it and continued, "—but then they got me, of course, and I suppose I filled that spot. Aunt Charlotte and Uncle Harold only had Crispin."

"If anything happens to him?" Wolfgang asked.

"If Crispin dies without issue, Uncle Herbert is next in line for the title. Then his eldest son, who is Francis. And after that it's Francis's eldest son, if he has one."

Which he probably would have. Constance was the maternal type, and only twenty-three, so there was plenty of time for her to pop out an heir and a spare, along with a girl or two for good measure.

"My grandfather had another son," Wolfgang said, somewhat reluctantly. "But he's dead now, too, along with my father and mother."

"I'm sorry to hear it," I said politely.

Wolfgang inclined his head. "There has been a lot of death in the past decade."

Yes, there had been. Between the war and the influenza epidemic, I had lost my father, my mother, and Cousin Robbie, and Wolfgang's story was likely similar. "Your uncle died without issue?"

"He was disowned and removed from the succession," Wolfgang said, which didn't answer the question, but which clarified enough of what had happened.

My lips twitched. "Did he fall in love with the wrong girl?"

"Eventually," Wolfgang said darkly, "but before that he read Karl Marx and threw off the fetters of the aristocracy in favor of living in communistic squalor and working with his hands."

He sounded as if such was a fate worse than death. "My father worked with his hands," I reminded him gently, "and I've read Marx. There's nothing wrong with either of those things."

He seemed to regain himself. "Of course not." He managed a smile, although it was a bit stiff. "And it's all water under the bridge, isn't it? He died during the war. There's only Opa and I left. When he passes, I will become the *Graf von und zu*

Natterdorff in truth, not just in title, and my son will become the *Erbgraf.*"

His son? "Do you have one of those?"

"No," Wolfgang said. "But I have hope for one in the future."

He smiled at me in a way that told me that he still hoped I would be the one to fulfill that wish. And although he didn't say so, I was certain that in addition to the son and heir, he'd most likely also want the requisite spare, and perhaps a daughter or two to boot, as well.

Unlike Francis's fiancée, I'm not particularly maternal. Or not yet, at any rate. Marriage and children at twenty-three might be all right for Constance and her ilk, but I wanted no part of it. And I certainly don't want to be responsible for the next generation of an aristocratic dynasty.

But I was at this table for a reason, and part of that reason was to make certain that Wolfgang was happy and didn't suspect that Tom and Crispin were standing by to follow him home after our meal. So I smiled back, and tried to make it look doting, as if raising his children was at the top of my list for how I wanted to spend the next twenty-five years.

We got through the rest of supper in the same manner. I simpered, and Wolfgang seemed to believe that I meant it. We spoke mostly of innocuous things. He asked me to tell him about growing up with Christopher, perhaps because he could sense that I had a hard time thinking of anything else, and although it was the last thing I wanted to talk about—what if I never saw Christopher again? Dwelling on what I had lost wasn't going to make me feel any better—I obliged. If nothing else, it was something safe to talk about, and assurance that I wouldn't let slip anything about any suspicions I might have had towards Wolfgang himself.

He certainly didn't behave suspiciously. Nothing he said

threw up any red flags in my mind, and his eyes were warm as he watched me expound on my close friendship with my cousin. He nodded sympathetically from time to time—especially when I lamented over how awful Crispin had been as a child, because I could hardly talk about growing up with Christopher without mentioning the best friend I had replaced in his affections.

The only thing I might say about it that wasn't complimentary to Wolfgang, was that he had asked me to talk about Christopher at all. Anyone else who cared for me would have tried to take my mind off my missing cousin and my worry for him by talking about other things. But we're all different, and perhaps talking his problems to death was how Wolfgang coped with them, and so he thought the same would be true for me. He might have been trying to do me a favor.

At any rate, we made it through supper and onto coffee and pudding without me having given anything away and without incident of any kind. And that was when things went sideways.

I suppose it was a case of various bits and pieces of information turning themselves over in the back of my head while I was talking about other things, such as the time when Crispin left me in the middle of the Sutherland Hall hedge maze at eleven, and Christopher had had to rescue me. The following year, I mapped out the maze with paper and pencil, so it wouldn't happen again, or so, if it did, I could rescue myself, and I suppose I was doing something of the same thing now, only subconsciously, while I was talking. Mapping out twists and turns and connections.

However it happened, a few disparate pieces of information seemed to bump into one another in the back of my head, with a noise like a click, and then, like magnets, they stuck together.

"My father—" I said, and it must have been enough of a

departure from the conversation that Wolfgang looked surprised, or perhaps discomfited, for a moment.

It was only for a moment, though, and then he smiled. "What about your father, *Liebling?*"

I ignored the blandishment, even though it was more familiar than what he usually called me. "You said you knew my parents. The first time we met, in the tearoom, you recognized me."

"You were only five or six years old the last time I saw you," Wolfgang agreed, "but I would know you anywhere. You look like your mother, but with your father's eyes."

Yes, I did. And as Christopher and I had decided at the time—because Germans didn't appear out of nowhere to claim kinship every day—he must have been telling the truth, because only people who knew my family would know which of my features I had inherited from which parent.

"We're related, you said."

He nodded, and this time I was fairly certain that I saw a flash of discomfort, or something very like it, in his eyes.

"Was my father your uncle, the brother who was disinherited?"

Wolfgang hesitated. I kept my eyes on him, and I suppose he came to realize that not saying anything was, for all intents and purposes, the same as saying yes. Only a resounding denial would have worked in this scenario, and for one reason or another, he was unwilling, or perhaps unable, to lie.

"He was," I said, "wasn't he?" It explained the Mensur scar —not because commoners had them too, as Christopher had postulated, but because my father hadn't actually been a commoner—and it also explained why my German, what little I could remember of it, had always been on the formal side. "Does that mean that I'm a *Gräfin?*"

"Your father was disowned," Wolfgang said stiffly.

Yes, of course he had been. I had grown up in a small flat, not a castle, and I had no memory of having met anyone in my father's family. Including Wolfgang himself, on that occasion he had told me about.

"Did we actually meet?" I asked. "You told me we had done, but I don't remember it."

"As a matter of fact," Wolfgang said, "we didn't. My father and mother were forbidden from associating with yours. I recognized you from having you pointed out to me on the street in Heidelberg when I was small, but not from spending time with you. I wasn't allowed."

"And all because my father wanted to make furniture?"

"That," Wolfgang said, "and because he didn't believe in the class distinctions that existed thirty years ago. Class distinctions are important to my—to our—Opa."

"Do they not exist anymore? The class distinctions?"

"The Weimar Republic abolished the class system," Wolfgang said, "and the aristocracy."

"But you're still a *Graf.*" And so was his—or our —grandfather.

He nodded. "But being a *Graf* doesn't mean much in Germany anymore. Not like it does in England. Everyone in Germany is poor these days."

Oh, really? "That's not much incentive to get me to marry you, you know," I pointed out, only half-jokingly, and he chuckled.

"Don't worry, *mein Schatz.* Grandfather has plenty of money. We won't starve."

No? "That presumes that your grandfather—or my grandfather too, I suppose—would accept me as your future wife. And if my father was disowned, I don't see him approving. Do you?"

There was a beat, and then— "Opa wants me to be happy," Wolfgang said.

That was nice. Whether he would allow that to happen with the daughter of a man he had disinherited, remained to be seen.

"Is it even legal for first cousins to marry in Germany? When you proposed, I had no idea we were so closely related." It didn't bode well for the next generation, I'd have to say. One does want ones children to grow up without hereditary issues, ideally.

"Of course," Wolfgang said. "It is legal here, as well, is it not?"

It was, actually. Not that I would ever consider it. When I had joked about marrying Christopher, if we were both single at thirty, having children of our own had not been part of that plan. The fact that we are first cousins by blood was only a small part of the problem, of course. The fact that we're closer to siblings emotionally was a big one, and so was the fact that Christopher doesn't like girls.

And after finding out that Wolfgang and I were more closely related than I had realized, there was no way that I would ever seriously consider marrying him, either. So at this point, I might as well move forward with my other questions.

"You've moved out of the Savoy," I said, "haven't you?"

This time something definitely flashed in his eyes, although it might have been simple surprise at the abrupt *non sequitur.* "How do you know that?"

"I came back here the other day," I said. "After we had had tea in the tearoom. After you received the note and after you loaded me into the Hackney and sent me home. I wondered why you seemed so determined to get rid of me, so I came back. And the doorman told me that you're no longer a guest here."

"That," Wolfgang said, "is not a crime."

No, of course it wasn't. A bit underhanded, with the secrecy and all, but hardly a criminal offense. "You've been trying to make me believe that you're still living here, though. Haven't you? You're still writing to me on Savoy notepaper."

"I didn't want you to think badly of me." He gave me a soulful look. "If you thought me poor, you might not afford me your hand in marriage, and I wanted to marry you. I know I should have told you, but I was..." He dropped his gaze, "—ashamed."

He wouldn't meet my eyes across the table, but kept his own down.

"I know all about being a poor relation," I told him. "I know it better than you, I daresay."

In fact, it was only because of Uncle Herbert's generosity and Christopher's love that I lived as well as I did. But that didn't excuse him having strung me along for weeks, if not months.

"Just out of curiosity," I said, "where do you live these days?"

He did look thoroughly ashamed, I have to say, when he told me that he had taken rooms in a house in Shoreditch, of all places.

I picked up my cup of coffee and drank what was left in it. "I think it's time I go home."

"Please allow me to explain," Wolfgang said.

I threw my hands up. "Explain what? What is there to say? You lied to me, Wolfgang. Not just once, but over and over. Every time we've met in the past month and a half, you've lied."

"By omission," Wolfgang said. "Not because I wanted to deceive you."

What poppycock. It had been precisely because he had wanted to deceive me.

And he wasn't the only one. Everyone had been deceptive, by omission if not directly. Crispin had lied to my face for years.

And yes, I probably wouldn't have handled it very well if he had told me the truth, but that was no excuse for his cowardice. And everyone else had known how Crispin felt, and no one had said anything about it. They had just watched me wander along, secure in my dislike of him and in my belief that he disliked me back, and no one had said a word to set me straight.

And now Christopher was gone, and might never come back. The Astleys might reject me. I might lose everyone I knew or loved, in addition to the lifestyle I had become used to. And of course it wasn't about the lifestyle; I'm not as mercenary as all that. But my whole life had been turned upside down over the course of a few days. My eyes were burning, and so was my chest, and I probably shouldn't have gulped that last half a cup of coffee the way I had done. Unless I was simply hyperventilating because my emotions were too much to handle, of course, and that was quite likely.

I pushed my chair back from the table and tried to force additional air into my lungs.

"What's wrong, my dear?" Wolfgang asked, from what sounded like a long way away. "Do you not feel well?"

I didn't, now that he mentioned it. The restaurant was doing a slow spin, and my fingers and toes were tingling. I blinked hard and managed to focus on Wolfgang. He was halfway up out of his seat, and he looked concerned. "Philippa? Are you all right, *Liebchen?*"

I opened my mouth, but nothing came out. There was one of him, and then two of him, and then they blended together into one again. I squeezed my eyes shut and opened them again, with some difficulty.

"Oh, dear." He pulled money out of his pocket to cover the bill before coming around the table. "Lean on me. I'll take care of you."

"St George—" I managed, my voice garbled and full of gravel. "Tom—"

They were both here somewhere, and I could count on either one of them to take me home.

"Not to worry, *mein Schatz*. Up you come."

He hauled me to my feet. The room did another slow spin, and my knees buckled, and that was the last thing I remembered for a while.

CHAPTER NINETEEN

THE FIRST TIME I woke up, it was only for a second, just long enough to blink my eyes open and recognize that I was alive and lying on a flat surface. My head was pounding, or perhaps the walls were, although it seemed more likely to be my head. I closed my eyes again and went back to sleep.

The next time I woke up was better, but still much the same. I had no idea how long it had been, but I was lying down in a room I didn't recognize, but which was most likely the same place I had been the last time I woke up. It was a small room, a tight rectangle with a low ceiling and no defining characteristics. And it was dark, so it was hard to make out any details beyond the basics. The walls were still pounding, and my head spun. I felt as if I were floating, as if the room was rocking back and forth. I closed my eyes and went back to sleep.

The third time I woke up was better. It was still dark, so I couldn't make out much I hadn't seen the first two times I had opened my eyes, but my head was filled with less cotton and I thought I was better able to think clearly.

Lifting my head made me feel dizzy, so I stayed flat on my back and took stock. Nothing hurt, other than my head, and even that didn't feel like an injury but more like I had drunk too much and was recovering. A slow probing over my temples and the back of my head found no injuries.

I was still dressed, including shoes, so that was a positive thing. No one had thought to cover me with a blanket, and that was perhaps less positive, although it didn't seem to have hurt me appreciably.

The surface I was lying on was somewhat squishy, so I decided that it was more likely to be a (low quality) mattress than the floor. I fumbled around and found the edge of the mattress, so yes, I was lying on a small cot somewhere in a room I didn't recognize.

A prison cell? It was certainly small and bare enough for that, but I couldn't recall doing anything that would have gotten me arrested. The last thing I remembered was dinner at the Savoy, and talking to Wolfgang about his grandfather.

Had something happened to me on my way home? Had I been kidnapped in the same way that Christopher had been?

Was Christopher here?

I rolled over on my side and peered down at the floor. The movement made a wave of nausea rise through my esophagus, and I swallowed it back, determinedly, and flopped onto my back again. The floor had been empty, and so was the rest of the room. I was alone, although that didn't mean that there couldn't be another room just like this one nearby, that had Christopher in it.

It was around this time that I realized that the knocking in the walls was real and not a product of my headache. The entire room vibrated, and there were banging sounds from outside the room, and the smell of... my nostrils flared. Was that petrol?

It was, wasn't it? The air stank of petrol and the floor was moving. It wasn't simply that I was dizzy and discombobulated from whatever had happened to me. The room vibrated and the floor moved.

It took much longer than it should have done to put those two things together—or three things: add the smell of petrol to the other two—and come up with an answer.

A boat. I was on a boat. On the water.

I had been here before, I realized, or at least somewhere very like it. Twelve years ago, my mother had put me on a boat bound for Southampton, and had telegrammed her sister in England to meet me there. It was a long time ago, and I had been small and distraught about leaving my mother and the only home I had ever known, so I didn't remember much about the trip. No details, just disjointed impressions. But I did remember the feeling of claustrophobia, and of being somewhere I didn't want to be. And the rocking, the constant rocking of the floor.

If I left the cabin and went above deck, would I see land, or only open water?

Could I even leave the cabin if I wanted to?

I sat up carefully—my head swam, but it helped to know that the unsteadiness was the water, not me—and got my feet under me. I wobbled a bit when I stood, and my head did a slow roll. The nausea reasserted itself, and I had to close my eyes and wait it out, but I stayed upright.

The door was four steps away. I made it there and leaned on the wall for several moments before I could fumble for the lock.

By now, things had started to come back to me, or if nothing else, I was beginning to reason a few things out.

I was still wearing my salmon frock, so I had been abducted before I could make it home from supper. I remembered going to the Savoy, and sitting across from Wolfgang at table. I also remembered, quite distinctly, Crispin telling me, not once but several times, that he and Tom would be on hand, in separate motorcars, to follow Wolfgang home.

I must have been taken by someone else, then. Perhaps Wolfgang had put me into a Hackney for the trip home, and then he had gone off to his... rooms in Shoreditch, wasn't it? I had a vague memory of him admitting to that. Unless I had imagined it, of course. My head was still fuzzy.

I was absolutely certain about what Crispin had told me, however. He and Tom would be outside the Savoy to follow Wolfgang to where he was going. One or both of them must have followed him home, then, and meanwhile, the Hackney driver had taken me... where? To the Royal Albert Docks? To Southampton?

Had I walked onto the boat under my own steam?

I couldn't remember doing that. I couldn't remember anything after talking to Wolfgang at table in the Savoy Restaurant. I had felt dizzy, hadn't I? And he had told me that he would take care of me?

I had a mental glimpse of a cup of tea—and of a man's hand knocking it over. And then déjà vu to another cup of tea, and... the same thing happening?

But no, I'd been drinking coffee last night, surely? The tea incident had taken place a long time ago, at least the first time. Crispin and I had reached for a cup of tea at the same time, one that Aunt Charlotte had poured for me. It had been just after I'd been shot, hadn't it? Late April at Sutherland Hall. He had been trying to help me, because the wound in my arm made it hard for me to reach for things.

Or perhaps he hadn't been helping. Perhaps he had knocked the cup over on purpose. He's not usually clumsy, so perhaps there had been something in it that he hadn't wanted me to drink. If Aunt Charlotte hadn't been above trying to shoot me, she wouldn't have hesitated to poison me, either. So I might owe him thanks for saving my life on that occasion. If I ever got out of here, I'd be sure to tell him so.

But that was a long time ago. More recently, Wolfgang had knocked a cup of tea practically into my lap. Not tonight, though. Tonight, we'd been drinking coffee.

No, that tea incident had been a few days ago. And like Crispin, Wolfgang wasn't usually clumsy.

It had been just after that, hadn't it, that the maître d' had delivered the note for Wolfgang? Perhaps Wolfgang had put something in my tea, and the maître d' had seen it, and then Wolfgang had aborted the mission once he knew that his action had been noticed?

And then he had tried again tonight, when another maître d' was on duty, a less observant one, and he had succeeded in getting me here?

I could have spent a long time pondering the past, but I thought the best thing I could do for myself was to try to find a way out of my predicament. Before we arrived in Germany (or perhaps somewhere else; perhaps we were not on our way back to the Weimar Republic) and certainly before Wolfgang could arrive at my door to—just as a possibility—force me into a wedding ceremony by sea captain, or alternatively, if I refused, toss me overboard.

I doubted I could make it to land if he did do. I can swim—now—but I'm not strong enough to want to brave the North Sea, especially at night. I still have something of an aversion to water after that incident in the Neckar when I was small, as well.

Or the plan might be something entirely different. I could be reading the whole thing wrong. Perhaps he didn't want to marry me or kill me at all. Perhaps he wanted something else.

But it didn't matter. The whole plan would be moot if I could just remove myself from the equation. So I grabbed the doorknob in my hand and twisted it.

I had been afraid that I had been locked in here. Such was not the case. The door opened easily from the inside, and I put my head out into a narrow hallway lined by half a dozen other doors.

It was possible—not likely, perhaps, but possible—that Christopher was behind one of them. The temptation to start opening doors in the hope that I might find him was almost overwhelming. A bit of sympathetic company in this situation would have been very nice. I didn't do it, however, for two reasons. Firstly, because I had decided that getting myself away would be the better part of valor, and secondly, because I was afraid that I would open a door and come face to face with Wolfgang.

Or if not Wolfgang, then whoever had brought me here. But it was most likely Wolfgang.

It was instinct to begin to take my shoes off before I set off, the better to move soundlessly, but a mere half second of thought told me that there was no point in trying to be quiet. The boat was already making so much noise that no one would hear anything I did. Nonetheless, I shut the door carefully behind me and headed down the hall towards the steep and narrow staircase I could see at the end of it. I walked quickly and with my heart in my throat, but I didn't run. At the bottom of the stairs, I started up, holding on to the railing the whole way.

There was another corridor and another staircase after that, less narrow and less steep. So far I hadn't seen a soul, and when I came out at the top of the second staircase, it was obvious why. The entire panoply of the sky arched above me, thousands of stars on a velvet background, with a waxing gibbous moon that would be full in a few more days. It was the middle of the night, and all I could see around me was water.

It was also freezing cold, and I wrapped my arms around myself to stop shivering. My wrap was below deck somewhere, no doubt—perhaps Wolfgang had it, along with my handbag, unless, of course, I was on this boat by myself, while Wolfgang was still on English soil.

I seemed to be on the deck of what was more a freighter and less a passenger conveyance. There were no deckchairs in sight, nor anything else you would expect to find on a passenger liner. The bridge was up ahead—I could see the lights and hear a faint murmur of voices from the seamen who were awake at this time of night. They didn't sound like they were speaking English—the words were more guttural, the consonants less refined—and after a few seconds of pricking my ears I could confirm that yes, they were speaking German. My own was no longer fluent enough to make out what they were saying, but I recognized the cadence and enough of the more basic words to verify it.

That seemed to take care of any question of what I was doing here, then. No one beside Wolfgang would surely think to carry me onboard a German freighter as a mode of abduction.

I had, it seemed, no good options. I could go back to my cabin and wait for Wolfgang to put whatever plan he had concocted into action, which might involve killing me or might only involve forcing me into marriage. I was honestly not keen on either of those choices, especially after this.

I could jump into the water and most likely drown, if I didn't die of hypothermia first.

I could approach the bridge and explain the situation, but there were no guarantees that the crew wasn't in cahoots with Wolfgang, or if not that, that they had at least been paid enough to look the other way. They'd more than likely give me back to him if I approached them. Or at least there was enough of a chance of it that I didn't want to take the risk.

I could try to hide. Leave the cabin empty and find somewhere else to stow away. Perhaps Wolfgang would believe that I had jumped overboard, and wouldn't look for me. Perhaps I could stay out of sight for long enough that the boat would reach shore somewhere. And once we got to where we were going—whether that was Bremerhaven or Kiel or somewhere further afield; hopefully this wasn't a cross-Atlantic voyage—I could attempt to make my way back home from there.

In fact, it might be better if we were going to America. The language would be easier there. I hadn't spoken German in more than a decade. And seeing as I was a German citizen, if I ended up in Germany, the authorities might even refuse to send me back to England.

If I made it to America, I could contact the Schlomskys for help. They owed me that, after I had figured out what happened to their daughter. And surely it couldn't actually be as far between New York and Toledo as I had been led to believe?

It was at this point that I heard the scuff of a shoe behind me, and then two hands grabbed my upper arms while a male voice said, "Got you!" in my ear.

I shrieked, of course, as if I had been stabbed. The voice—or more accurately, the man it belonged to—muttered something (likely a curse) and moved one hand up to slap over my mouth. He was wearing gloves, or I would have bit him.

His other arm went across my chest so he could haul me backwards and then shake me. "Quiet!"

There wasn't anything else I could do, of course. Or rather, I did my best to scream, but the hand across my mouth stopped anything but muffled outrage from escaping.

"Should have let him do it himself," the voice muttered, and my blood chilled as I realized that Wolfgang might have accomplices onboard. Not just sailors he had paid to look the other way, but actual accomplices. Perhaps he wasn't even here. Perhaps he had loaded me into a motorcar outside the Savoy, and someone else had taken me to the boat, while Wolfgang himself led Tom and Crispin on a merry chase all over London. They may not even have noticed that I was missing yet.

Perhaps this had nothing to do with marriage at all. Perhaps Wolfgang was part of a white slavery ring, and he had abducted both Christopher and myself and was shipping us off to darkest Arabia for some sultan's harem.

I renewed my efforts to get free, to the obvious irritation of the man holding me. He gave me a shake, the way a terrier might shake a rat it had caught. "Stop it! We're the Royal National Lifeboat Institution, and we're here to rescue you. You're going home."

I was?

"Here. You take her." He shoved me at someone else, whose scent and tweed coat was familiar.

"It's all right, Pippa," Tom's voice said. "Come with me. We'll get you off the boat."

That was the point when my knees buckled, of course, and he had to put an arm around my waist to keep me standing. There was no going anywhere, not while I was like this. And he must have realized it, because he stayed where he was while I buried my face in his tweed coat and hung on, shaking.

"Christopher?" I managed after a few seconds, my teeth chattering.

His head came up alertly. "Is he here?"

"I haven't seen him. I thought maybe you—"

But he shook his head. "I'm afraid not. We'll find him. I

need you to pull yourself together and walk with me, all right? There's a lifeboat off the side of the ship."

He nudged me into moving, and then shuffled with me across the deck before he stopped at the edge of the boat where a ladder led downward. I peered over the edge. There was icy black water below, as well as a smaller boat tied up to the bigger freighter, bobbing along.

And there was a dark figure on the deck of the smaller boat, and a familiar pale face smirking up at me. "There you are, Darling."

"St George," I said, and I'll admit that I was happy to see him, if only because he was here to rescue me. Certainly not because I had been concerned that I would never see him, or anyone else in the family, ever again.

"Would you like for me to climb up and fetch you? You can hang around my neck like a monkey on the way down."

"Thank you, but no." If this was what it took to get me onto the ladder and down to the lifeboat, I would take it. "You'd probably drop me. Just step aside."

Tom assisted me onto the ladder and made sure I had a solid grip on the top rung before he let go. "It's not that far," he informed me. "Just move slowly and carefully."

"Yes," Crispin agreed from below, cheerfully, "no need to rush. The view is lovely from down here."

That probably implied that he was taking the opportunity to peer up my skirt. Or perhaps not, perhaps he was just watching my derriere coming down. Either way, it gave me incentive to keep going. By the time I was almost at the bottom, he grabbed me around the waist and swung me the rest of the way down, and then he wrapped both arms around me, a bit too tightly, and buried his nose in my hair.

I was too shocked to say anything, to be honest. It was something Christopher would have done, and for a moment it was comforting to lean into the embrace and imagine that it was he who was holding me instead of Crispin. But of course it wasn't. Tweed is tweed, but Crispin smells differently than Christopher does, and aside from that, he was also engaged to be married and too much closeness in this situation would be a very bad thing.

I freed myself and took a step back. "Thank you, St George."

"Don't mention it," Crispin said and had to clear his throat. It must have helped him get his usual acerbic self back in line, because the next thing out of his mouth was, "Bloody hell, Darling, could you be any less careful?"

"Whatever do you mean?"

I wrapped my arms around myself, because I was standing in a boat on the open water in a short-sleeved silk crepe gown with short sleeves in October, and he made an exasperated noise before shrugging out of his tweed coat and wrapping it around me. "Come sit down."

He pulled me over to a bench against the small wheelhouse midships of the lifeboat, and pulled me down next to him. And proceeded to wrap his arm around me in an effort to share some of his own body heat.

"Thank you," I muttered. Thanking Crispin for anything goes against the grain, but under the circumstances he deserved it, and I'll do what I have to do when there's no other choice.

"As I said, don't mention it. How could you have been so careless?"

As to allow myself to be doped, I supposed.

"You were the ones who were supposed to keep an eye on me," I said indignantly, instead of admitting that I had allowed Wolfgang to dope me and kidnap me without any suspicions as to his motivations whatsoever. "Why didn't you rescue me?"

"What do you call this, Darling?"

He gestured to himself, and the lifeboat, and Tom, somewhere on the freighter, looking for Christopher and Wolfgang.

Since he had a point, I told him, "I didn't think he would do something like this. All my focus was on keeping him busy until after supper, when the two of you were supposed to go after him."

"As we did," Crispin said, "when he hauled your lifeless body out of the Savoy and loaded you into a Hackney."

"I'm surprised you didn't fall on him right then and there."

"I wanted to," Crispin said. "Tom held me back. He thought Wolfie might be taking you to where Christopher is."

Trust Tom to prioritize finding Christopher over rescuing me. And trust Crispin, I suppose, to go along with it. He might love me, but he loved Christopher, too.

Not that I wouldn't have done the same, of course.

"It's possible that he's in one of the other cabins," I said. "I didn't open any of the other doors, just in case I found Wolfgang instead. I didn't want him to realize that I was awake."

"If Kit's there, Tom will find him," Crispin said. After a moment, he added, "I'll be surprised, though. I'm fairly certain that this was a Gretna Green situation, and the thing with Kit is something else."

Yes, I was fairly certain of the same thing. Wolfgang had no reason to want to take Christopher to Germany with him. I wasn't even sure what his reason was for wanting to take me. It wasn't for love of me. No one who loves someone else would dope their cup of coffee and load them onto a freighter bound for foreign parts without their consent.

No, whatever this was, the reasons for it were a lot colder and more calculating than love.

"I ought to let Tom tell you," Crispin said when I expressed as much, "but I'm not certain I quite understand it either."

"Then why don't you tell me what you know, and I'll tell

you what Wolfgang told me, and perhaps we can figure it out from there."

"Certainly," Crispin said. "The chap from the Natterdorff constabulary—the one Tom spoke to yesterday morning—rang back during the time you and I were at the flat. Tom told me about it while you were inside the Savoy with Wolfie."

"And what did the constable know?" Whatever it was, it must be good, because Crispin had *Schadenfreude* written all over his face.

He smirked. "Quite a lot, as it happens. Wolfie left the castle three months ago, after a heated argument with the old man. No one's seen him since. Six weeks ago, the old man changed his will—"

Oh, dear. "Did he cut Wolfgang out?"

Crispin nodded. "And it seems he also cut off the money at the same time. That would explain the Savoy Hotel situation, wouldn't it?"

It certainly would. The cash flow had stopped abruptly, and Wolfgang had had to move elsewhere, to conserve what money he had left.

"He told me that he's been living in rooms in Shoreditch," I said. "I don't know whether it's true or not."

"I don't know that I care," Crispin answered, "other than that of course it's wonderful, imagining him living in squalor in rented rooms in Shoreditch. But he couldn't keep Kit there, so I don't know if it matters."

No, of course he couldn't keep Christopher there. Too many people around for that. That was why the Schlomsky parents had been made to pay for the flat in the Essex House Mansions as well as for the 'country cottage' in Thornton Heath. A nice flat for 'Flossie' to occupy, and a secure place to keep the real Flossie while her kidnappers bled her parents dry.

That same thought as last time buzzed through my head

again, and this time I took it out and looked at it. But before I could say anything, Crispin had continued. "Apparently, the old man is on his deathbed. Any chance to get him to change that will back is dwindling by the minute. I suppose that's why Wolfie decided to head home."

I made a noncommittal little noise, and he added, "I can't imagine why he'd want to take you with him, though."

His tone indicated that nobody with any sense would want me around given the choice.

"It's one thing if he needed a wife to get back into his grandfather's good graces," Crispin continued peevishly. "Perhaps the old man likes women, or he thinks Wolfie ought to give up philandering and start producing heirs. Perhaps he has a habit of tomcatting around—"

"You would know all about that," I said sweetly, and he shot me a look.

"I'm engaged, remember? If anyone's settling down and producing heirs, I am."

I made a face, and he added, "But why on earth would he want *you* badly enough to dope you and carry you onto a boat to smuggle you out of the country and back into Germany with no one the wiser? No offense, Darling, but you're not exactly the type to drive men mad."

"And here I always thought I drove you mad," I said. "I can explain that, actually—"

Or at least I thought I could, if my suppositions were correct. He didn't let me do so, however.

"It'd be one thing a hundred years ago. A forced marriage might stick then. But you'd either marry him willingly or not at all, and if he forced you, you'd leave him and then divorce him. Thank God that's an option now."

I nodded. Yes, indeed. If the worst had come to the worst, and the captain of the freighter had agreed to facilitate a ceremony once we were in international water, at least I wouldn't have had to stay married afterwards.

"So" Crispin said, "I don't see the sense in forcing you. Unless he thought you'd be so enamored with his castle that you'd accept him after all? Although if he thinks a castle will sway you, he doesn't know you very well."

No, he didn't.

"I'm fairly certain I know why he did it, St George."

He gave me a dubious look. "You do?"

"I might. The old man changed his will, did you say? Who is the new heir?"

"A cousin," Crispin said. "Born on the wrong side of the blanket, or some such thing." He wrinkled his nose. "Common as dirt, most likely. The child of some disgraced younger son from a generation or two ago, who—"

"Yes," I interrupted, "thank you."

He looked at me. And then—I always knew he was quick—his eyes widened. "No."

"I'm afraid so."

"You..." He seemed to have lost his breath, and it took a moment for him to regain it. "*You* are the new *Gräfin von und zu* Natterdorff?"

"It appears I am. Wolfgang told me that my father was his father's younger brother, disinherited for reading Marx and wanting to work with his hands."

"Dear Lord," Crispin said faintly. He buried his face in his hands and hunched over, moaning. I patted him on the back while I wondered, half-heartedly, whether the shaking under my palm was from tears or laughter, and whether, ultimately, it mattered.

CHAPTER TWENTY

TOM FOUND us like that a few minutes later, when he swung down the ladder to the deck of the lifeboat and landed lightly on his feet.

He opened his mouth, and then closed it again. After a look at Crispin and then one at me, he inquired, "Is everything all right?"

"Fine," I said. "St George is simply overcome with emotion. His entire worldview has changed. It turns out that I'm not beneath him, after all."

Crispin straightened his back and dislodged my hand. I removed it to my lap as he dropped his own from his face.

I still couldn't tell whether the pink splotches on his cheeks were from too much laughter or some other strong emotion, although I could make a guess. If I were the granddaughter of the *Graf von und zu* Natterdorff, Uncle Harold could no longer claim that I was either common or poor. I was still German, of course, so that probably wouldn't have been enough to change his mind about allowing Crispin to pursue me either way, but I could quite understand why the latter might be thrown for a loop, and perhaps not entirely sure whether he ought to laugh or cry about it.

"For the record," he told me, "I never thought you were beneath me. That was my father and mother."

I shrugged. "It doesn't matter at this point anyway, does it?"

"Doesn't it?"

"Well, you're—"

Engaged, I was going to say, but that was only until I realized that saying anything like that would give away the fact that I knew how he felt about me, and that wasn't a conversation I wanted to have. Not now, and preferably not ever.

He gave me a suspicious sort of look. "I'm what?"

"A better man than your father, it seems. Thank you."

"Don't mention it," Crispin said, and ignored, magnificently, the muttered comment from Tom that included the words 'beneath' and 'different way.' I decided not to dignify it with a response, either, but I'm fairly certain that both Crispin and I blushed.

"What's going on?" I asked Tom instead, to get the conversation back onto safer ground, and also because I sincerely wanted to know.

He turned to me. "I brought your wrap and handbag." He handed them over. "But there's no sign of Kit. The crew said they haven't seen anyone fitting his description."

"You can speak German?" I shrugged out of Crispin's jacket and handed it back to him with thanks before I wrapped my own coat around myself. I'm certain we were both grateful to have our own back, and to both be warmer than we had been.

"I picked up a bit during the war," Tom said. "Enough to get by."

"And you described Kitty," Crispin said, "as well as Kit himself, I presume?"

Tom nodded. "I asked, but we also looked around. They were upfront about seeing Pippa being carried onboard. I think they would have mentioned it, had it happened before, as well."

"Wolfgang would have no reason to bring Christopher to Germany anyway," I said.

"He might have wanted to throw him overboard somewhere in the North Sea, though."

I looked at Crispin, aghast. "What a horrible thing to say!"

He stared back. "How do you know that wasn't what he planned for you, Darling?"

"I assumed he wanted the money," I said. "He would have gotten it by marrying me. Not by throwing me overboard."

"What's this, now?" Tom looked from one to the other of us for clarification, but we were both too busy bickering to answer him.

"He might have thought that without you in the picture, his grandfather might relent," Crispin said. "If there was no one else left with the Natterdorff blood."

Granted. But— "He'd be better off marrying me now and killing me later, if he wanted me out of the way."

"He doesn't seem too particular about needing you alive," Crispin pointed out. "It's been... what? Three murder attempts now? Four? Perhaps five?"

"Murder attempts?" Tom echoed.

I scoffed. "I don't know where you're getting your information, St George, but there hasn't been anywhere close to five."

"The fall into the underground," Crispin said, lifting a finger. "The Hackney that barely missed you and Kit the other evening. Tonight—"

"You don't know that tonight was a murder attempt."

"I don't know that it wasn't," Crispin retorted, and raised another finger. "The bullet that barely missed you."

"That was your mother."

He rolled his eyes. "Not that bullet. The one at Marsden Manor last month."

Oh, of course. That bullet.

"That wasn't Wolfgang," I said.

"How do you know that it wasn't?" Tom wanted to know. Academic interest, I assume.

"She doesn't," Crispin told him. "No one else ever admitted to doing it."

"It was most likely Geoffrey," I said. "Another attempt at getting rid of Cecily."

"Geoffrey didn't try to get rid of Cecily," Crispin said. "He only wanted to get rid of the baby. A bullet wouldn't have done that."

"That doesn't mean that it was Wolfgang."

"Who else could it have been?" Crispin said, throwing his hands up. "It wasn't Laetitia. I was next to her the whole time. And don't you dare accuse me of shooting at you!"

"I wasn't going to," I said.

He sniffed. "Well, nobody else had a reason for wanting you—or Francis or Kit—dead."

He was right about that, of course. I had chalked that whole thing up to a misunderstanding due to the fact that I looked a bit like Cecily Fletcher from a distance, but that was before I knew that Wolfgang had had ulterior motives for many of the things he did. It was quite possible that Crispin was right and Wolfgang had taken a potshot at me as long as a month ago.

"So three attempts," Tom said, "if we leave tonight out of it."

"Four," I said reluctantly, "actually. He upended a cup of tea in my lap a few days ago. Given tonight's occurrence, there might have been something more than tea in it. Perhaps not poison, but—"

"An earlier attempt to knock you out so he could kidnap you." Crispin nodded. "Where is he, Gardiner?"

"Coming," Tom said, "and don't even think about going after him. He's handcuffed and under guard, and I do not want to have to arrest you for attacking a man who can't fight back. Do you understand me?"

Crispin glowered, but nodded.

"Neither of you is to talk to him," Tom continued sternly, "or to approach him or to do anything else to him. In fact—" He glanced at the small wheelhouse, "I want you to go inside, and preferably down below. And I don't want to see either of your faces again until we're docked at Ramsgate and I have put *Herr* Albrecht into a police car."

Herr Albrecht, was it? I smirked.

Crispin couldn't contain himself either. He sniggered. "Do you call him that to his face?"

"I have it on good authority," Tom said, "that he has been disinherited by his grandfather. That makes him just like the rest of us, doesn't it?"

He didn't wait for either of us to respond, just flapped his hands at us. "Off you go. Into the wheelhouse where I can't see you. Shoo."

We shooed, into the darkest corner we could find, where we curled up side by side and waited for the prisoner to be brought out and down.

"There he is," Crispin muttered a minute later, when a pair of legs came into view on the freighter's ladder, descending slowly.

I nodded. "Stay here. You heard what Tom said."

He shot me a glance. I could see the light reflect off his eyeballs for just a second in the dark. "It would be worth it. I only want to get one good lick in. Just one. You can't say he doesn't deserve it."

"He deserves a lot more than that," I said. "But I certainly don't want you ending up in jail over it. Let the police deal with him."

He sighed. "You're a better man than I am, Darling."

"We've always known that," I told him. "Listen, St George."

"Yes, Darling?"

"Do you have your motorcar at Ramsgate?"

He nodded. "We both followed him. All three of us, actually; Detective Sergeant Finchley was there, too. See, there he is."

He pointed. I looked, and there he was, Tom's colleague, making his way down the ladder after Wolfgang. The latter was at the bottom now, turning towards Tom, and as opposed to what Tom had told Crispin earlier, Wolfgang was in fact not in handcuffs. It would have been difficult for him to navigate the ladder with handcuffs on, I supposed, so that may have been why Finchley had taken them off. As we watched, Wolfgang took a step forward and then pivoted to present Tom with his back. He put both arms behind himself. Tom reached towards them, handcuffs in one hand... and just as he was about to make contact, Wolfgang took off, straight for the side of the lifeboat.

Two steps later, he was in the water. We both saw and heard the splash when he hit.

Tom surged forward—I imagined he was on his way over the side of the boat, too—but Finchley's hand on his shoulder stayed his momentum.

"Light!" the latter called, and elsewhere in the wheelhouse, a switch flicked on and a powerful search-lamp illuminated the water in front of the boat.

Crispin made a move to get up, but I grabbed onto his sleeve. "We promised."

"He's off the side and in the water," Crispin objected. "He won't see us." He tugged on his arm so I would free him.

I held on. "Just wait. They may pull him up again in another moment."

But they didn't. The lifeboat pulled away from the freighter and began circling, search-lamp sweeping from side to side across the choppy water. Tom and Ian Finchley had gone to the stern, one on each side, and were peering intently into the dark. They had been joined by most of the crew of the lifeboat, everyone who wasn't necessary to actually maneuver the craft.

"Let me up," Crispin said irritably. "I want to see."

"It's better if you stay here."

I certainly didn't want to watch them fish Wolfgang back out of the water, and then add evading arrest to his list of crimes. I wanted even less to watch them fail in fishing him out because he had drowned. I wanted to stay here, in the dark corner of the wheelhouse, where I could pretend that every-thing was well.

In the end, they gave up. Wolfgang was nowhere to be seen. The lifeboat circled the freighter several times, just in case he had made it to the other side of it and was climbing out of the water there, but there was no sign of him. He was either a very strong swimmer, or he had decided that drowning was prefer-able to hanging. It was hard to say whether he was right or wrong. I can't imagine that either is pleasant, really.

"Take us back to Ramsgate," Tom told the lifeboat crew, "and then you can go back out and look for him one more time, if you want. But I need to get the victim to shore and get her checked out by a physician."

The coxswain nodded, and the boat turned towards shore, although he kept the search-lamp going.

"This is silly," I protested. "I'm fine. I don't need to be looked at by anyone."

"You were doped, Miss Darling," Finchley said, "and now you've been sitting here in the cold..."

I rolled my eyes. "I slept it off, Finch. I woke up on my own. And I'm not cold. St George gave me his jacket, and then Tom brought me my own. I'm fine."

"No injuries?"

I shook my head. "Nobody hurt me. I drank a cup of laced coffee and fell asleep. Now I'm awake. The only thing I want, is to go home. If you'll just let us off at Ramsgate, St George can escort me to London while the rest of you go back out to search for Wolfgang."

They exchanged glances, but in the end, that's what ended up happening. The lifeboat crew didn't want to leave Wolfgang for dead, I supposed, and Tom and Finchley were still hoping that they might arrest him. Nor were we as far from shore as I had been afraid of. I probably wouldn't have been able to swim it, but perhaps Wolfgang could do. At any rate, it didn't take forever to get there. The crew set Crispin and myself off on the dock, and turned the boat around. Tom left with a promise to come and find us when he was back in London, to tell us what had been the eventual outcome.

"This way," Crispin told me as the boat pulled away from the dock again. He put a hand to my lower back and guided me in the direction of the car park outside the lifeboat station, where the Hispano-Suiza was waiting. The knocking of the lifeboat's engine faded slowly across the water as we picked our way across grass and gravel.

"They'll find him," he added after a moment, as if he knew in which direction my thoughts had strayed.

I flicked him a look out of the corner of my eye. "What if they don't?"

"Then they don't," Crispin said, and flicked one back. "Do you care?"

I did, but then again I didn't. "He kidnapped me, and I suppose he did try to kill me. Or if not that, at least there was a concerted effort to maim."

Crispin nodded.

"I suppose it would be only fair that he should pay for that."

"More than fair," Crispin agreed.

"Although I think I'd rather he pay in prison than by drowning."

"Of course you would." His tone said that he, personally, was good with either outcome.

"On the other hand," I said, "facing him across the Old Bailey and having to detail all the things he said and did, sounds like rather an onerous time. So perhaps it would be better if Tom and Finchley didn't find him."

Crispin grunted something noncommittal. Up ahead, the Hispano-Suiza came into view, the blue color making itself clearer as we got closer, and he stopped beside the passenger door and opened it for me.

"But then there's the fact that he's my cousin," I said as I got in, "and I'd hate to lose what little family I have left."

He stared at me. "What on earth do you mean by that?"

I told him what I meant, in a shaking voice that got progressively shakier as I went along. "Christopher's missing, and what if we can't find him? And if Christopher's gone, Aunt Roz and Uncle Herbert might blame me, and so might Francis, and then they won't want to see me anymore. And you're marrying Laetitia, so you won't be allowed to have anything to do with me after December—"

"Aunt Roslyn would never do that," Crispin interrupted. "She's not the type to abandon a child over something he or she can't help. Not like some people."

He shut my car door with a slam, and under normal

circumstances I would have tried to pursue the topic, since there was clearly some underlying bitterness there, judging from his tone. But he was on his way around the motorcar before I could say anything else. Once he arrived on the other side, he continued as if nothing had happened, and I forgot all about what he had said earlier. "And as for me, it's not as if I'll be a loss to you, Darling. You'll be happy to see the back of me, I'm sure."

He slid behind the wheel and closed the door behind himself without looking at me.

I snorted. "Don't be ridiculous, St George. I'll admit that we haven't had the easiest time of it. But we're doing better now. We haven't tried to kill one another once today."

Or yesterday, either.

"That's only because I was worried about you," Crispin said, inserting the key into the ignition. "Once we get back to London, I'm certain we'll be bickering as usual."

No doubt. And on that topic— "Would you happen to know where Thornton Heath is located?"

He glanced over at me, eyebrow arching at the sudden change of subject. "South of London? Yes, of course I do."

"Is it on the way back? Can you take me there?"

"To Thornton Heath?" His brows drew together. "Why?"

"It was where they kept Flossie Schlomsky during the time she was gone," I said.

He nodded. "And?"

"It occurred to me that it's a ready-made place to keep someone who's missing. Boarded up windows, extra locks on the doors, everything someone might need for an extended involuntary stay."

"Kit?" He looked brighter for a moment, before he must have thought it through. "They're in prison, aren't they? The people who took Flossie? So how would Kit end up there?"

"Wolfgang was there," I said. "When Mrs. Schlomsky remembered that she and Hiram had agreed to pay for a 'country cottage' in Thornton Heath—"

Crispin snorted, since Thornton Heath is about as far from a picturesque country cottage as one can get.

I nodded "Precisely. But when we went to the Savoy to pick up Hiram, Wolfgang was there. And I invited him along."

Or perhaps he had invited himself along; I couldn't recall at this point how the conversation had gone. It had been during the time that he had been ingratiating himself with me, before he started shooting at me and trying to run me over, so he might have been playing nice.

"It was quite helpful having him," I added, begrudgingly, "seeing as all three of the kidnappers were there when we arrived."

"But he'd been there. So he knew where it was located."

"And he would have known that it was sitting empty, since the Schlomskys had paid for its use, but all the occupants were either dead or headed to prison."

A shadow crossed his face at the thought of Flossie's murder, but it cleared a moment later, and he yanked on the gearshift. "We should certainly take a look, then. Although it can wait until we've had some rest, I suppose. And perhaps when Gardiner is available to come with us."

"I've had plenty of rest," I said. "All I've done since we left London, is sleep. You're the one who has gone the past two nights on no sleep at all."

"It's not as if I've never done that before, Darling."

No, of course it wasn't. He and his cohorts in the Society for Bright Young Persons frequently pull all-nighters of wild parties and treasure hunts across London.

"If you'll allow me to drive," I said, "you could take a nap—"

He stared at me, and the H6 veered dangerously to the right. "Over my dead body."

"That could be arranged," I said. And quite easily, if he didn't keep his attention on the road."

"You wouldn't."

I sniffed. "Of course I wouldn't. You're a constant thorn in my side, St George, but I'm not going to murder you. You're about to run off the road."

"Oops." He adjusted the wheel. "Be that as it may, you are not getting behind the wheel of my motorcar."

"I'm in better condition than you are. I wasn't the one who almost had an accident."

"I'll be fine." He peered out through the windshield, into the darkness beyond. "The sun will be up soon. That'll help."

"Fine," I said. "But if you kill us on the way there, I'll never forgive you."

"No worries, Darling. I'm used to this. It'll take more than a few nights of less-than-stellar sleep to impair my abilities."

"If you say so. Although I'm keeping my eye on you. And at the first sign of drooping eyelids, I'm going to pinch you. Hard."

"Of course, Darling." He flashed me a grin. "No more or less than I would expect."

"To Thornton Heath, then. The sooner we find Christopher, the better."

I settled back into my seat for the drive to London.

CHAPTER TWENTY-ONE

"THERE IT IS," I said, some two-and-a-half hours later.

The sun was up by then, but of course we had been headed west, so it had been at our backs the entire way. And Crispin was right: he had been just fine. His eyes were a bit red, but there had been no sign of drooping eyelids, nor even a yawn, and I had had no excuse for pinching him.

Not that I felt particularly like pinching him at the moment. He had been rather wonderful, both yesterday and so far today. More so than I would have expected, given the source. We were back to bickering, of course, just as he had predicted, but he hadn't been unkind, and also hadn't twitted me too terribly about being taken in by a murderer, or at least by a kidnapper, since there was no reason to think that Wolfgang had murdered anyone. He had perhaps tried to murder me, but then again, perhaps not. The shot at Marsden Manor might not have been intended to hit anyone, and the fall down the stairs to the tube wasn't likely to have been fatal. And the Hackney that had come so close to clipping Christopher and myself in the street the other night... well, it hadn't actually hit us, had it? Nor had there been actual poison in my coffee last night, so perhaps there hadn't been anything worse than sleeping draught in the tea the other day, either. And the dose in the coffee had been small enough to allow me to wake up after just a few hours, so it clearly hadn't been an attempt on my life. Perhaps not even on my virtue.

And I absolutely refused to believe that Wolfgang had murdered Christopher. There was no reason for him to do so, not even if Christopher had discovered that Wolfgang lived in rented rooms in Shoreditch. That was not a killing matter. And the idea that we might get to the cottage in Thornton Heath and find Christopher dead was one I would not countenance. So no, Wolfgang was not a murderer. Call him a kidnapper and leave it at that.

At any rate, the drive had not been unpleasant. We had discussed our hopes of finding Christopher alive and well. I had regaled him with a description of what had transpired during my last visit to Thornton Heath, since Crispin hadn't been there for that. We had talked about the likelihood (or lack thereof) that Tom and Finchley and the lifeboat crew would find Wolfgang alive—poor in Crispin's opinion, a bit more hopeful in mine—and whether it was possible that he might have made it back onto the freighter after the lifeboat navigated away with us onboard.

The possibility that Wolfgang had survived the water and was on his way to Germany even as we spoke was a bit of all right with me, I'll admit. I didn't much like the idea of his being dead, but having him out of the country—and out of my life— was better than the possibility that he had made it back to shore and that I would see him again.

"You're too soft," Crispin complained when I said as much.

I scoffed. "Don't be ridiculous. No one knows better than you how well I hold a grudge."

He slanted me a sideways look. "I'm not seeing a grudge in this case."

"It's only because it's a choice between this and death," I said. "I'd rather have him be alive than dead. I don't wish death on anyone. And I'd rather he be alive in Germany than in England, so I don't have to deal with him."

"I'd rather him be alive in prison," Crispin grumbled, and I supposed I had to give him that. Besides, if anyone in the family was better at holding a grudge than me, it was him.

At any rate, the sun was up and warming our backs when we drove into Thornton Heath and began to look for the rental cottage. I could no longer remember the address, although I did recall that the cottage was termed Ivy Cottage, and of course I knew I would recognize it when I saw it. But that was different from knowing where to go to find it. We ended up spending fifteen minutes just driving around peering at houses, in the hopes that I would see something I recognized, until that actually happened.

"Right there," I said, and he peered out the windshield.

"Where?"

"At the corner. Turn. There!"

"Oh." He turned the corner, a bit too abruptly. "I thought you meant—"

"I know what you thought. But this is the road. At the end of it, there's a cottage on the right that sits a bit apart from the others. The drive is on the right before the house itself."

Crispin nodded. "Just point to it when we get closer."

By then I was on the edge of my seat, with both hands braced on the console, trying to make the H6 move faster. Not that it couldn't move faster than it did—a Hispano-Suiza H6 had set the Brooklands record in 1924—but it wasn't wise to employ those kinds of speeds in the middle of Thornton Heath.

"There! There!"

I pointed. Crispin followed the direction of my finger, and wrinkled his nose. "Not very picturesque, is it?"

It wasn't. I had noticed the same thing the last time I was here, as a matter of fact. You would expect a house with a name such as Ivy Cottage to be a lovely, rambling sort of place, covered with greenery and climbing roses. Here, there was a squat brick house—and not attractive brick, either—behind a sagging gate, with a barren front yard and a pockmarked drive that led back to a dilapidated garage. The last time we had been here, the garage had held a black Hackney, and the occupants of Ivy Cottage had been frantically packing their belongings preparatory to making their getaway. This time, the garage doors stood open and the space inside was empty but for some debris and empty petrol cans.

"I suppose the police probably took the motorcar," I said as Crispin brought the Hispano-Suiza to a stop beside the back stoop.

He shot me a look. "What's that?"

"There was a motorcar here back in August. A black Hackney. I suppose the police must have taken it."

"Or Wolfie did," Crispin said, which made sense now that I thought about it. He would have needed a way to get back and forth to London, and it explained the black Hackney that had come so close to running Christopher and myself down the other night. "It's parked at Ramsgate, as it happens. It was the vehicle he used to get you there."

"Was it really? And nobody thought anything of it?"

"I don't know what Gardiner and Finchley thought," Crispin said as he turned off the motor. "They were in the police issue Tender. I was alone in the H6. And I had no idea that there had been, or ought to be, a black Hackney here."

I glanced at him. "I do appreciate you coming after me, you know. In case I didn't say it already. You didn't have to do that."

He glanced back. "Yes, Darling, I did. Kit would kill me if I hadn't done whatever I could do to get you back in one piece."

"Christopher wasn't there," I pointed out. What I didn't say, was that he might not be there again.

"He'll hear about it. And he'd have had something to say about it if I hadn't stepped up."

He pushed his door open before he added, "Besides, I'm not going to let you be doped and abducted and not do something to stop it. You're part of the family, Darling, whether I like it or not."

He slammed his door shut as a sort of final word on the sentiment.

"How extremely gracious of you," I muttered, but I opened my door and stepped out onto the drive to stand beside him and contemplate the house without saying anything else about it. Instead, I pointed to the upstairs corner window in the back. "See that? Boards nailed across the window."

He nodded. "That's where they kept her?"

"So we assumed. She wasn't here anymore at that point." She had been in the morgue, after having been murdered the previous night.

Crispin looked around. "It looks deserted."

Yes, it did. "I could be wrong, and there's nothing here. It simply struck me as enough of a possibility that we ought to—"

"Yes, Darling. Of course we ought."

He eyed the house for a second, with all of the enthusiasm of a man presented with a dead fish.

"I'll do it," I said, and stepped forward.

The last time I had been here, the backdoor had been locked and we had had to pick the lock to get inside. Or rather, Wolfgang had done, using two of my Kirbigrips, and I don't know why his ability to do that hadn't presented itself as more sinister at the time. It ought to have done. But back then, I had simply been grateful that one of us had had the ability to get the rest of us inside.

This time, the handle moved under my hand, and the door opened smoothly. That didn't make it any more likely that anyone was kept hostage here, of course, but neither of us mentioned it.

We stepped into the same ugly kitchen as last time, only more dusty and depressing now. Dead flies littered the windowsill and mouse pellets decorated the corners of the floor. There was also a horrible stench in the air, one that made Crispin's nostrils flare.

"Struth," he complained, "didn't anyone think to take out the rubbish before they left?"

"That's not the smell of rubbish," I told him tightly. "Not even rubbish that's festered for two months."

He glanced at me. "No?"

I shook my head. "Let's hope it's a rat and not something worse."

He turned pale—paler—and for a second, it appeared as if he were thinking of running ahead of me. I wrapped my fingers around his wrist and kept him where he was. His skin was warm under my hand, and I could feel his pulse jumping.

"Are you certain?" he asked. As if he wasn't perfectly capable of recognizing the odor of decomposing flesh for himself.

"Positive," I said. "Come on."

I took a step towards the door to the dining room, tugging him behind me.

He resisted the pull. "Hold on, Darling. Shouldn't we contact the local constabulary and let them deal with it?"

I eyed him. "It's going to take them at least twenty minutes to sort themselves out to come here. Perhaps longer. Do you really want to stand outside—" because there was no way I'd breathe this air for any longer than I had to, "—and wait? Without knowing who or what is dead?"

He didn't answer, and I added, "We're here. Let's just keep going and hope for the best."

If the worst had happened, and Christopher was here, dead, I'd rather know it now than later.

Crispin hesitated, but eventually he gave a tight nod and followed me into the dining room.

"This was where we fought the kidnappers," I told him, softly, as we crossed the room on our way to the front door and the staircase to the first floor. The furniture was still suffering from the altercation two months later, with overturned chairs and drops of blood here and there on the rug. "Hiram Schlomsky had a sword stick, did I tell you? And he went absolutely mad and swung it at anyone who came within range."

"And Wolfie had to save your life," Crispin said disagreeably.

I shot him a look. "Is that what Christopher told you? It wasn't quite like that. It was a bit of a brawl, with a lot of fists and hair pulling and the like. And while I'm certain that fake Flossie would have liked to murder me, Mrs. Schlomsky was equally determined to murder her. I was never in any real danger. Besides, then Tom and Christopher showed up, and it all turned out quite all right in the end."

"Kit made it sound like Wolfie swooped in like a knight on a white horse and swept you out of danger," Crispin said with a grumble, and I giggled.

"Hardly. I mean, I'm happy he was there. The Schlomskys and I were no match for Sid and the two women. Without Wolfgang, they may have overpowered us. They had nothing to lose at that point, after all. They had already murdered the real Flossie. So I'm grateful that he was there to help us. But I wouldn't have said that he saved my life. I'm not sure my life was ever in any real danger, and besides, as I said, it was only a few minutes before Tom and Christopher turned up."

Crispin nodded and took a look around the sitting room. "This is depressing."

It was. The furniture was old and worn, and here, too, everything was covered with dust and dead flies and mouse droppings. There were dead plants on the windowsill, and that permeating odor of sweet rot.

"The stairs," I pointed. The corpse—rat or otherwise—must be up there, because it wasn't down here. This was a small house, just the three rooms downstairs and, I assumed, two bedrooms and lavatory on the first floor.

We stopped at the bottom of the staircase and peered up. It was narrow, and would allow only one of us to ascend at a time.

"I'll go first," Crispin said.

"I'm older," I countered.

"I'm the man."

"I'm older."

"I don't want you to see this, if—" He stopped before saying it.

"I don't want to see it, either," I said, "but there's simply no way, if Christopher is up there, that I'm not going to look at him. I'll be one step behind you. But if you insist, you can go first."

He nodded tightly and turned to contemplate the staircase again. After a moment, he squared his shoulders and started up. I followed.

The stench got worse and worse as we got closer to the top of the stairs. I stopped breathing through my nose as soon as we got halfway up, and began to draw air through my mouth instead. The idea of that was unpleasant, of course, but it made the smell a little easier to take.

Crispin reached the top of the stairs and stepped aside to

give me room. We stood side by side on the landing, looking at three closed doors.

"That's most likely the lavatory," I said nasally, pointing to the one in the middle. "We know that that one—" on our right, "—is the back bedroom. That's the one with the boarded-up window. The one on the left must be the front bedroom."

Crispin nodded.

"Bathroom first," I said.

He shot me a look. "Do you have to vomit?"

I did, of course, or it felt as if I could easily do, but I shook my head. "Least likely place for a body. Let's eliminate it."

"Be my guest." He gestured to the door.

"So much for being the man," I told him, as I pushed past him and took hold of the handle. There was a moment of squaring of shoulders, and then I pushed the door open.

The lavatory was small and dinky and dirty, with a pedestal sink and toilet, but it was corpse free. I breathed out and pulled the door shut again.

We locked eyes for a second across the small landing, and then we both turned to the door to the back bedroom. If Christopher was anywhere in this house, it was likely that he was there.

"I'll do it this time." Crispin crossed to the door and wrapped his hand around the handle. I put a hand against his back—for support—and peered over his shoulder as he pushed the door open.

And gagged as he slammed it shut again. "Oh, God." The toilet was right there, of course, but I swallowed hard, and did it again, and kept myself from sicking up.

"Could be worse," Crispin managed. He was pale and looked clammy, but he wasn't vomiting either.

"How?"

"It wasn't Kit."

No, it hadn't been. It had been a man in a dark suit, not someone wearing my serge skirt and high heels.

"Did you look at the rest of the room?"

"I mostly just slammed the door shut as soon as I could," Crispin admitted.

It had been an understandable reaction, of course. It's instinctive, to put a barrier between ourselves and something unpleasant. But we needed to know that Christopher wasn't in there, too.

I put out a hand. "Lend me your handkerchief, if you don't mind."

"Are you going in there?" But he handed me the silk square.

"I have to," I said, accepting it. "We have to make absolutely sure that there's nothing we can do."

"He was dead, Philippa. There was absolutely no question about that."

No, there hadn't been. "Just let me look," I said and turned to the door. "You can open the other door if you'd like. If the body is behind this one, it's not likely that there's anything unpleasant in the other room."

He gave me a look and a mutter, but he stalked across the landing to the other door and pushed it open. I took the opportunity to do the same while his back was turned.

The bedroom in the back was small and dark. As it would be, when there were wooden boards nailed up across the window. I squinted into the darkness, but saw no sign of anything other than the very obvious body on the floor. There was a bed up against the wall—it must have been where Flossie had slept while she'd been kept here—and a wardrobe and a few other odds and ends, but no other sign of life. The bed had a few drops of blood on the pillow, I noticed when I inched closer. Nothing at all like the puddle that covered the floorboards under the corpse, though; just a few drops, as if someone had had a tiny scratch or puncture. The blood was dry, of course, as it would be, if it had been here since before Flossie died.

From this angle, I got a slightly better look at the dead gentleman, and caught my breath quickly.

"What?" Crispin wanted to know. He had returned from the other bedroom and was loitering in the doorway.

I eyed him. He didn't have the look of a man who had come across anything else unpleasant. "Nothing?"

He shook his head. "Do you recognize him?"

"It's hard to be sure, with him on his front like that." And when all the blood in his body—the part of it that wasn't in the dried puddle on the floor—had migrated to the lowest point and had turned his face purple. "But he looks like the maître d' from the Savoy."

"Not the chap from last night?"

"The chap from three or four days ago. The one who brought the note to the table after Wolfgang had dosed my tea."

"Ah." Crispin took another look at him. "Yes, I can see that. He saw what Wolfie did, and tried to extort money. And when Wolfie couldn't pay, he—Wolfie—killed the bloke instead."

I nodded. It was as good an explanation as any. "There's no sign of Christopher in here."

"Nor in the other room. There's a suggestion that someone has been using it—more recently than two months ago—but it's more likely to have been Wolfie, I'd say."

"No rented rooms in Shoreditch, then?"

"Why pay for lodging if he could stay here for free?" Crispin said savagely. "Let's go."

He turned towards the staircase.

"We have to tell someone about the body." I glanced at it on my way past.

"Gardiner," Crispin said over his shoulder. "Best not to involve the local constabulary when it's Scotland Yard's case. Or when we don't want to be detained."

"So we just leave him there?" I shut the door behind me, but I couldn't help one last look over my shoulder at the dead man.

"I'm not picking him up and taking him with us," Crispin said. After a moment, he added, "He's been there for several days already. A few more hours won't matter to him."

He started down the staircase.

It seemed like something we ought to take care of sooner rather than later, but perhaps he was right and it would be better to pass the responsibility on to Tom and Scotland Yard instead of involving the local Thornton Heath chaps.

"Wait for me," I told his back and scurried to the top of the stairs and down on his heels.

CHAPTER TWENTY-TWO

"WELCOME HOME, MISS DARLING," Evans greeted me when we, at long last, made our way into the foyer at the Essex House. "My lord." He gave Crispin a bow.

"Evans." Crispin nodded back.

We were both a bit the worse for wear at this point. Crispin still hadn't slept. I was still wearing the same gown and wrap I had left in last night, but now I had slept in it, traveled in a boat in it, and found another dead body in it, this one a malodorous one. I would never wear this gown again, as it clearly carried with it awful luck. All I wanted was to get upstairs, into a bath and a different set of clothing, and to sit down with a cup of tea and breathe. I imagined that Crispin wanted much the same thing, and hopefully Christopher's wardrobe would be able to provide.

"Any messages?" I inquired on my way to the lift.

Evans shook his head. "But Detective Sergeant Gardiner arrived twenty minutes ago and went upstairs."

Oh, really? Part of me wanted to chastise Evans about

letting people other than Christopher and myself up to the flat without announcement—first there had been Crispin, and then there was his father, and now there was Tom—but I didn't have it in me to argue. Besides, Tom probably had information I would want to hear, so it was just as well that he was here, really.

"Did he seem upset, Evans?"

"No more than usual," Evans said, which seemed fair.

"Thank you, Evans." Crispin shoved me into the lift and pulled the grille shut behind us.

"There's no need to manhandle me," I told him, but without any heat whatsoever. "I was going. I want to see Tom just as much as you do."

"I'm sure you do, Darling." He mashed his finger on the button for the second floor and stood back. "I want to get out of this suit. And bury it somewhere. I can't get the smell out of my nostrils, and I'm certain it must have permeated the fabric."

He gave his sleeve a sniff and made a face.

"At least you didn't sniff me," I said. "Although I do know exactly how you feel. This is the first time I've worn this frock since the night Flossie was killed, and I'm never wearing it again."

He gave me an up-and-down look as the lift rose. "That's just as well. It's not very flattering, is it?"

"Says you," I said, offended, and he grinned.

"Sorry, Darling. I like the Bramley. It matches your eyes."

"It does not." My eyes are more emerald or forest green than apple, and if he was referring to the second definition of green-eyed—as in jealousy—he couldn't be more wrong.

We reached the second floor, and the lift stopped with a jolt. Crispin pulled back the grille and pushed open the door. I headed down the hallway towards the flat.

"At any rate," I told him over my shoulder, "I'm certain Christopher has something that'll fit you. At this point, he might not even need it back."

I stopped in front of the door and fumbled in my handbag for the key.

"Don't say that," Crispin said, coming to a stop behind me. "We'll get Gardiner on the case. Perhaps there really is a Shoreditch flat, and perhaps Kit's in it. Perhaps Natterdorff had information about it in his luggage. I'm sure Gardiner and Finchley between them gathered up all of Natterdorff's things..."

"Perhaps." I turned the key in the lock and pushed the door open. "It's just difficult, Crispin—"

And that was as far as I got before a shriek cut through the air, loud enough to pierce my eardrums, and the next second there was a rush of feet and then I found myself knocked back into Crispin—who had the wherewithal to hold on to me— while Christopher flung his arms around both of us.

"HE WAS HERE WHEN I ARRIVED," Tom said ten minutes later. "Otherwise I wouldn't have been able to get in, don't you know."

No, of course he wouldn't have done. I didn't know why that thought hadn't occurred to me before now.

I was curled up next to Christopher on the Chesterfield, close enough that our bodies were mashed together from shoulder through arm to hip, while Crispin exhibited a bit more restraint. He sat on Christopher's other side, but not so close that they actually touched. Just close enough that he could reach out and reassure himself that Christopher was there if he wanted to.

"Where were you?" Tom added.

"We stopped off in Thornton Heath on our way back," Crispin told him, while Christopher alternated between sipping tea from a cup and water from a glass, and alternating that again with eating.

"Did he not feed you?" I asked, and Christopher shook his head.

"A glass of water in the morning and evening, whenever he gave me another dose of sleeping draught, but no food."

After a second he added, with a shrug, "I was asleep most of the time, so I didn't notice how hungry I was."

But he clearly noticed it now. There was a stack of toast on the table in front of him, and he was making his way through it at a rapid pace.

"What happened?" I wanted to know, and he flicked me a look.

"It's a long story. Let me eat, and then I'll tell you. I'm certain you have other things to discuss with Tom."

I was certain we did, too. Crispin and Tom had continued the conversation while I'd been speaking to Christopher, for one thing.

"I already know that," Tom said. "I'll be taking Finch and Curtis and Pendennis out there as soon as we're finished here."

They must be talking about the body. But how could he know about that already, unless—

"Were you in the house in Thornton Heath?" I asked Christopher.

He nodded, mouth full of toast.

"You must have left just before we got there."

Christopher swallowed. "Halfway through the night. The sleeping draught wore off. He'd usually give me a dose at night, but he didn't come back for it last night."

No, Wolfgang had been busy carrying me onto a freighter

bound for Germany last night. I supposed he thought that once Christopher woke up, the ship would have sailed, quite literally, and there would be nothing he could do to get me back.

"So you just walked away?"

"Stepped over the body and headed down the stairs." He reached for another piece of toast.

"But you didn't stop at the local constabulary on the way?"

"I was still dressed in your skirt and jacket," Christopher said as he lifted the piece of toast to his mouth. "I didn't want to risk it."

He bit into it while I nodded. No, that made sense, actually.

"What did you want?" I asked Tom, who blinked at me. "You came to the flat for something. Were you looking for us?"

"Yes, of course." He had taken off his jacket at some point, to get comfortable—he had been up all night too, hadn't he?—and it was hanging over the back of one of the chairs. Now he went to it, reached into one of the pockets, drew something out, and came back to the table, where he put it in front of Crispin. "Here you are."

When he took his hand away, the gaudy Sutherland engagement ring sparkled on top of the wood, next to a pair of matching earrings and a string of pearls. I winced as a refracted beam of light hit me in the eye.

"Natterdorff stole it?" Crispin asked, without making a move towards picking any of it up.

Tom nodded. "We have to keep it in evidence for now. You'll get it back once it's been processed. But I thought you would want to see that it has been recovered."

"Thank you." The look he slanted at it wasn't that of a man happy to see his heirlooms, but more like someone who wished he would never see the items again.

"I also need you to formally identify them. I know what I'm looking at, but they're yours, so I need it to be official."

"Of course." Crispin cleared his throat. "That's the engagement ring that I gave to Laetitia in August, with the matching earrings. They're part of the Sutherland parure. They're the same pieces that were stolen from Marsden House on Friday night."

"And the pearls?"

"You'll have to ask Laetitia," Crispin said. "I didn't give them to her. And one string of pearls looks very much like another."

Tom nodded. "Thank you." He scooped it all up. "I'll get it back to you as quickly as I can."

"No hurry," Crispin muttered, but I'm not sure Tom heard him.

"Did you find Wolfgang when you went back out?" I asked Tom when he had made his way back to the table.

He shook his head. "I'm afraid not. He wasn't in the water. And we didn't find a body, so it's possible he's still alive. We searched the freighter again before we let it go, and didn't find him, but it's possible that he may have stowed away somewhere we didn't look. He could be on his way home. If not, I suppose we'll find out in a few days."

When the body washed up on shore. Right.

"I would rather not think about it," I said. "But you recovered all the jewelry?"

"Most of it. We'll have to show it to the victims once we've dealt with the dead body in Thornton Heath, but I expect it will all match up. Except for the peacock brooch. Although there are a few other emerald and sapphire pieces that might explain it."

Such as the engagement ring he had offered me, I supposed.

"It's the maître d' from the Savoy Restaurant," I said.

"Who is? The corpse at Thornton Heath?"

I nodded. "I'm fairly certain. I didn't get a good look, and he wasn't looking quite like himself when I saw him—" A brief vision of the bloated, discolored face appeared in front of my inner eye, and I swallowed, "—but I think so."

"He met with the chap after luncheon at Sweetings," Christopher said. "I followed him across the street to the church—"

"St Mary Aldermary?" I exchanged a glance with Crispin, who winced.

Christopher nodded. "The bloke was waiting for him there. They must have arranged it beforehand, because neither of them looked surprised to see the other."

No, that had probably happened on the Saturday afternoon after tea. The maître d' had handed Wolfgang a note. Wolfgang had put me in a Hackney and gone back inside the Savoy. By the time I got back to the hotel, the maître d' had not been at his post outside the restaurant. They must have been together, arranging their next meeting.

"I got the impression that Natterdorff was supposed to give the other bloke money," Christopher added. "He handed him a brown bag and told him to count it, and when the chap's attention was elsewhere, Natterdorff hit him on the back of the head with something."

I winced. "And you?"

He made a face. "He realized I was there, and came after me. I couldn't run fast enough in the stupid strap shoes to get away."

Well, no. It's difficult to run in high heels, and Wolfgang was quite a few inches taller than Christopher to begin with, with correspondingly longer legs. "What I meant," I said, "was whether he hit you too."

He shook his head. "At first I think he thought I was a woman. I gave that away when I opened my mouth, and after that, he knew who I was."

"But he didn't hurt you."

"He told me that you wouldn't like it," Christopher said, "and that as long as I cooperated, I would be fine."

"So you cooperated?"

This was Tom's question—it would never occur to me to question it—and Christopher's brows lowered. "Was I supposed to not do?"

"No, of course not," Tom said. "I'm glad you did." He shot a look at me, and then one at Crispin. "We're all glad you did."

I nodded. "Of course," Crispin said. "Whatever kept you safe, Kit."

"Well, he made me get in the back of the motorcar with the bloke, and then he drove us to the house in Thornton Heath. By the time we got there, the bloke was dead."

He shuddered. "I'm sorry we made you sit in the back of the motorcar with Frederick Montrose's body that time in June, Pippa."

"It's all right," I said, although I was glad for the sympathy. It had been a rather harrowing experience. "And then he locked you in the room upstairs?"

"And doped me to the gills," Christopher nodded. "I asked for a chance to write you a note, but he said no. I think he was afraid that I would manage to get you a message in code or something. He didn't seem to realize that having me write and tell you I was all right would have been preferable to not telling you anything, since that would only make you more frantic."

I nodded, fervently.

"And then he said that he was going to put me to sleep, but it would only be for a few days, and as long as I cooperated he wouldn't hurt me, so I cooperated. Until I woke up and he wasn't there, and then I made tracks."

He reached for another piece of toast. We all watched as he folded it into his mouth and chewed.

"I suppose that's it," Tom said after a moment. "It explains it all, I think. His grandfather cut him off, so he began stealing to keep himself afloat financially. He spent the money, no doubt, but it seems he held onto most of the jewelry. Perhaps he planned to pawn it in Germany, where it was less likely that anyone would recognize it."

I nodded. That made sense, actually.

"The maître d' at the Savoy tried to blackmail him," Tom added, "and Christopher saw it happen, so that explains both Christopher's disappearance and the dead body."

Christopher nodded, still masticating.

"He wanted to marry you," Tom said, eyeing me, "to keep the Natterdorff money in the family. If you wouldn't accept him, then he wanted to kill you so he could be the only heir. He went back and forth between the two because...?"

"Probably because I went back and forth between being conciliatory and not," I said with a sigh.

Tom nodded. "After his grandfather formally disinherited him, it became even more imperative that he sew up the inheritance, so he came up with the freighter and the elopement."

"It was hardly an elopement," I said, but at that point Christopher had swallowed wrong and was coughing hard enough to expel a lung. I turned to smack him on the back only to find that Crispin had got there first.

"There, there. Breathe, old chap."

"What—?" Christopher croaked.

"We were cousins," I said. "You know that, Christopher."

"Yes, of course. But—"

"As it turns out," Crispin said dryly, "the relationship was a bit closer than we thought. You're looking at the new *Gräfin von und zu* Natterdorff."

Christopher's eyes widened. "You're joking?" He was still breathing hard from his choking fit, but at least his cheeks were nice and rosy now. And for the record, he had directed the question to Crispin, not me.

"I'm afraid not," Crispin said. "What a time to find out, eh?"

Christopher nodded. "Indeed."

Neither of them explained this exchange, of course. Then again, they didn't have to, although if I hadn't known what I now knew, I would have asked them about it. As it was, I didn't. Nor did Tom, so he probably knew, too.

"Will you be going to Germany, then," he inquired instead, "to meet your grandfather?"

"And deliver myself right into Wolfgang's hands, if he managed to get onto that freighter?" I shook my head. "I think not."

"And you don't want to take your rightful place in the family?"

This was Crispin, and I faced him. "Not at all. I'm British, not German. I don't care that I would have been a *Gräfin* in Germany. The Weimar Republic did away with all of that in 1919."

"But your grandfather—" Christopher began.

"The grandfather who disowned my father for wanting to be a craftsman? The grandfather who disowned Wolfgang and made him turn to theft, and then to kidnapping and murder, to save himself? No, thank you. Let the old man reap what he sowed. Or let him choose to take Wolfgang back, if he makes it home. I can do without that kind of family."

There was a pause. Then Christopher leaned his head on my shoulder. "I'll be your family, Pippa."

"You're already my family," I told him. "Marriage at thirty if we haven't married anyone else, remember?"

"Marriage at thirty," Christopher echoed, with a glance across the table at Tom, "if we haven't married anyone else by then."

Next to me, Crispin said not a word.

Dear Reader,

First, the ubiquitous note about the language. As always, this book is a mess of British and American English. There's color and valor, and curb instead of kerb, but there's also lift instead of elevator, and Kerbigrips instead of bobby pins. I try to make it sound like Pippa is British, but the spelling is mostly American. If there are mistakes, and I'm sure they are, I'm hopeful that they simply fade into the rest of the mess and that no one cares.

Now, for a few historical references, mostly because I like research:

The Criterion Restaurant has been a fixture of Piccadilly Circus since March of 1874. So has the Criterion Theatre, nicknamed the Piccadilly Jewel Box. Back in the fall of 1926, *The Scarlet Lady* by John Hastings Turner was playing, starring Marie Tempest (1864-1942) and Ernest Thesiger (1879-1961). The actress Millicent Tremayne is entirely of my own invention.

The Piccadilly Circus tube station opened in 1906. By 1907, 1.5 million people used it every year, a number that grew to 18 million by 1922. At that point, it was decided that the original station, planned and built by British architect Leslie Green—best known for a long line (pun totally intended) of London underground stations, all tiled in shades of green and white—needed to be upgraded. Work began in February 1925 and was completed in 1928. During the process, the statue of Eros was removed from Piccadilly Circus to the Victoria Embankment Gardens for safekeeping. There are images of the original, now defunct tunnels on the link below, if you're interested in seeing what Pippa saw before she tumbled down the stairs. The tunnels really were round, and looking at them, it's easy to see why the London Underground was nicknamed the Tube. https://alondoninheritance.com/under-london/ hidden-london-piccadilly-circus/

The Cave of the Golden Calf operated in the draper's basement below 3-9 Heddon Street, on the edge of Mayfair. It was opened by Frida Strindberg in 1912 as the first gay bar in London. Of course it wasn't advertised as such; it was a nightclub, and women as well as men frequented the place. So did the police: there were regular raids on the area as well as on the nightclub itself.

The club went bankrupt in 1914, and then, of course, the Great War came. Things changed, and changed again. In 2025, a restaurant called Heddon Street Kitchen occupies the space above the old nightclub. Across Heddon sits another restaurant called The Star-man. It takes its name from David Bowie's 1972 record, *The Rise and Fall of Ziggy Stardust and the Spiders from March*, the cover photo of which was taken at 23 Heddon Street. In the background of that photo, you can see 3-9 Heddon as it looked in the early 1970s. The album back cover photo gets you a little closer: it was taken in the cul-de-sac outside 3-9, which can be seen on the left behind the telephone booth. That particular booth didn't go into production until 1927, so in October of 1926, when Pippa and Tom were there, there would have been no red telephone booth in that corner.

There's no reason to think that Lady Austin, who was a real person (if not a real lady) who hosted drag balls in London in the late 1920s, would have used the old Cave of the Golden Calf for that purpose. Given the club's past, it would have been safer not to, I imagine. But I like history, so I decided to dust it off and make use of it for book purposes.

Sweetings really is everything Pippa says it is, the oldest oyster bar in London, and it really does sit in the Albert Building, which is where the incumbent government offices were located in 1926. St Mary Aldermary Church is located across the street, and everything Pippa says about that is true, as well.

Gretna Green, for those of you who didn't grow up reading Barbara Cartland, is the first easily reachable village across the Scottish border from England. It's a place whence young English couples would elope. Scottish law allowed for 'irregular marriages,' meaning that almost anybody had the authority to conduct the marriage ceremony as long as the declaration was made before witnesses. As a result, the blacksmiths of Gretna Green became known as 'anvil priests.' The best known was Richard Rennison, who performed 5,147 marriage ceremonies. When Crispin references Pippa's abduction as a 'Gretna Green situation,' he means that it's an elopement.

The Royal National Lifeboat Institution was a bit like the coastguard, but more concerned with search and rescue than patrolling the English Channel for invaders. Their lifeboats are not the little rubber dinghies you may be thinking of, the kind that hang on the deck of a larger ship, but were big wooden boats in their own right. Pippa is rescued by lifeboat No. 697, the *Prudential*, which was a 1925 vessel paid for by the

Prudential Insurance Company. She worked out of the Ramsgate RNLI station in southeast England for 28 years. In 1940, the *Prudential* was the first RNLI lifeboat to respond to the call for volunteers to help out at Dunkirk. She saved 800 men on her first night, and by the end of the botched invasion, had helped save 2,000 more. *Prudential* Coxswain Howard Primrose Knight was awarded the D.S.M./Distinguished Service Medal for the part that he and his crew played in the evacuation of Dunkirk.

The boat still exists, but under the name *Trimilia*, and you can learn more about her here: https://trimilia.co.uk/

ABOUT THE AUTHOR

New York Times and *USA Today* bestselling author Jenna Bennett has written more than fifty books, most of them in the genres of mystery and suspense.

For more information, please visit her website, www.jennabennett.com

———

To purchase Jenna's books, please visit her store, www.jennabennett.myshopify.com
or your preferred ebook/print book vendor.